The Attenbury Emeralds

**Center Point
Large Print**

**This Large Print Book carries the
Seal of Approval of N.A.V.H.**

The Attenbury Emeralds

JILL PATON WALSH

CENTER POINT PUBLISHING
THORNDIKE, MAINE

This Center Point Large Print edition
is published in the year 2011 by arrangement with
St. Martin's Press.

The text of this Large Print edition is unabridged.
In other aspects, this book may vary
from the original edition.
Printed in the United States of America
on permanent paper.
Set in 16-point Times New Roman type.

ISBN: 978-1-61173-021-0

Library of Congress Cataloging-in-Publication Data

Paton Walsh, Jill, 1937–
The Attenbury emeralds / Jill Paton Walsh.
p. cm.
ISBN 978-1-61173-021-0 (library binding : alk. paper)
1. Wimsey, Peter, Lord (Fictitious character)—Fiction.
  2. Vane, Harriet (Fictitious character)—Fiction.
  3. Aristocracy (Social class)—England—Fiction.
  4. Private investigators—England—Fiction. 5. Emeralds—Fiction.
  6. Large type books. I. Title.
PR6066.A84A95 2011b
823'.914—dc22

2010050672

For Judith Vidal-Hall,
With gratitude for many years of friendship

ACKNOWLEDGEMENTS

I would like to thank the following for help in the writing of this novel. First the trustees of Dorothy L. Sayers, for allowing the use of her characters; Anne Louise Luthi for lending me books about jewellery and putting me in touch with Diana Scarisbrick and Judith Kilby-Hunt who generously advised me on the subject of heirloom jewels. To Mr Christopher Dean I am particularly indebted for making available to me his dramatic transcript of the proceedings of the trial of the Marchioness of Writtle; my account of that trial is substantially derived from his. Phyllis James made a very fruitful suggestion to me about the line of the plot. Sir Nicholas Barrington found and translated for me at a moment's notice the lines from the Persian poet Hafez which are used in the narrative. The fate of Bredon Hall is modelled on the fate of the Manor House at Hemingford Grey. I have constantly consulted Stephen P. Clarke's *Lord Peter Wimsey Companion*, and have enjoyed the support and encouragement of Dr Barbara Reynolds and of Mr Bruce Hunter.

As always my debt to my husband is beyond acknowledgement and I offer him my heartfelt thanks.

JPW October 2009

THE CHARACTERS

(in order of appearance)

Lord Peter Wimsey

Harriet, Lady Peter Wimsey, née Harriet
Vane: his wife

Arthur Abcock, Earl of Attenbury: a recently
deceased peer

Mervyn Bunter: Lord Peter's manservant

Honoria, Dowager Duchess of Denver: Lord
Peter's mother

Lady Charlotte Abcock: daughter of Lord
Attenbury

Gerald, Duke of Denver: Lord Peter's brother

Helen, Duchess of Denver: the Duke's wife

Roland, Lord Abcock: eldest son of the Earl
of Attenbury

Bredon Wimsey: Lord Peter Wimsey's eldest
son

Peter Bunter: son of Mervyn Bunter

Hope Bunter: wife of Mervyn Bunter

Paul Wimsey: middle son of Lord Peter
Wimsey

Roger Wimsey: youngest son of Lord Peter
Wimsey

Claire, Lady Attenbury: wife of the Earl of
Attenbury

Lady Diana Abcock: her middle daughter

Lady Ottalie Abcock: her youngest daughter

Captain Ansel: an army friend of Lord Abcock, guest at Fennybrook Hall

Mrs Ansel: his wife

Mrs Sylvester-Quicke: guest at Fennybrook Hall

Miss Amaranth Sylvester-Quicke: her daughter

Reginald Northerby: Lady Charlotte's fiancé

Freddy Arbuthnot: guest at Fennybrook Hall

Sir Algernon Pender: guest at Fennybrook Hall

Lady Pender: his wife

Mrs Ethel DuBerris: a widow, guest at Fennybrook Hall

Ada DuBerris: her daughter

Inspector Sugg: a policeman from Scotland Yard

Nandine Osmanthus: an emissary from the Maharaja of Sinorabad

Mr Whitehead: an employee of Cavenor's Bank

William DuBerris: deceased nephew of Lady Attenbury and husband of Mrs DuBerris

Jeannette: Lady Charlotte's maid

Sarah: Lady Attenbury's maid

Sergeant Charles Parker: a policeman from Scotland Yard

Harris: Lord Attenbury's butler

Salcombe Hardy: a journalist

Constable Johnson: a policeman

Mr Handley: a pawnbroker

Mr Handley's son: who unexpectedly inherits his father's business

The Marquess of Writtle: husband of Lady Diana Abcock

The Lord Chancellor

Sir Impey Biggs: a distinguished barrister

Mrs Prout: a cleaner at the House of Lords

Edward Abcock, Lord Attenbury: grandson and heir of Arthur, Lord Attenbury; son of Lord Abcock

Mr Snader: a director of Cavenor's Bank

Mr Tipotenios: a mysterious stranger

Mr Orson: an employee of Cavenor's Bank

Miss Pevenor: a historian of jewellery

Lady Sylvia Abcock: widow of Roland, Lord Abcock

Frank Morney: husband of Lady Charlotte Abcock

Captain Rannerson: owner of the horse Red Fort

Lady Mary Parker: wife of Commander Charles Parker of Scotland Yard and sister of Lord Peter Wimsey

Verity Abcock: daughter of Lord Abcock and Lady Sylvia Abcock

Lily: an ayah

Joyce and Susie: workers at the Coventry Street mortuary in 1941

Mrs Trapps: cook in the London House
Rita Patel: volunteer at the mortuary
Mrs Smith: a visitor to the mortuary
Miss Smith: her daughter
The Maharaja of Sinorabad
Franklin: maid to the Dowager Duchess of
  Denver
Thomas: butler at Duke's Denver
Dr Fakenham: physician to Duke's Denver
Cornelia Vanderhuysen: American friend of
  the Dowager Duchess
Jim Jackson: gardener at Duke's Denver
Bob: another gardener
James Vaud: a London detective inspector
Mr Van der Helm: a retired insurance valuer
Mr Bird: a retired insurance company owner
Mrs Farley: housekeeper at Duke's Denver

1

'Peter?' said Lady Peter Wimsey to her lord. 'What were the Attenbury emeralds?'

Lord Peter Wimsey lowered *The Times*, and contemplated his wife across the breakfast table.

'Socking great jewels,' he said. 'Enormous hereditary baubles of incommensurable value. Not to everyone's liking. Why do you ask?'

'Your name is mentioned in connection with them, in this piece I'm reading about Lord Attenbury.'

'Old chap died last week. That was my first case.'

'I didn't know you read obituaries, Peter. You must be getting old.'

'Not at all. I am merely lining us up for the best that is yet to be. But in fact it is our Bunter who actually peruses the newsprint for the dear departed. He brings me the pages on anyone he thinks I should know about. Not knowing who is dead leaves one mortally out of touch.'

'You are sixty, Peter. What is so terrible about that? By the way, I thought your first case was the Attenbury *diamonds*.'

'The emeralds came before the diamonds. Attenbury had a positive treasury of nice jewels. The emeralds were very fine—Mughal or something. When they went missing there was uproar.'

'When was this?'

'Before the flood: 1921.'

'Talking of floods, it's pouring outside,' said Harriet, looking at the rainwashed panes of the breakfast-room windows. 'I shan't be walking to the London Library unless it leaves off. Tell me about these socking great baubles.'

'Haven't I told you about them already, in all the long years of talk we have had together?'

'I don't believe so. Have you time to tell me now?'

'I talk far too much already. You shouldn't encourage me, Harriet.'

'Shouldn't I? I thought encouragement was part of the help and comfort that the one ought to have of the other.'

'Does help and comfort extend to collusion in each other's vices?'

'You needn't tell me if you don't want to,' said Harriet to this, regarding it as a deliberate red herring.

'Oh, naturally I want to. Rather fun, recounting one's triumphs to an admiring audience. It's a very long story, but I shall fortify myself with the thought that you asked for it.'

'I did. But I didn't contract to be admiring. That depends on the tale.'

'I have been warned. It's undoubtedly a problem with being married to a detective story writer that one runs the gauntlet of literary criticism when

14

giving an account of oneself. And the most germane question is: is Bunter busy? Because I think explaining all this to you might entail considerable assistance from him.'

'When is Bunter not busy? This morning he intends, I believe, to devote himself to dusting books.'

Lord Peter folded his copy of *The Times*, and laid it on the table. 'A man may dust books while listening, or while talking. We shall join him in the library.'

'Bunter, where do I start on all this?' Peter asked, once the project was explained, he and Harriet were settled in deep armchairs either side of the fire, and Bunter was on the library steps, at a remove both horizontally and vertically, but within comfortable earshot.

'You might need to explain, my lord, that the occasion in question was your first foray into polite society after the war.'

'Oh, quite, Bunter. Not fair at all to expect you to describe my pitiful state to Harriet. Well, Harriet, you see . . .'

To Harriet's amazement, Peter's voice shifted register, and a sombre expression clouded his face.

'Peter, if this distresses you, don't. Skip the hard bit.'

Peter recovered himself and continued. 'You know, of course, that I had a sort of nervous collapse after the war. I went home to Bredon Hall, and cowered in my bedroom and wouldn't come out. Mother was distraught. Then Bunter showed up, and got me out of it. He drew the curtains, and carried in breakfast, and found the flat in Piccadilly, and got me down there to set me up as a man about town. Everything tickety-boo. I'm sure Mother will have told you all that long since, even if I haven't. Only as you know all too well, it wasn't entirely over. I have had relapses. Back then I couldn't relapse exactly, because I hadn't really recovered. I felt like a lot of broken glass in a parcel. Must've been hellish for Bunter.'

'I seem to remember your mother telling me some story about Bunter overcome with emotion because you had sent away the damned eggs and demanded sausages. Rather incredible, really, but I always believe a dowager duchess.'

'Expound, Bunter,' said Peter.

'The difficulty about breakfasts, my lady, was that it entailed giving orders. And his lordship in a nervous state associated giving orders with the immediate death of those who obeyed them. The real responsibility for the orders belonged to the generals who made the battle plans, and in the ranks we all knew that very well. But just the same it fell to the young men who were our immediate captains to give us the orders to our faces. And it was they who saw the consequences in blood and guts. All too often they shared the fate of their men. We didn't blame them. But his lordship was among those who blamed themselves.'

'That really must have made him difficult to work for,' said Harriet.

'It was a challenge, certainly, my lady,' admitted Bunter, blowing gently on the top of the book in his hand to dislodge a miniature cloud of dust.

'But by the time I knew him he had got over it,' continued Harriet. 'I don't remember seeing him having any difficulty in giving you orders in recent years.'

Bunter replaced the book in the run, turned round and sat down atop the library steps. 'But back in 1921 his lordship was very shaky, my lady. We had established a gentle routine for life in town—morning rides in Rotten Row, a few concerts, haunting the book auctions, that sort of thing. And at any moment when boredom or anxiety threatened we went suddenly abroad. Travel is very soothing to a nervous temperament. But his lordship had not resumed the sort of life in society that a man of his rank was expected to lead. He couldn't stand even the rumble of the trains on the Underground Railway, because it evoked the sound of artillery, so we felt it would be better not to attend any shooting parties. I had been hoping for some time that a suitable house-party would occur, at which we could, so to speak, try the temperature of the water.'

'What an extraordinary metaphor, Bunter!' said

Lord Peter. 'The temperature of the water at a house-party is always lukewarm, by the time it has been carried upstairs by a hard-pressed servant and left outside the bedroom door in an enamel jug.'

'Begging your pardon, my lord, but I always saw to your hot water myself, and I do not recall any complaints about it at the time.'

'Heavens, Bunter, indeed not! I must be remembering occasions before you entered my service. That vanished world my brother and all seniors talk so fondly about. When wealth and empire were in unchallenged glory, and to save which my generation were sent to die wholesale in the mud of Flanders. I wasn't the only one,' he added, 'to find the peace hard to get used to.'

'That's an odd way of putting it, Peter,' said Harriet, contemplating her husband with a thoughtful expression. 'I can see that horrible flashbacks to the trenches might have undermined you. Might have haunted you. But the peace itself?'

'The peace meant coming home,' Peter said, 'finding oneself mixing with those who had stayed at home all along. Listening to old gentlemen at the club, who had waved the flag as eagerly as anyone when their own prosperity was in danger, complaining once the danger was past about ex-servicemen who according to them thought far too much of themselves and what they had done. Reading in the press about unemployment and poverty facing returning soldiers, and employers grumbling about being asked to have a mere 5 per cent of their workforce recruited from ex-servicemen.'

Harriet said, 'I remember a visit to London when there was a man on crutches selling matches in the street. My mother gave me a penny, and said, "Run across and give this to the soldier, Harry, but don't take his matches." I shook my head when he offered me the matches, and he smiled. My mother said when I went back to her side, "They're not allowed to beg, but they are allowed to sell things." I remember that very clearly, but I'm afraid most of it passed me by.'

'You were just a girl, after all,' said Lord Peter, smiling at his wife, 'and a swot, I imagine. What were you doing in 1921?'

'Head down over my books preparing for Oxford entrance exams,' said Harriet. 'I think, you know, that it's just as well I didn't meet you then, Peter.'

'You'd have been a breath of fresh air compared to the girls I did meet. And you never know, you might have liked me. Wasn't it my frivolity that put you off for years? I hadn't yet got into the way of frivolity so much then.'

'Is that true, Bunter?' asked Harriet, affecting doubt.

'His lordship never perpetrates falsehoods, my lady,' said Bunter, straight-faced.

He descended the library steps, moved them one

bay along, and gave his attention to the next column of books.

'Bunter, do get down from that thing, and face forward somewhere. Come and sit down and tell Harriet properly about those lost years.'

'Yes, my lord,' said Bunter stiffly, doing as he was asked.

'Well, come along then, your most excellent opinion, if you please.'

When Bunter hesitated, Harriet said gently, 'How did *you* find the peace, Bunter?'

'It was very easy for me, my lady. I had escaped serious injury. I had a job for the asking, and it was a well-paid position with all found. Many of those I had served with, especially the seriously injured, came home to a cold welcome, and were soon forgotten. People turned away from mention of the war as from talk of a plague. His lordship's sort of people threw themselves into pleasure-seeking and fun. My sort had longer memories.'

'The awful fact was,' Peter put in, 'that all that suffering and death had produced a world that was just the same as before. It wasn't any safer; it wasn't any fairer; there were no greater liberties or chances of happiness for civilised mankind.'

'Working men were beginning to toy with Bolshevism,' said Bunter. 'And it was hard to blame them.'

'The very same people,' Peter added, 'who were refusing to employ a one-armed soldier, or who

20

were trying to drive down miners' wages, were horrified at a rise of Bolshevism, mostly because of the massacre of the Romanovs. Well, because the Russian royals were disappeared, supposed dead.'

'I remember Richard King in the *Tatler*,' said Bunter, 'opining that the mass of men will gladly sacrifice themselves for the realisation of a better world, but would never again be willing to sacrifice themselves merely to preserve the old one.'

At which both his employers objected at once.

Peter: 'Even you, Bunter, cannot expect me to believe that you have remembered that verbatim for something like thirty years!'

Harriet: 'In the *Tatler*, Bunter? Surely not!'

Bunter met both sallies with aplomb. 'It happens, my lord, my lady, that I began to keep a commonplace book at that time. I was so struck by those words of Richard King that I cut out his article, and pasted it on to the first page of the book. My eye lights on it again every time I open it to make a new insertion.'

'Worsted again,' said Peter. 'I should have realised long ago that it is useless to argue with you.'

Bunter acknowledged this apology with a brief nod of the head.

'Uneasy times,' said Peter. 'There was a coal strike that spring—quickly over, but with hindsight it was rumbling towards the General Strike. And what Bunter calls my sort of people were carrying on like the Edwardians become hysterical. Dancing, dressing up, getting presented at court, throwing huge parties, racing, gambling, prancing off to the French Riviera or Chamonix, chasing foxes, shooting grouse . . . I was supposed to be a good sport, and join in. It seemed meaningless to me. I found my station in life was dust and ashes in my mouth. I might have been all right with a decently useful job.'

'Couldn't you just have gone and got one?' asked Harriet.

'Of course I could. I was just too callow to think of it. I think I went for months with no better purpose in life than trying not to disappoint Bunter. If he made breakfast, I ought to eat breakfast. If he thought I needed a new suit, I ought to order one, and so forth. If he kept showing me catalogues of book sales, I ought to collect books.'

'If I may say so, my lord,' said Bunter, 'I believe the book-collecting was entirely your idea. I have been your lordship's apprentice in anything to do with books.'

Harriet looked from one of them to the other. They were both struggling to conceal emotion. Whatever had she stirred up? Should she have guessed that the emeralds would open old wounds in this way?

'You see, Harriet,' said Peter, 'that if my life was

a stream of meaningless trivia, I was affronting Bunter. He was far too good a fellow to be a servant to a witless fool. I could just about manage to do what Bunter appeared to expect I might do, but I knew, really, that I was frittering both of us.'

'I shouldn't think Bunter saw it that way,' said Harriet. 'I imagine he saw you as a decently useful job. I hope we aren't making you uncomfortable, Bunter,' she added.

'Not unusually so, my lady,' said Bunter gravely.

His remark brought a brief blush to Harriet's face. All three of them laughed.

'So as Bunter was saying,' Peter continued, 'he and my mother between them—that's right, isn't it, Bunter?—were on the lookout for a suitable occasion, a kind of coming-out for me, when I might show my face in public again, and try to behave normally. And they chose the Abcock engagement party. A party to present Lady Charlotte Abcock's fiancé to Lord Attenbury's circle.'

'Abcock is the Attenbury family surname, my lady,' said Bunter helpfully.

'Thank you, Bunter,' said Harriet. She thought wryly that she would find all that easier to remember and understand if she had ever been able to take it entirely seriously.

'It seemed just the right sort of occasion,' said Bunter, 'with only one drawback. It wasn't very large, but on the other hand large enough to seem like being in society. The Earl of Attenbury's family were long-established friends of the Wimsey family. The event was not in the shooting season. His lordship had been at school with Lord Abcock—Roland, the Attenburys' eldest son—and had known the eldest daughter as a girl. Fennybrook Hall, the Attenburys' seat in Suffolk, was not a taxing journey from London, as I supposed. I thought we would go by train, my lady. I had not anticipated that his lordship would insist on driving us, a circumstance that certainly made the journey memorable.'

'That I can well imagine,' said Harriet sympathetically. 'What was the drawback?'

'Oh, just that brother Gerald, and my dear sister-in-law Helen were among the guests,' said Peter.

'1921,' said Harriet thoughtfully. 'Surely Helen was not yet the full-blown Helen of more recent years?'

'Much the same, if a little less strident,' said Peter.

'In the event, my lady, another drawback emerged when we had already accepted the invitation, and it was too late to withdraw,' said Bunter. 'The family decided to get their jewels out of the bank for the occasion, and the press became aware of it. There was a great deal of most unwelcome publicity about it, and it seemed likely that the party would be besieged.'

'I have never been able to see the point of jewels

24

so valuable that they have to be kept in the bank,' said Harriet.

'The thing about such possessions is that their owners don't really regard them as personal property,' said Peter. 'They are part of the patrimony of the eldest sons. They go with the title, like the estates and family seat. Unlike the estates and the family seat, however, they can be entailed to go down the line of daughters. They are a family responsibility. Nobody wants to be the one during whose tenure they were lost, stolen or strayed.'

'The Attenbury emeralds were, or rather are, in the strict sense heirlooms, my lady,' said Bunter.

'Yes,' said Harriet doubtfully, 'but it must greatly limit the enjoyment they can give.'

'You married me wearing Delagardie earrings,' said Peter mildly.

'That was to please your mother,' Harriet said. 'She had been so kind to me; and she thought they would look good with that golden dress.'

'She was right,' said Peter, smiling.

'My mind was on other things that day,' said Harriet, 'but I wouldn't normally like to wear something that wasn't really mine, but only on loan from history. It would be like going to the ball in a hired gown.' Not for the first time she felt thankful that Peter was the younger son. She glanced at the blazing ruby in her engagement ring. That was completely hers.

'On the other hand,' said Peter, smiling—he

must have seen that glance—'it lends occasions some éclat when everyone puts on their glory only now and then.'

'Many families solve the difficulty by having paste replicas made for less august occasions,' said Bunter.

'And the Attenburys had done exactly that,' said Peter, 'which added to the complexity. But, Bunter, we're getting ahead of ourselves. Time we took the King of Heart's advice: begin at the beginning, go on till you get to the end and then stop. That last is the most difficult, isn't it, Harriet?'

'Rough hewing our ends being easier than divinely shaping them, you mean? We seem to me to be having difficulty beginning at all,' she said.

2

The difficulty beginning at all was greatly increased by the unexpected arrival of the two eldest sons of the house, Bredon Wimsey and Peter Bunter. When Mervyn and Hope Bunter had christened their son 'Peter' it had been a conscious tribute, but now that the boy was growing up in the Wimsey household, in a world where distinctions between master and man were increasingly precarious, it had become a source of confusion, and young Peter was known as 'PB'.

'To what,' demanded Peter of these two, 'do we owe the honour of your presence in term-time?'

'Research, Father,' said Bredon. 'We were sent to sit in the spectators' gallery in the House of Commons. To make notes, of course. And we do have permission to stay overnight at home. If it's all right by you, of course.'

'Hmm,' said Peter.

'Well, the food is pretty foul at school,' said his son hopefully.

'Very well then. It's a pleasure to see you both. You may report on your impression of the Mother of Parliaments when we sit down to dinner together. Run along now and find your younger brothers and beat them at ping-pong or something.'

'It's easy to beat Paul,' offered Bredon, 'but little Roger is a demon player.'

'Do your best,' said Peter. 'And off you go. The grown-ups are story-telling.'

'Thanks,' said Bredon.

But they stood in the doorway waiting.

'You too, PB,' said Bunter.

'Oh, thanks, Dad,' said PB over his shoulder as the two disappeared down the stairs.

Harriet said, 'I really like to see what good friends those two are.'

'Well, effectively they have grown up together,' said Peter.

'Does that always make friendship?' asked Harriet. 'I don't know. There's such a lot an only child doesn't know.'

'Hope and I are very grateful, my lord, my lady,' said Bunter, 'that our only son has had the companionship of your sons.'

The three of them hesitated on the brink of the treacherous social gulf that yawned between them.

'You know that we love him like one of our own,' said Harriet, full of daring.

'As long as it doesn't give him ideas,' said Bunter gruffly.

'I hope it does,' said Peter. 'I hope it does. And I hope his ideas make my sons buck up. It's a changing world now. But we were in the past, weren't we? Where were we?'

'You were arriving at the Abcock girl's engagement party,' prompted Harriet. 'Can you pick up the thread?'

'We arrived safely, my lady,' said Bunter, rising to the challenge. 'His lordship was given a room at the corner of the house, and I was assigned a place below stairs.'

'Do we have to explain to Harriet the layout of the bedrooms?' Peter asked.

'Perhaps we should first describe the family and the other guests,' said Bunter.

'Righty-ho. Well, Lord Attenbury was a traditional old stick. About fifty. Honourable to a fault. A bear of very little brain. But Lady Attenbury was cut from another cloth altogether. A graceful and intelligent woman. Kept her brains strictly undercover, brains not being the done thing, you know, but never missed a thing. She was a great friend of my mother's, by the way.'

'Was your mother at the party?' asked Harriet.

'No. She had been invited and declined, all for my sake. One can hardly demonstrate one's independence while hanging on to Mother, after all. The Attenburys had four children. First a son: Roland, Lord Abcock, remarkably obtuse sort of fellow, but a good sport. I knew Roland well at school: he used to fag for me. Often had to do his prep for him. You could tease him all day long, and he never noticed. He had married his childhood sweetheart, but she wasn't present. Looking after her sick mother in Wiltshire or something. Then a daughter, Charlotte, the one just recently engaged. Knew nothing much about her really, although I had seen her now and then before the war, when she was much younger. Then a second daughter, the joker in the pack, Diana, who was at finishing school in Switzerland on the occasion of this party. We'll come to her later. Lastly, quite a bit younger, an after-thought, Ottalie. Sweet little girl in white pinafores with a playmate in residence. That's the family. Now the guests. Well, I'm blowed if I can remember most of them, but the ones that matter were the ones who had been given rooms in the main wing. Help me out here, Bunter.'

'Captain and Mrs Ansel,' said Bunter, 'army friends of Lord Abcock. Mrs and Miss Sylvester-Quicke; Mr Northerby, the lucky fiancé; Mr

Freddy Arbuthnot; Sir Algernon and Lady Pender; Mrs Ethel DuBerris, a young war widow, and her daughter, Ada, a child about Ottalie's age. The Duke and Duchess of Denver. And yourself, my lord.'

'The only names I recognise apart from your brother and sister-in-law are dear Freddy and Sylvester-Quicke,' said Harriet. 'The dreaded Amaranth. Is that where she first took a shine to you?'

'I suppose it might have been. She was very young, and posing as a blue-stocking. Her mother thought my brains might make me susceptible.'

'The word posing is harsh, Peter.'

'Accurate. Now where were we?'

'With a catalogue of guests. I observe that you have a problem familiar to novelists. A large cast list to be introduced to the audience, and no reason why they should wish to know or remember any of it until the story starts.'

'It starts slowly, my lady,' said Bunter, 'with arriving at our rooms. There was, of course, a servants' wing, and as I said a room had been assigned to me there. But it was a long way from the room allocated to his lordship. I was unhappy about being out of call; naturally there were bells in the servants' wing, one for each room in the main house, but they would serve to summon somebody, most likely one of the house servants, not me. I therefore discreetly removed the sheets and blankets from the bed in the room I had been given, and made up the couch in the dressing-room opening from Lord Peter's room. We did not want to draw attention in any way to this arrangement. The whole experiment would be negated if anyone observed an undue dependence on his lordship's part. I persuaded the housemaid for the room not to mention this below stairs. That was quite easy, because the servants' hall was in a state of sullen resentment about the presence of the police. The young woman had been annoyed by Inspector Sugg, who had told her to report anything unusual to him. She was very eager to disoblige him.'

'Inspector Sugg!' exclaimed Harriet.

'Yes, that was the first time we encountered him,' said Peter. 'He was in charge of a posse of policemen who were staking out the house and grounds in case of trouble over the emeralds. Attenbury had hired them for the purpose—that wouldn't have been unusual.

'At dinner the first night the party had not yet completely assembled, although Mr Northerby was present, and paying very conspicuous attentions to Charlotte Abcock,' said Peter.

'So were these attentions welcome?' she asked.

'Seemed to be,' said Peter. 'Yes, I thought so. Rather charming show, really. Stung me a bit, at the time. Green-eyed monster stuff.'

'You fancied Charlotte yourself?'

'Not specifically Charlotte. Just the general

picture of love returned, and no war looming to spoil the prospect.'

So it was about Barbara, Harriet realised. She who had jilted Peter while he was away fighting. These emeralds really were a dangerous subject. Too late to avoid them now.

'In the morning all the men went riding, or playing a round of golf at a course a little distance off. I decided on browsing in the library. Attenbury had a famous collection of old atlases and naval books I thought I'd like a peek at. Wonderful room, designed by Inigo Jones. So I was the only man around when the mysterious visitor showed up.'

'A plot thickens at last,' said Harriet. 'Who was the mysterious visitor?'

'Called himself Nandine Osmanthus, and presented himself as an emissary from the Maharaja of Sinorabad. Said he had urgent business with Lord Attenbury. Lady Attenbury had him shown into the library with a request that I would entertain him until her husband returned. He was quite jolly company, actually. Very suave and confident. Wellington and Sandhurst. Didn't blink an eyelid when I couldn't find Sinorabad on the atlas I had open on the table. Though since it was a Mercator from 1569 I couldn't claim it was definitive. Although he was mysterious, and quite unexpected, he wasn't suspicious. Or I didn't think so at the time. He told me quite openly what his business was. His Maharaja owned a spectacular Mughal jewel, a carved emerald which had once been part of a necklace. The present Maharaja's grandfather had sold a number of jewels to fund relief in a famine eighty years before, including the emerald that they thought must be the one now owned by the Attenbury family, and the Maharaja would now like to buy it back. Nandine Osmanthus had been sent to compare the jewel they had retained with the one in the Attenbury emeralds, to establish whether they were from the same bauble in origin.

' "How is the comparison to be made?" I asked him.

' "I understand the Attenbury emeralds are to be worn in public for the first time in many years," said he.

' "Well, not in public," said I. "This is a party for the family and their guests." It was beginning to occur to me that perhaps the policemen shouldn't have let him in.

' "I shall not intrude in private festivities," said Osmanthus, "but if the jewels are in the house, the comparison is as easy as this." And he took out of his waistcoat pocket a silk handkerchief, and unfolded it on the table. And there was an almighty great emerald, before my very eyes.'

'You've got me hooked, Peter,' said Harriet. 'What was it like?'

'Strange,' said Peter. 'Huge. Nearly an inch

square—well, like a square with the corners off, and quite thick, about as thick as two sovereigns. Very dark. And carved intaglio with a flower and twining leaves. The thing is, Harriet, emeralds are very difficult to carve. They are very hard, and very frangible. That's why they are usually table-cut rather than rose-cut, to protect them against knocks when being worn. An intricately carved emerald is a masterpiece. Beauty draws us—I reached out a hand towards it . . . "You may hold it," said Nandine Osmanthus. I picked it up and felt the heft of it in my hand. I held it up between finger and thumb against the light. It was translucent. Not sparkling, you understand, but holding the deepest possible green lights, like a dark, clear river. Green as a dream and deep as death. I turned it over, and the back was inscribed in an oriental script, in exquisite fine calligraphy.

' "The Koran?" I asked my companion.

' "As it happens, no," he replied. "It is a quotation from the Persian poet, Hafez. Well, what do you think of it, Lord Wimsey?"

' "It is very beautiful," I told him. "And daunting. But you said it was a Mughal jewel? With a Persian inscription?"

' "It was made for Akbar," he said, with a note of reverence in his voice. "And Akbar had a Persian mother. From her he must have known of the Persian poets. This inscription is in Arabic script, and in the Persian tongue. I can read it to you."

'He intoned the words—you know what it's like, Harriet, to hear the sound of poetry in an unknown tongue. Very impressive and mysterious.

' "When did the jewels come into the possession of your Maharaja?" I asked him.

' "Long ago. They should not have been divided."

' "Didn't you say it was done for the relief of a famine? An act of mercy?"

' "Even a virtuous action may be regretted when its consequences are seen," said Osmanthus. "Those who were fed are dead now. Now it seems right to try to reunite the stones."

' "Well, I wish you luck," I said. "But I shouldn't think for a minute Lord Attenbury will wish to part with something that has now been in his family for several generations." I was thinking that by this man's account the thing had been sold, not looted or prised from its owner as tribute. Attenbury owned it with a clear conscience.'

'It was no moonstone, you mean,' said Harriet.

'Exactly. Not a curse about it anywhere. And yet . . .'

'Yet?'

'There was certainly charisma about it. I was longing to hold it when he gave me permission, and I was reluctant to put it down.'

'Did you see it, Bunter? Did it have this effect on you?' asked Harriet.

'I did not see the one that Mr Osmanthus brought

to the house, my lady. But I was very struck by his lordship's account of it. Very struck, and concerned.'

'You were concerned, Bunter?' asked Peter. 'Why exactly? Did you say so at the time?'

'I imagine not, my lord,' said Bunter.

'Can you explain now?' asked Harriet.

'A small object of very great value is a responsibility, my lady. And the servants in a household carry a large share of that responsibility. They are in the limelight as soon as anything goes wrong.'

'Suspected, you mean?'

'I do. A lady's maid has access to her jewel box. To her secrets. It goes with the job. A manservant knows where keys are kept, and what is worth locking up, in the eyes of his employers, at least.'

'So if a policeman like Sugg comes along, and asks who could have stolen a gem of great price, and the answer is that one of the servants could, then that is often enough for him. Off with her head! Or off with her to jail anyway,' said Peter. 'The very trust that has been reposed in a servant can be held against her. Or him.

'So by and by the riders and golfers returned to the house, and Lord Attenbury appeared in the library, still in riding gear, to see what was what. Nandine Osmanthus repeated his request. He would be infinitely grateful if it were possible to put his stone down beside the Attenbury emeralds,

36

and see if they were alike. Attenbury took it rather well, although I saw his eyebrows go up. "I don't see any problem with that," he said, "do you, Wimsey?" I didn't actually like to say, "Not as long as you watch him like a hawk." Not with the man standing there. But I promised myself I would be the hawk in question. Just in case.

' "However," said Attenbury, "the jewels are not in the house yet. We are expecting Mr Whitehead from the bank to bring them at about four. Look here, I suppose it wouldn't do to compare yours with the paste copy? That would be easiest, don't you think?"

' "Unfortunately there is the matter of the inscription on the back," said Nandine Osmanthus. "I doubt if that could have been carved into a paste copy."

' "Stuff on the back?" said Attenbury. "Didn't know that."

'Osmanthus produced his stone again, and Attenbury said, "Good lord! Haven't a clue whether ours has a scrawl on it like that. I suppose you'd like to wait and see the real one?"

' "I would be obliged to your lordship if you would allow that," said Osmanthus.

'I could see that Attenbury was in an agony of indecision about something, and indeed, he said, "A word with you, Wimsey," and drew me away to the other end of the library.

' "Dammit," he said, *sotto voce*, "do I have to ask

the fellow to lunch? What will the others think?"

'And I'm afraid I didn't know what to say. I could have said, "There were brave Indian soldiers fighting with us in the trenches." I could have said, "Ask him to lunch by all means. Your guests in your house must accept anyone you have invited." What I did say was, "That would be kind of you." What Attenbury did was to have a lunch laid for Osmanthus in a little breakfast-room, where he would eat alone. The official guests sat down to lunch together in glory. Well, in the kind of glory represented by white linen and family silver. Even so, one of them remarked on having seen "one of our black brethren" walking on the terrace. I ate up my potted shrimps and lamb chops, and removed myself for a toddle around the grounds. Lady Attenbury was keen on gardens, and had had Gertrude Jekyll laying them out for her. Charming.

'It was there among the lilies and roses that I hit the first difficulty of the weekend. I had a little set-to with Mrs DuBerris, or, rather, I was set upon by her. I rounded a large bush and found her seated in a little bower made of a bench and boughs. She was very tense; fists clenched in her lap, and sitting bolt upright. "May I join you?" says I, trying, don't you know, to be civil in a normal sort of way.

' "If you must," says she.

'Well, I didn't know what to do. I was thunder-struck, so I just stood there like a great big ninny.

38

It seemed as though I would offend her if I did sit down, and would insult her if I just walked away. Not the sort of dilemma I had any practice at back then. After a brief interval she said, "Well, make up your mind then, poor Major Wimsey. And don't expect any sympathy from me. Every single nurse who volunteered for war service saw worse things than you did, and had to deal with them too. I don't recall a single woman getting shell shock as you please to call it, and footling around being feeble and needing sympathy." She spoke with great bitterness in her tone. And of course she floored me, because I thought exactly that myself; that the state I was in was a form of unmanly weakness, of which I ought to have been ashamed. And it hadn't escaped me that her emphasis on *"poor* Major Wimsey" sounded like a quotation from somebody else; I was excruciated by the thought that I had been talked about with that form of compassion that is indistinguishable from contempt.

'I just stood on, rooted to the spot. I only needed a coat of whitewash to have served as a piece of garden statuary. I didn't answer her. And then I was rescued. Lady Attenbury appeared, with a trug of cut flowers over her arm and a pair of secateurs in her hand, seemingly from behind a large rose bush just behind the bower. She put her arm through mine, and walked me away briskly down the path away from the house, without a word spoken to Mrs DuBerris.

' "Peter, I'm so sorry," she said to me as soon as we were safely out of earshot.

' "Not your fault," I managed to say.

'We walked a little further. "You might be wondering why I invited her," Lady Attenbury said. "Not quite our sort of person."

' "It's not for me . . ."

' "She is a sad case," Lady Attenbury continued. "She was indeed a brave volunteer nurse. She encountered my nephew, William DuBerris, when he was lying horribly wounded in a field hospital, and accompanied him on a hospital train to a town behind the lines. He recovered enough to be escorted home, but before he reached England he had married her. His family refused to accept her, and disinherited him. He died a few months later in poverty, leaving his wife to bring up their daughter—little Ada, whom you might have seen playing with Ottalie. He left his wife only a few bits and pieces, and she is struggling."

' "And you don't feel inclined to follow the family line?" I said.

' "My brother deems her a fortune-hunter who took advantage of his son. But I think my nephew might genuinely have loved her. She is a handsome enough woman of some education. Isn't it perfectly possible?"

' "It might be hard to distinguish love from gratitude and dependency in that situation," I told her. "But there is nothing criminal about gratitude."

40

' "In any case," she said, "Ada is my great-niece. I am entitled to take an interest."

' "Rather hard luck when your lame ducks start pecking each other," I said.

' "She should not have spoken to you like that. I shall have a word with her and it will not happen again."

' "I wish you wouldn't take it up with her," I said. "Rather reinforces the idea that I can't look after myself, don't you think? Best left alone."

' "If you think so, Peter," she said. "Now, I must be off with these flowers. The staff need them for the table setting." '

3

'I didn't see Osmanthus again until I got back from my walk. The party were at play—the young at tennis and the older at croquet, and Attenbury himself was playing a round of bowls when Mr Whitehead from the bank arrived. Attenbury asked me to see to Osmanthus's little business with the jewels, and bid him farewell. He didn't want to break off his game.

'So I galloped back into the house, and intercepted Whitehead and took him to meet Osmanthus in the library. It was dashed awkward. Whitehead was very reluctant to open the jewel case for anybody except family. Quite right, I suppose. Anyway, in the end I got Lady Attenbury to come and lend her authority to the proceedings. Whitehead got a written receipt for the jewels he was carrying, and we opened the case. The Attenbury emeralds were a parure—a complete suite of jewels. There was an ingenious setting which could be worn as a necklace with the Mughal jewel hanging from it, or inverted as a tiara with the jewel suspended in it at the centre. There was a separate clip with a pin on it, so you could wear the centre stone as a brooch if you liked. There was a bracelet and pendant earrings and three rings. They were all big emeralds, mounted in platinum with a snowstorm of tiny diamonds—quite dazzling things, in which to be honest the big square carved centrepiece looked rather sombre. Obviously the big stone could be detached from the setting, because it could be suspended either way up, depending if you were wearing it as necklace or tiara. It had not been drilled, but was mounted in a gold clip with a little loop.

'Anyway, Osmanthus put down his jewel, and Lady Attenbury unhooked the one in the parure, and they were laid side by side. They were identical from the front. A swirl of leaves and a single flower had been cut into each. When they were turned over there was indeed an inscription on the Attenbury jewel, partly obscured by the mount. Osmanthus expressed regret that he could not read it all, and Lady Attenbury picked up the jewel, and unclipped it from the mount.

Osmanthus took a jeweller's loupe from his pocket and examined it carefully.

' "What does it say?" I asked him.

'He said, "It means: *'I will not cease striving until I achieve my desire . . .'* This is indeed one of the jewels we are trying to trace. I think my master the Maharaja will offer to buy this stone from you, Lady Attenbury."

' "It is not for sale, Mr Osmanthus," she said.

'So he bowed, and made fulsome thanks and said that at least the family he served could be sure that the jewel was safe. There were many Indian princely families sending their jewels to Cartier and others to be re-cut in western style, he said. Obviously nothing of that kind would happen to the Attenbury jewels.

'Lady Attenbury made no reply to this remark. She replaced the jewel in the clip and put it back in the silk-lined box, and courteously but firmly bade Osmanthus goodbye.

'She offered Mr Whitehead tea, but he declined, having a train to catch, and the two of them were shown out of the house together.

'I was glad to be done with dealing with this for Attenbury; I didn't think it was quite the thing, although I was an old family friend. Lady Attenbury didn't think so either. "We have been imposing on you, Peter," she said. "Although of course, Arthur is very busy with so many guests in the house."

' "A pleasure, I assure you," I said. "I am lucky to have seen the things so close up. What dazzlers."

' "I can't imagine what Arthur was thinking of, letting that fellow near them," she said. "And as it is, we should perhaps have left them in the bank. Charlotte doesn't want to wear them. She says they are grim and horribly dated, and couldn't she just borrow my pearls."

' "All the girls like pearls," I said, foolishly. Privately I rather agreed with Charlotte.'

'Why, Peter?' asked Harriet.

Bunter, presumably having decided the conversation would be long and rambling, had resumed dusting books.

'Well, Charlotte was certainly a beauty,' said Peter, 'but of a pallid kind. Very light brown hair, pale hazel eyes, slender and willowy. There wasn't much substance to her. She became a fine figure of a woman, but she was a wispy sort of a girl back then. And those great jewels take a bit of wearing, Harriet. They take a bit of carrying off. If they are more striking than the woman wearing them they quench her fire. You could have worn them . . .'

' "Nobody asked me, sir, she said." And I would have been as reluctant as Charlotte. Green is not my colour.'

'Well, there we are. Lady Attenbury told me she had told Charlotte sharply that the emeralds were to be her father's marriage gift to her, and she must wear them when she was told to. Then she took the jewels from the library to the little safe in her bedroom, and we all pottered about until it was time to dress for dinner.'

'There was an element of showing off the dowry?' Harriet asked.

'Precisely. Well, so we all went down for drinks at the appointed hour. Charlotte didn't appear, but I supposed she could be forgiven for wanting to make a grand entrance. I had time to study the prospective fiancé. He addressed a few nondescript remarks to me, but naturally his chief concern was to be charming to his future parents-in-law. Discreet flattery was his line of talk. Asked me about my regiment. Asked Gerald about the estate at Duke's Denver. Asked Freddy about prospects for investing in South American railways. Thoroughly presentable chap. Awfully boring. Attenbury seemed pleased with him. Lot of talk about how the golf had gone. I could hardly have endured it if Lady Attenbury hadn't noticed my difficulty and plied me with questions about the books in the library. Well, everyone had been assembled for some time. Even little Ottalie was there, done up Adèle-style, with her nanny sitting in a corner beside her. Special dispensation—she was allowed to stay to see Charlotte in glory, and then she had to scamper back to the schoolroom. She told me that herself.

'Time went on, and both Lady Attenbury and Lord Attenbury began to glance discreetly at their watches. I saw Lady Attenbury beckon the butler, and speak to him quietly. In his turn he spoke to a maidservant, who put down her tray of glasses and left the room. Miss Sylvester-Quicke eased her way through the crush and said to Mr Northerby, "Where are your people, Reggie? I should have thought we might have seen them tonight."

' "My father has retired from the army, Miss Sylvester-Quicke," said he, "and is now in charge of extensive tea plantations on the lower slopes of the Himalayas. My parents are sorry not to be here. They are delighted at . . . all this," he finished lamely, stopping himself from making an announcement that Lord Attenbury would shortly be making.

' "Good heavens!" said she. "Delighted? I should rather think they would be!"

'On that far from tactful remark there was a hush, as Charlotte entered the room. She was indeed all festooned about with emeralds, her cheeks were flushed, and she looked very flustered. As she moved towards her father the gong was sounded, and we all went in to dinner. Freddy and I were placed at the foot of the table, with a good view of the company. I wondered what had upset Charlotte, though whatever it was had transformed her—she didn't look pallid one bit.

' "A lovers' tiff?" suggested Freddy, *sotto voce*.

' "If so, he's a cool customer," said I. For Reggie Northerby didn't seem perturbed at all. He hadn't been late coming down, he had had two glasses of champers at least before the gong went. And he was now regarding his girl with a combination of admiration and puzzlement, seemed to me. Granted, a man may smile and smile and be a villain, but it takes nerve. Anyway, I knew only too well how over-heated one can get in the feelings department when it's young love at stake.

'Dinner ran its course after course, and at our end of the table the talk was quite jolly. Freddy asked Amaranth what she thought of the emeralds. She turned her head to look down the line of candlesticks to where Charlotte was sitting, and thought for a moment. Then she said, "They're big."

' "Don't know that they quite live up to their reputation," said Freddy thoughtfully. "Isn't that centre stone very famous? Reggie had better watch his step."

' "It's hard to see from here," I said, kicking Freddy under the table. Mrs Sylvester-Quicke, who was sitting next to him, had a reputation as a terrible gossip. A friend of that woman columnist in the *Tatler*. And it was true—what with the silver and the candlelight, and the chiaroscuro from the Bohemian glass chandeliers overhead, we couldn't see clearly. Though I thought I saw Charlotte's eyes bright with tears.'

'Doom, doom!' said Harriet.

'What?' said Peter.

'A comment on your narrative technique,' said Harriet. 'We have reached the *Little did they know* juncture.'

'So we have,' said Peter. 'On, on. We got to speeches and toasts. Attenbury talked very nicely about Charlotte, the apple of her parents' eyes, the very pineapple of perfection, as sweet-tempered as she was beautiful, to make a perfect wife for the lucky young man. Excellent fellow. Welcome addition to the family—that sort of thing. Reggie made a short speech expressing his thanks for the welcome he had received, and the trust reposed in him, above all by Charlotte whose love he would endeavour to deserve. He read out a telegram from his father and mother in Darjeeling, conveying pride and joy. Calloo, callay all round.

'Then Lady Attenbury rose from her seat, and led the ladies off to the drawing-room, and the port and cigars were brought in. A lot of manly talk then—a bit of politics. Denver was worrying about the drought. The young wheat was dying in the fields, and even fruit orchards were dropping the prospective fruit. Ansel grumbling about the first woman to become a barrister. What was the world coming to? Pender wondering if Chamberlain would be tough enough on strikers. But of course by and by the talk came round to those emeralds.

' "It's a damn generous wedding present, Attenbury," said Sir Algernon Pender.

' "No more than she deserves," said the proud father.

' "Course, people have a thing about emeralds," Pender went on. "My wife prefers sapphires, thank God."

'Captain Ansel said to Freddy, "Aren't you something of an expert about emeralds? Didn't I read a piece of yours from my stockbrokers about investing in them?"

'Freddy humphed modestly, and said that yes, advising on investing in gemstones was one of his lines.

' "Well, tell us all!" said Sir Algernon. "What's so special about them?"

' "They are green," said Freddy feebly, to gales of laughter. "No, I mean it. They are greener than sapphires are blue or rubies are red. And they are rare. Old emeralds all come from Colombia. The Spanish tortured the natives to find the location of the mine. That way they found the Chivor mine. Then they looked for others nearby, and they found the Muzo mine. They used native labourers in murderous conditions to dig the stones out. They couldn't use explosives, because that would have shattered the stones. The suffering was horrible, but the stones were wonderful, the deepest green, clearest, gem-quality emeralds. These are called 'old mine' stones. They are the finest, and the original Muzo stones are the next best."

' "You surprise me, Arbuthnot," said Pender. "I've

49

always thought of emeralds as coming from India."

' "Ah, well, Pender," said Freddy sagely, "the Colombian emeralds were all sent to Spain, naturally. But gems don't stay put. They go where the money is. And at that time the wealthiest people on earth were the Indian princes, great maharajas and Mughal nabobs among them. They had acquired a taste for emeralds from the small bright stones found in Afghanistan or Egypt. They paid fabulous fortunes for the Colombian glories. So by the time the Colombian mines had given of their best the loot was in India, for the most part."

' "That's all very interesting, Arbuthnot," said Captain Ansel. "But I still don't see why emeralds are so expensive. Damn things cost more than diamonds."

'I had noticed that Mrs Ansel was wearing an emerald brooch, and I thought he was speaking with feeling.

' "It's rubies that time is more precious than . . ." I offered, but nobody took me up on it. I needed a literary soul for that game, and there was none present. Freddy launched into an attack on diamonds.

' "There's lots of fun in diamonds," he was saying. "And they do come in various tints and colours. But the fashion is for clear-water stones, so the more valuable they are, the less distinctive. Whereas emeralds—highly recognisable. With large stones no two are the same."

' "One can tell where they were mined, you mean?" asked Ansel.

' "Much more than that," said Freddy. He was enjoying all the attention. "There's no such thing as a flawless emerald. Emeralds have flaws and inclusions. Little crystals of pyrite, calcite and actualité. Drifting veils within the stone—the French call this *jardin*. Lots of personality. Someone who has looked closely at an emerald could tell it again even if it has been re-mounted, or carved or re-cut."

'By this time everyone within earshot of Freddy was listening to him. The estate talk continued at the other end of the table, where Gerald and Attenbury were deep in their landed concerns, but Northerby, who was sitting halfway down the table, was now riveted by Freddy, and leaning forward to catch every word.

' "I say, Arbuthnot," said Pender, "do you mean to say that you could identify one of Attenbury's emeralds even if it was out of the set, just from the stone alone?"

' "I couldn't," said Freddy cheerfully, "but I know a man who could. And if one of those stones were to go walkies, there would be a man in London who knew it by sight, and a man in Paris, ditto, and several chaps in Amsterdam, and someone in Geneva . . . need I go on?"

'Northerby was giving Freddy a very fishy look, I thought. "Surely not, Arbuthnot," he said.

51

"Haven't these things been kept in a bank vault since time began? Surely very few people indeed have seen them. Even the sort of people you refer to. What is all the excitement about, with the press at the gate, except that the emeralds are hardly ever seen?"

' "They've been seen to be valued for insurance, I imagine," said Freddy.

'And at that point Attenbury rose to his feet, and said, "Shall we join the ladies? Mustn't keep Reginald too long from Charlotte."

'So that was that. Off we all trooped to the drawing-room, where Mrs Ansel was playing briskly on the piano the latest hits from Irving Berlin, and Charlotte was surrounded by a sisterhood, motherhood, and all rabbit's friends and relations. It was Freddy who went straight across to talk to her, I noticed, while Northerby went to sit beside Lady Attenbury. Mrs DuBerris was the only lady available to be sat beside, so I thought I would rise above our little spat, and I sat beside her.

' "I hear you have seen two emeralds close up, this afternoon," she said.

' "Yes. Attenbury asked me to."

' "And the only difference between them was the inscription?"

'I said that it was.

' "But you don't read Persian, do you, Lord Peter?"

' "Fraid not."

'I was distracted being stung by the strains of "Ain't misbehaving, all by myself", because it was all too true—I wasn't, and I was. And I'd had much more than enough of my fellow men and women by then. I thought of pushing off to bed early, just for some solitude, but instead I went to the billiard-room to footle around a bit, and by and by Freddy joined me, and we played a round. Still absolutely oblivious of what was going on. Not a clue.'

'That's a good teaser, Peter,' said Harriet appreciatively. 'I'm enjoying this. I should stay home and demand a story from you more often.'

'What precisely is a teaser?' asked Peter.

'Another form of doom. A page-turner. You were absolutely oblivious of what?'

'Bunter shall tell you that, because he didn't have the luxury of oblivion. But before he does I have one more remark of Freddy's to get into the tale. I asked Freddy while being soundly beaten at billiards what he had meant about Northerby needing to watch his step, and he told me that Northerby was on hard times. Something about the tea trade that had gone wrong. "There's been some raised eyebrows in the City about this match, because Attenbury is rolling in it, and Northerby is on cheese-ends. Of course the old chap can afford to bankroll a son-in-law, but mostly men in his position want the wench to marry wealth. Very generous of him, what?"

' "Well, he's a soft-hearted fellow underneath all that barking formality," said I. "With a particular soft spot for Charlotte."

'Freddy just looked at me enquiringly.

' "She's a devil of a sport on a horse," I told him. "Only one of the family to share Attenbury's passion for hunting. I believe that's how they met Northerby."

'Right. If you have no more comments to make I will hand over to Bunter.'

'I have one comment, my lord,' said Harriet. 'Unless you have been making half of this up, you have an extraordinary memory. How long ago is all this?'

'Thirty years. Of course I'm not remembering everyone's remarks verbatim, I'm making a good deal of it up, but the drift of what they said, and when they said it is all right. There is no more such a thing as a forgetful sleuth than there is such a thing as a flawless emerald. Now, Bunter, old fruit, stand not upon the order of your going, or on those library steps. Come and sit down and relate matters as they befell on your side of the baize door. Here is Harriet, all agog. You are agog, Harriet, I take it? It doesn't sound like a pleasant state to be in. What exactly is it?'

'I am very much agog,' said Harriet. 'We shall look it up later.'

'Well, my lady,' said Bunter, 'I cannot make claims for my memory such as his lordship makes, but as I remember, it was upon this fashion . . .'

Goodness! thought Harriet. How like Peter Bunter has become . . .

4

'When Lady Charlotte came to dress for dinner,' Bunter continued, 'she found that the emeralds laid out ready for her to wear did not include the carved central stone. They used to call it the king-stone, I believe. She at once rang for her maid. The maid was Jeannette, a French young lady who had been with the family some three or four years, ever since Charlotte graduated from the care of the governess. She came at once expecting to help her mistress dress, and was thunderstruck to find that the jewels were not complete on the stand, as she swore she had left them. She had fetched them from Lady Attenbury's room, carried them down the corridor to Charlotte's room, and laid them out ready only an hour since. The two women panicked—Jeannette with very good reason—and began to run around shouting for help.

'The senior manservants of the household were in attendance on the guests assembling for dinner, but Jeannette fetched Lady Attenbury's own maid, who opened the safe in Lady Attenbury's bedroom of which she was trusted with the keys, to see if the emerald had become detached and was lying there loose, Jeannette all the while asserting passionately that it had been with the parure when she left it. When it was found not to be in the safe the panic escalated. Agitated voices reached me in my lordship's dressing-room, and a couple of footmen and the valet of Captain Ansel had also heard the commotion. A little parliament of the servants assembled. At my suggestion we began a systematic search of both the bedrooms—Lady Charlotte's and her mother's—and along the corridor between the two, which by unhappy chance was carpeted in dark green Axminster.

'Time was passing, and Lady Charlotte was distraught. She was supposed already to be downstairs among the guests. Jeannette suggested that she simply put on her pearls, and go down. The stone must be somewhere near, and it would be found before her father or mother could ask questions. This simply provoked anguish from Lady Charlotte. She had already incurred her father's displeasure by reluctance to wear the emeralds; they had been brought specially from London for her, and if she showed her face downstairs without them her father would interpret this as flagrant defiance. He might even suppose that the very absence of the Mughal stone was a trick of some kind that she herself had got up to in order to avoid doing what he asked of her.

'There was now only some five minutes left before the dinner gong would sound. Crying woe was not getting anywhere, and the Axminster was greenly refusing to yield a dropped jewel. Sarah, Lady Attenbury's maid, a lady of about her mistress's age and with long service in the family, solved the immediate problem. I think she was as much concerned to avoid a public debacle and a scandal, which would certainly get into the press, as she was about the whereabouts of the jewel.

' "Stop crying at once, Miss Charlotte," said she. "You must wear the paste, and get downstairs immediately. Come here." She produced the paste replica from a drawer of Lady Attenbury's dressing-table, and put it round Lady Charlotte's neck herself. "Run!" she said to the girl.

'Meanwhile all the commotion had attracted the attention of the policeman who was posted on the upper corridor, who went and fetched Sergeant Parker, my lady—'

'Goodness!' said Harriet. 'Charles?' She was charmed to find that her brother-in-law had a part to play.

'And he took over the direction of the search, which proceeded in an orderly manner. Of course he also reported the matter to Inspector Sugg.

'When Sugg appeared, he was very confident. The gem could not possibly have left the house— he had men posted at every door. It would be recovered, and the culprit brought to justice. We might be sure of that. I must admit that I was not reassured very greatly by this, my lady.'

'I should think not!' said Peter indignantly.

'You are running ahead of yourself, my lord,' said Bunter reproachfully. 'Until his investigation began you had no knowledge of Inspector Sugg, and no reason to think ill of him.'

'Your capacity for being in the right is beginning to irritate me, Bunter,' said Peter petulantly. 'Shouldn't you make a mistake or two, to soothe my feelings?'

'I made a mistake at the time, my lord. But I do not recall your finding it soothing. You reproached me for it rather severely. You came to bed very late, and wearied by the unusual excitements of so much society. I did not tell you what had been happening until the following morning.'

'At least you did tell me when I woke,' said Peter. 'The other guests learned only when they appeared for breakfast that the house was in purdah and that no matter what plans they had made, no matter who they were, they would not be allowed to leave until the mighty Inspector Sugg said they could. It was not a very jolly breakfast, that I do remember. It was a very troubled morning, come to that. Alarums and excursions on every side.'

'Alarums indeed, my lord. But no excursions,' said Bunter. 'The whole household below stairs was thrown into crisis. If nobody could leave, then everyone including all their visiting servants required the usual three meals a day. The provisions had not been laid in for anything on that scale beyond breakfast of that day; the cook was distraught, the butler harassed, and those of us who were ourselves visitors, the personal servants of the upstairs guests, were attempting to help and getting in the way. "One thing we may all be sure of," Mr Harris, the butler, told me. "They'll be trying to pin this on one of us. I wouldn't be in Jeannette's shoes for all the port in the cellar."

'There was confusion on every side. The hall was full of bags which had been packed the previous night, or very early that morning, ready for guests' departure. I regret to admit, my lady, a small detail escaped my notice entirely at the time; that is, a set of very expensive golf clubs being carried through the hall just before all movement of the luggage was suspended. It turned out that nearly every one of the guests had a very urgent appointment to meet later in the day, and they all fussed and blustered and threatened at the thought of being detained. But Inspector Sugg stuck to his guns, so to speak, and there was a confrontation between him and Lord Attenbury in the lobby, with voices raised loudly enough to be heard in the hall where several of us were struggling to sort out the luggage. Mr Northerby's man was in the hall, and it stopped him in his tracks. It was very entertaining, my lady. A major row in which one is not oneself directly involved has a theatrical quality, and is capable of giving a perverse sort of pleasure, like the pleasure conferred by the gruesome events of a Shakespearean tragedy.'

'How very Aristotelian of you, Bunter,' said Harriet. 'You mean pity and fear, I suppose.'

'I mean excitement, my lady.'

'Well, do tell me,' said Harriet, 'what the row was about—no, wait, let me guess. It was because Lord Attenbury didn't want his guests to be questioned.'

'Exactly, Harriet,' said Peter. 'His lordship had reluctantly accepted that since no amount of searching had produced the emerald, there was a possibility it had been stolen. He was happy to have Sugg arraign the servants, any and all of them. But as for the smallest aspersion cast on any of his house guests, it was unthinkable that any of them were involved. They were under his roof, and under his protection and it was an outrage beyond bearing to subject them to questioning.

' "I can take them to the local police station for questioning if you prefer," said Sugg.

'Attenbury had brought me with him to confront Sugg, because he was convinced that "that odd Indian chappy" might have something to do with it, although I told him I couldn't see how. "You may take their names and addresses before they leave," he told Sugg. "But that is all. I absolutely forbid you to subject them to interrogation."

' "It is as witnesses I need to question them, my lord," said Sugg. "Not as suspects. But question them I will."

' "You will not!" said Attenbury. "You are dismissed. Remove yourself and your men from my property immediately."

' "I'm afraid I cannot do that," said Sugg.

' "I hired you, and I am firing you!" said Attenbury, at the top of his not inconsiderable voice.

' "I have reason to believe that a felony has been committed," said Sugg stubbornly. "This is no longer a private arrangement with the police to protect your property. This is now a criminal investigation. I must remind you, my lord, that obstructing the police in the course of their enquiries is itself a serious offence." '

'Well, so far, bully for Sugg,' said Harriet.

'Oh, he's not short of guts,' said Peter. 'Just brains. I thought Attenbury would bust a gasket. He stormed off to telephone the Chief Constable, who was, he declared, a friend of his. "And we shall see!" he said as he went.

'Well, he did see. The Chief Constable backed up his man, and the enquiry went ahead as Sugg wished. Perversely, you might think, he decided to question the servants first. Attenbury made one last rather muted protest, saying that if the guests were questioned first they would then be free to leave, and the servants could wait. But Sugg said that when he had questioned the servants there would be in all probability no need to question the guests, and since his lordship had expressed himself forcefully opposed to questioning the guests . . .

'So Sugg commandeered the gunroom as an interview room, and the servants were called in one by one.

'As you can imagine, Harriet, there was an atmosphere of discomfort in the house. Mrs Ansel and Mr Pender had attempted to go out for a walk in the grounds, rather than stay caged up in their rooms. A policeman at the door had stopped them. The ladies had gravitated to the conservatory where they were playing a desultory round of whist. We gentlemen gathered in the billiard-room. I was very agitated—too excited to play. Abcock played a round with Freddy. I was fidgeting about, distracting him.

' "Look here, Wimsey," he said, in a while. "You're putting me off my stroke. What's the matter?"

' "I wish the hell I knew what was going on downstairs," I said.

' "Oh, don't let it bother you," said Abcock. "It isn't bothering me. If the damn thing has gone missing Papa will clean up on the insurance money, and make it up to Charlotte."

' "It's just that I have a feeling something may be going horribly wrong for somebody," I said.

' "If you want to know what's going on in the

gunroom," said Abcock, "that's no problem. It used to be the dining-room—the main hall—when the house was much smaller, and there's a ladies' peephole into it." '

'Enlighten me,' said Harriet, 'into the nature and uses of a ladies' peephole. If you please.'

'In the high and far-off times, O Best Beloved,' said Peter, 'it let the ladies enjoy the bawdy uproar at the tables without being seen to be part of it. I know one or two houses where such a thing remains. Anyway, Abcock led us to it. The old hall had a solar at one end of it, now used as a linen store. It had a sliding panel that opened into the room below, between one bit of carving and another on the panelling. We all three crouched down at it and slid it open a crack. Sugg's voice came clear as a bell to us. Abcock left at once—he really wasn't interested in his sister's emeralds at all. The family diamonds would in due course be his, and those were still in a bank vault in London. Freddy didn't like it either—too much a gentleman to fancy overhearing by stealth. So I sat down on a bale of sheets by myself, and listened in. Luckily Bunter found me very shortly, having looked for me in the billiard-room, and been sent along by Freddy, and he brought me pencil and paper, and joined me on the floor.'

'So you were in effect spying on the police? Shame on you, Peter! Shame on you both!' said Harriet, laughing.

'I didn't get where I am today,' said Peter, 'by evincing undue respect for the police.'

'But Charles was there,' protested Harriet.

'We'll come to Charles later,' said Peter. 'When I began to spy Inspector Sugg was in full cry, and Sergeant Parker was bringing in his witnesses one by one. He had the indomitable Sarah, Lady Attenbury's personal maid, in front of him. I was hampered by being able to see rather little, but I heard him summing up her evidence to her, and offering her a statement to sign. There was only one key to the safe in Lady Attenbury's room. She, Sarah, was entrusted with it, and never let it out of her sight. Last night when Jeannette came to fetch the jewels for Charlotte, she had opened the safe herself, and given Jeannette the box, exactly as it had come from the bank.

'Had she personally opened the box and seen for herself that everything was in order?

'Yes, naturally.

'And she trusted Jeannette?

' "The servants here are one family," she had told Sugg. "We work together and we look after each other. Jeannette is in a position of trust here, and I have seen nothing in her time with us to make me doubt the propriety of that."

' "Now," said Sugg to her, "when the alarm was raised about the missing jewel you first instituted a search, and then adopted a ruse—the wearing of the paste replica—which delayed by some perhaps crucial minutes the commencement of the police enquiry. Why did you not immediately inform the police? What were you covering up? Who were you protecting?"

'When this met with no answer, he went on: "You say that Miss Jeannette Mondur is trustworthy. Would it surprise you to know that she has a clandestine lover who she meets on her afternoons off?"

'At this Sarah lost her composure. "No, it would not surprise me!" she exclaimed. "I and everybody else in the servants' hall know all about it. I expect the family does too. Clandestine? It is nothing of the sort! And it is not against our terms of employment here."

' "All right, all right, my good woman, keep your hair on," said Sugg. "I ask you again—why all that diversionary business with the false jewels? And why did you delay in informing the police? It is not clear to me that you would have informed the police at all had not raised voices and a commotion drawn attention to what was going on."

' "I assumed that the missing gem was just that— missing," said Sarah. "I knew all too well the scandal and disturbance that would arise if there was a hue and cry after it during dinner last night when the house was full of guests. I thought the delay would allow us time to find the jewel. I was mistaken, that is all."

' "So you put your supposed loyalty to the family ahead of your duty to assist the police?"

' "I did, and I do," she said coldly. "Lady Attenbury has favoured me with a lifetime of kindness, and I put her interests before those of anyone else, myself included."

' "Oh, do you?" said he. "Well, your room will be searched. What have you to say to that?"

' "You will no doubt do your duty, Inspector, as I shall do mine," she told him. "May I go now? I have work to do."

' "Hoighty-toighty," said Sugg. "Off with you, then. Parker, fetch me this Jeannette woman."

'I was pretty horrified at the tone of all this. Sergeant Parker was too. He actually suggested to Sugg that a gentler approach might elicit more information.

' "I know how to deal with people like these, Parker," said Sugg. And he proceeded to deal in the same inimitable fashion with Jeannette.

'She told him simply that when Sarah had given her the box, she had taken it along to Lady Charlotte's room, and laid out the entire parure on the stand. She had laid Lady Charlotte's dress on the bed, and her shoes ready on the floor. Then she had left, to wait for the bell. Lady Charlotte was late coming upstairs to dress. When she did ring for Jeannette it was in distress, to ask what had been done with the central stone in the array. Jeannette saw at once that it was not where she had left it. She had no idea what had happened to it.

'Well, Sugg weighed in very heavily. He told Jeannette that nobody would believe her. She was the person who had seen the jewel last, she was the person with the best opportunity to steal it. Her room would be searched, and she was as of this minute under arrest. Jeannette was immediately in tears, and crying, "But I didn't do it, monsieur! I didn't do it! I shall lose my job, and never get another one!"

'Parker said, "Sir, wouldn't it be better to postpone arresting anyone until we have taken statements from everybody in the house?"

' "Why so, Sergeant? It must have been one of the servants, and this girl is the obvious suspect. We might be able to avoid annoying the high and mighty ones. The Chief Constable himself asked me to tread carefully, after all."

' "But we need above all, sir, to recover the jewel. And it seems it was laid out for anyone to see, in Lady Charlotte's room, behind an unlocked door for the best part of an hour. That is right, isn't it, Miss Mondur?"

' "Yes, it is, sir," she said.

' "And who was in the habit of trampling through Lady Charlotte's bedroom?" asked Sugg sardonically. "Apart from yourself, that is?"

' "The chambermaids keep the room clean, and the footman makes up the fire. And the family. Nobody else."

' "Between the time when you put the jewels out ready and the time when Lady Charlotte went up to dress, did you actually see anyone enter her room?" asked Sugg.

' "No, monsieur. I had retired to the servants' sitting-room to wait for the bell."

' "Shouldn't you have been dressing the girl?" asked Sugg.

' "Lady Charlotte likes to dress herself. I help her just with her hair, and the finishing touches."

' "Hmph," said Sugg. "Off you go now. And don't make any attempt to leave the house, or communicate with anyone outside, or it will be the worse for you."

'As she left, he said to Parker, "Search all the servants' rooms, starting with hers!" '

5

'I'm afraid this is awfully Ancient Mariner, Harriet. I shall cut the tale short. Nothing was found in any of the servants' rooms. But ransacking their rooms left the entire household below stairs resentful, wouldn't you say, Bunter?'

'Resentful and triumphant, my lord. There was much talk about the respectable nature of people in service, and the not so respectable affairs of some of their supposed betters above stairs. I felt as much myself, my lady. I was enraged by one of Sugg's men who insisted on searching for the emerald by opening the back of my camera and ruining the half-exposed spool of film. To make it still worse he put a huge thumb-print on the lens while doing so.'

'Well, what then?' continued Peter. 'Nothing for it but to start interviewing the guests. Sugg's manner of doing so was cringe-makingly respectful, peppered with sirs and madams and my lords and my ladies, and met with outraged indignation, suppressed with difficulty for the sake of Attenbury, who had asked them to help the police. In the end they realised that if they ever wanted to be allowed to go home, cooperation was the only policy.'

'And were you crouched on a pile of sheets eavesdropping all this time, Peter? Weren't you missed from the company?'

'Yes, I was, almost all the time, and no, I wasn't missed as far as I know. As the ineffable Mrs DuBerris had made clear to me they all thought of me as a queer fish. Poor Peter, war's done for his nerves . . . good cover, in fact. The servants all knew where I was, of course, because the chambermaids came in and out for clean linens. They seemed very happy to discover a conspiracy against Inspector Sugg. I had a worse fright when Lady Attenbury herself arrived, overseeing something domestic, I assumed, although perhaps a maid had alerted her. My brother Gerald was huffing and puffing below, perfectly willing to say where he had been between five and seven, and naming half the company as witnesses, and furiously refusing to say where he had been all night. Sugg was after discovering not only who had had a chance to lift the emerald, but where they might have had a chance of concealing it before the hue and cry was raised in the morning. Who was where overnight was proving very interesting. I could have made a fortune by selling the dirt to that news-hound Salcombe Hardy, except that I hadn't yet met him, and wouldn't have known where to find him.'

'You diverge. What did Lady Attenbury think of finding you *in flagrante*?'

'*Flagrante*? Not much *delicto*, though. She slid the panel shut, and said to me in a low voice, "Have you heard anything useful, Peter?"

' "No," I told her. "I rather doubt if anything useful can come of this."

' "I understand our poor Jeannette has been threatened. If I am any judge of character . . ."

' "I think you might be better at judging character than Inspector Sugg is. Do you mind my poking my nose into all this? Obviously impertinent, you know. Under your roof."

' "Weren't you in intelligence in the war, Peter?"

' "Yes. Rather different sort of thing, though."

' "Do you think our Indian visitor might have anything to do with this?"

' "It's odd, certainly. I hate coincidence, it demolishes rational causation." '

'That's interesting,' said Harriet. 'You can't have coincidences in detective stories, either. Readers simply can't accept them. Though in real life they do keep happening.'

'And this was real life,' said Peter. 'I told Lady Attenbury that I didn't see how Nandine Osmanthus could have had a hand in it. She and I both had seen the gem back in the box. I admitted to having been watching Osmanthus carefully. Mr Whitehead had been sitting there watching too. She nodded.

' "I shall regard you as a son of the house in this matter, Peter," she said. And then perhaps because she had betrayed herself just a little she added, "It isn't really Roland's sort of thing, I think."

' "You are about to have reinforcements in the son department," I said to her. "A new son-in-law."

'She moved away and turned her back to me, looking out of a small window. She made no comment about Northerby's intelligence, but she said, "He has a kind heart, I think. I have seen him walking in the garden with Mrs DuBerris, and playing with little Ada, when Charlotte has been busy with something or other. None of our other guests has paid her the least attention, and they don't have the cause she has given you, Peter, for keeping clear of her."

'Then she turned back into the room, reached past me, and very quietly opened the panel again. She smiled at me and left. Silent permission to sleuth. Changed my life, now I come to think of it. All down to Claire Attenbury.

'She had opened the panel further than I had had it before—I could now see quite well. I was looking over Sugg's head and facing the witnesses sitting opposite him. Their voices rose up to me. When I resumed spying my sister-in-law was asserting with icy fury that Gerald had been with her all night. Poor Helen; how was she to know that Gerald had just been confessing to a midnight ramble in search of a bite to eat?

'He wasn't the only one, of course. Northerby and I were about the only fellows present who slept well all night, or who at least didn't open their doors and prowl the corridors.'

'After a full formal dinner, Peter? Can everyone have been hungry?'

'Oh, not at all. Merely rearranging themselves in the bedrooms. But what can you tell a policeman? Hardly that you have been sleeping with another man's wife, with that man's connivance and consent. Chivalry obliges you to lie. Anyway, the long and the short of all this was that everybody with rooms on the main corridor had an alibi that could be corroborated if they were prepared to tell the truth. And the truth thus told would have ruined reputations and set the London beau monde ablaze with scandal. Sugg had put a policeman in the broom cupboard, who had watched all the coming and going and written it down. Attenbury's party was turning into a general catastrophe.

'But Sugg wasn't much further forward. Because the crucial time was not overnight, when the thief might have hidden his pelf, but the hour before dinner when he might have taken it. And during that time everybody had been milling about in the public rooms downstairs, and alibis and corroborations were thick as autumnal leaves that lie in Vallombrosa. But just before the gathering for dinner every single guest had returned to their rooms to dress. There had been coming and going all along the corridor, and then throngs of people descending the main stairs. But the copper in the broom cupboard had reported seeing nobody enter Lady Charlotte's room between the time Jeannette came with the jewel box, and left again, and the time Lady Charlotte came up to dress. Impasse! Sugg proceeded to have all the luggage returned to the bedrooms and searched. Indignation and discomfiture on every side.'

'And nothing was found?' asked Harriet.

'No missing emerald appeared. Plenty of nice jewellery, but not the dark, mysterious Mughal stone.'

'What then?'

'I had a stroke of luck. I was tired of being cooped up with the linens, and sickened, rather, at the stuff I was hearing. I had a sudden fit of nausea. I left Bunter doing the dirty work, and went for a walk. Well, only a prowl, really. Nobody was allowed into the open air. I made for the conservatory, where at least there was sunshine showing through, and some greenery. Right at the far end of the thing—it was massive on account of Lady Attenbury's passion for plants—there was a wrought-iron bench among the tendrils of a vine, and I sat down and stretched my legs. Hadn't been there a minute when little Ottalie came up to me, and stood in front of me.

' "Are you a lord?" she asked.

' "Fraid so," said I.

' "So what do I call you?" she asked.

' "I'm also a family friend," I told her. "You call me Peter."

' "Uncle Peter?"

' "Just Peter."

' "I want to ask you something, Peter."

' "Fire away."

' "If that emerald came back, would all the horribleness go away?"

'I considered my position. The easy thing would have been to say yes—but I have never been any good with children. I just deal with them as though they were adults. Sheer ignorance. So what I actually said was, "It depends, Ottalie, on how it 'came back', as you put it. If you know anything about it, you ought to tell, even if it makes the horribleness worse for a bit."

' "Do you think Charlotte would stop crying?" she asked.

' "She might," I said cautiously. "But it isn't Charlotte who is in the worst trouble, is it? It's probably Jeannette."

' "Jeannette didn't take it," said Ottalie decisively.

' "How do you know that?"

' "Because she made me put it back," she said.

' "*Put it back?* When and why, Ottalie?"

' "Well, my friend Ada and I were in the nursery playing being at court," said Ottalie, sitting down beside me. "We were all dressed up, and it was still ages before we could go down and watch the grown-ups. So I went to see if Charlotte was back in her room yet, and then I just borrowed the emeralds. I wanted to show Ada how you could turn them into a tiara. And I put them on, and posed in the mirror. So then Ada wanted a turn."

' "I can see that she would have done," said I.

' "So I went and borrowed the other ones, so that Ada could wear some too."

' "The other ones?"

' "The paste ones. Mummy keeps them in her boudoir. She wears them sometimes. We borrowed those. It was only going to be for a minute . . . I suppose we lost track of the time. We were pretending to pose for the court photographer. I was using Mummy's ivory fan, and Ada had her ostrich feathers."

' "So then what?"

' "Jeannette found us. She was very angry.

People were already coming up to dress for dinner. We put the king-stones back the right way up, and I ran and put the necklace back in Charlotte's room. And it was all right because Charlotte still hadn't come up. But if Jeannette was a thief why would she have made me put it back?"

' "So where is the other necklace now?" I asked, privately noting that Jeannette had protected the children when giving her evidence to Sugg.

' "Jeannette put it back in Mummy's room."

' "Let's go and look at it. I'll come with you," I said.'

Harriet was looking at him quizzically. 'Peter, do you mean to say that in this famous first case you didn't have to do any detecting at all, just listen to a pretty little girl?'

'Aha!' said Peter. 'Not so fast, Harriet. I went and found Lady Attenbury's maid, and we fetched out the other necklace, the paste one, from her jewel box. This was what Charlotte had worn. Sarah opened her mistress's jewel drawer for us, with a sort of grim triumph about her—that policeman was going to be wrong-footed—and there indeed was a gorgeous emerald rivière, with a big dark stone in the middle. No mistaking it for paste, close up. But my rapture was very rapidly moderated, because with it wasn't the real king-stone—no inscription on the back.'

'Gosh, Peter, what then?'

'Well, it shifted the game completely. Those

naughty children and the panicked maid had mixed up the things; they must have put the real king-stone on the paste necklace, and put that in Charlotte's room. But since during the hour before the dinner gong the jewels had all been in the nursery, which was along a bit and up one floor, everybody had answered the wrong questions about their whereabouts.'

'Is that what made Sugg so angry with you? That you told him his whole enquiry was off beam?'

'No; because that's not what I did. I made very sure that when they scampered to return the jewels there had been two king-stones. They were certain of that. They were also mistakenly sure they had put everything back exactly as they found things. I swore young Ottalie and Jeannette to secrecy. I told them I was a secret agent and they could leave the whole thing to me, but everything depended on nobody getting to know what we three now knew.

'Having got that far I went to look for Charles. Sergeant Parker, as I then knew him. I gathered he was off-duty.

'I found Charles in a tiny room assigned to a lowly sergeant in the hierarchy of a grand household, up in the attics. He was sitting in an armchair, reading Origen. I admit, Harriet, I was surprised. The Church Fathers didn't strike me as the expected reading material for young policemen. I was even more surprised when he looked up as I entered his room—he had called

"Come in!" to my knock—and put the book down on the bed. It didn't have the Attenbury library binding. It was his own copy. He moved to sit on the bed, and gestured me to sit in the chair.

' "What can I do for you, Lord Peter?" he said.

' "Purification by fire," said I, nodding at his book. "Makes the difference between heaven and hell almost notional, seems to me."

'Charles said cautiously, "I would not have expected an English lord to be interested in theology."

' "The English lord in question would not have expected a policeman to be reading the Fathers. But it's jolly encouraging, Sergeant Parker, because what I've come to talk to you about is a moral dilemma. Can I put it to you?"

' "I'm off duty for a couple of hours while Inspector Sugg chews the cud," said Charles. "So you may put something to me, if you like. But even an off-duty policeman is a policeman, remember, my lord."

' "The thing is, I can guess where that emerald is. I think it could be returned to its rightful place, on the quiet. And that would be my duty to my old friend Lord Attenbury. We could just 'find' the thing, and send Sugg and co packing, and have a quiet word with somebody, and that would be that."

'But, Peter!' said Harriet indignantly, 'the real king-stone was gone and you *didn't* know where it was!'

'I was guessing, I admit. Put it down to irresponsible youth. But also remember that nobody in the family actually liked the king-stone . . . no, that's a red herring. Anyway, Charles thought about it.

' "In your position, that is probably what I would do, Lord Peter," he said. "But if you were easy in your mind about it, and certain that that is what you want to do, you would not be talking to me about it. And since you are talking to me, I must tell you that I think such a course of action would be deeply immoral."

' "Deeply immoral? That's going it a bit, isn't it?"

' "Let me put this to you. If you recover the jewels without incriminating the thief, do you think the person in question might do it again? If they could continue to be the trusted guest or servant of wealthy people, whose trinkets are worth several years' wages for ordinary people? Another thing: if you recover the loot by stealth in this way where does that leave the current suspect? Could the girl ever clear her name?"

' "Lady Attenbury trusts her," I said.

' "And what of her standing among the below-stairs people of whom she is one? Will everyone here trust her, once she has been accused?"

'That left me thinking. I said, "If I went to Lord Attenbury and asked him if he wanted his property back with no scandal and no fuss, or if he wanted the thief caught and exposed, I know what he would say."

' "I imagine you do," said Charles icily.

' "Oh, come, Sergeant, give a fellow a break," I said. "You must see I'm in a quandary."

' "But, my lord, you put me in a quandary too," Parker said. "Now that I know that you know something relevant to our enquiries, I ought to interview you, to subpoena you if necessary, to make sure that you divulge what you know to Inspector Sugg."

' "The devil you ought!" I said. "But you see I have acquired a strong dislike of Inspector Sugg."

'Charles said, "I do not see how you could have reasonable grounds for that opinion, my lord."

' "He bullies his witnesses," I said.

'Charles said quietly, "How could you know that?"

'Now I'd put a cat among the pigeons. Charles and I just sat staring at each other. I contemplated simply lying to him, simply telling him that the servants had been talking afterwards about their ordeal in the Suggery, and that my trusted manservant had conveyed to me . . . I don't know what Charles was thinking.'

'Well, you had put him in a difficulty, Peter. His duty was to Sugg. And he didn't know you from Adam. Why should he risk his career by trusting you?'

'Why indeed? But after we had been eye-balling each other for some time, that is what he decided to do, all the same.

' "Eavesdropping, Lord Peter?" he said at last.

'I was quiet—just thinking about what to say.

' "I can easily find your spy-hole, my lord," he said.

'I said, "It's dashed uncomfortable balanced on a pile of sheets. I wouldn't need to do it if I could see the witness statements."

' "That would be against every possible police procedural rule," he said.

' "But might have advantages," said I.

' "What would those be, my lord?" he asked.

' "Well, I'm an insider in the world you are investigating. I know how these chaps and their ladies live; I know how they think. I might be able to help."

' "So you might. But who would you be helping? You might dish the police enquiry to protect your friends. You have just told me you are tempted to do that."

' "And you just convinced me that that would be an immoral thing to do."

'Stalemate. I knew just how two dogs feel when they are walking round each other in the park.

' "I don't think I'll feel very pally about whoever pinched the thing," I said. "Let's flush him out together, or her, of course, and I'll gladly expose the wretch to the law and the press." '

'I imagine Charles was just as worried that if he helped you detect, you might shop him,' said Harriet.

'I'll bet he was,' said Peter. 'But I said, "Look here, Sergeant Parker, I'm really bothered that your superior officer may be going to pin the thing on the wrong person."

'He didn't actually say, "So am I," but his face said it as clearly as a subtitle in a French film.

'So then I gave a dog a bone. I said, "Look, I happen to know that those jewels weren't where everyone thinks they were at the time Inspector Sugg is asking about. Sugg put one of your colleagues watching Lady Charlotte's room, but someone—I'd rather not say who at the moment—fetched them out of there for a crucial forty minutes in the hour before dinner. Sugg is staking out the wrong territory."

' "Are you telling me that Constable Johnson fell asleep? How could the emerald be taken somewhere else without his seeing and reporting it?"

'No, no, I've got nothing against Constable Johnson. He has an excuse. But the crucial thing is that during most of the hour before dinner the place we should be thinking about isn't the main corridor, but the one above; the western end. So all the witnesses have been asked about their proximity to the wrong place. Or if you like, the wrong time. There were only a few minutes between the return of the emeralds to Lady Charlotte's room, and the sounding of the dinner gong. By which time nearly all the guests were already milling about downstairs in their glad rags."

'But I take it,' said Charles, 'that this private information does not enable you to lay your hands on the missing jewel?"

' "Fraid not. It really has been taken."

' "And where was it in the hour between five and six?"

' "In Miss Ottalie's nursery."

'Charles chewed that over a bit, and then he said, "But if that is the case, Lord Peter, of what possible interest to you can the witness statements be that we have already taken? As you say, they contain answers to the wrong questions."

' "It was any that are still to be taken that I was hoping to see," I said.

'Charles said, "The most I can do for you, Lord Peter, is to continue to talk to you as we are doing now, privately and in my time off. And in doing even that I am taking a risk, as I am sure you realise."

' "Thank you," I said. The man had put himself in my hands. I appreciated that. "But the first thing you will have to do is convince Sugg that the damn thing had wandered, and that he must not interview—"

' "The little girl?"

' "She must on no account be bullied."

' "Indeed not," said Charles. "We shall have to have the maidservant bullied instead."

'That was his first indiscretion, Harriet. It let me see that he agreed with me about Sugg.

'Well, I took myself off, and a few minutes later I had a visit from Constable Johnson, knocking discreetly on my door. Sent along by Charles, of course. And I asked him if he remembered seeing Ottalie running about. He did. She was with the tiny girl, Ada. Of course he hadn't taken any notice of them, being doggedly fixed on seeing potential thieves. He turned out to be a sharp enough young man. The moment he realised that Ottalie came into the picture he was remorseful for not having noted her down in his book, and was racking his brains to help me. He had seen Ottalie running along the corridor, and entering her sister's room. She had left again almost at once, and he had not written it down. Then a crowd of people had come up the stairs—Captain Ansel, Mrs Ansel, Honourable Freddy, Mrs Sylvester-Quicke—and passed along to their rooms in a burst of conversation. Then Mr Northerby had come up the stairs with Lady Charlotte, and seen her to the door of her room. For a brief moment they had stepped inside, and partly closed the door—the constable assumed they had been kissing. Then Charlotte had opened her door, and walked briskly along the corridor to the foot of the stairs, where she called, "Ottalie, are you there? Do you want to see me dress, or not?" Mr Northerby said, "See you in a minute," and entered his own room. Charlotte returned to her room without seeing Ottalie, and the hue and cry among the servants was raised almost as soon as she had closed her door. He could give me an exact time when Charlotte came up: five forty-five. That was all he could tell me. But it was enough.'

'It didn't tell you where the king-stone was.'

'Well, by now, Harriet, I was full of dire suspicion. I expect you are too, at this stage in the story.'

'Such suspicions as I have, Peter—and remember all this is shadowy compared to having been there, and seen and known the participants— are subject to a profound sense of puzzlement about motive.'

'Ah, motive. You know I don't believe in that.'

'You don't think people have motives for their evil deeds?'

'Or for their good ones. Of course they do. I just don't think they have reasonable, thought-out motives that a rational person could deduce and base a line of detecting on. Or, no: you provoke me, Harriet, into overstating my case. I don't think people always have rational motives. Of course, sometimes they do, I'll grant that.'

'Thank you, my lord,' said Harriet drily.

'But if you are asking about motive, then you have penetrated deeper into all this than I supposed you could from my fancy story-telling. I imagine you are going to ask me why someone should steal something that is about to be theirs anyway.'

'Naturally one wonders that. It seems so stupid a thing to do that one wonders if one is mistaken in one's suspicions.'

'All will become clear. Unless, that is, you have had enough, and wish to go about your day as planned. I think it has stopped raining. It is positively sunning. Would you like to walk in the park with me? I am well able to narrate while perambulating.'

'Good idea,' said Harriet. 'Just let me get a coat on.'

But Bunter was already bringing their coats over his arm, and holding scarves and hats at the ready.

6

The Serpentine made a pleasant sight for walkers. It was now a bright, rain-washed late spring afternoon, but still sharply cold. Harriet and Peter, strolling arm in arm, looked, it must be said, just like the sort of Londoners who figure in tourist posters. Harriet was wearing her fur coat, and a Liberty silk scarf, and a pair of two-tone brogues, and Peter still wore a hat out of doors, a practice that was becoming steadily less common. They looked both smart and old-fashioned in the world of the Festival of Britain, which they had resolved to visit as soon as it opened. When they reached the pleasant path along the bank of the lake, Harriet said, 'Tell on, tell on.'

'The next thing was Sugg's great *coup de théâtre*. He stopped me on the stairs as I came down to dinner.

' "I understand, Lord Wimsey, that you have been taking a particular interest in this case," he said.

' "Who told you that?" I asked. I hoped it wasn't Charles—Sergeant Parker I should call him. "I can't help keeping an eye on things, Inspector," said I. "I was an intelligence officer. It comes with the rations."

' "War's over now, in case you haven't noticed, sir," he said. "However, it does no harm to humour a young gentleman. I have solved the case. Lord Attenbury's guests are free to leave. I'm just on my way to tell him so."

' "Have you recovered the jewel?"

' "Not yet, sir. But we have a warrant for the arrest of the thief and the search of his premises. I have no doubt the recovery of the jewel will follow. The key to the whole thing"—he was preening himself, Harriet, positively preening—"was finding the link between the thief and his inside conspirator. I have arrested *her*. This was a clever plan, Lord Wimsey, laid well in advance."

' "You have arrested Jeannette?" I said, with a sinking heart.

' "And even as we speak," he said, "officers from the Yard are seeking to apprehend Mr Osmanthus, in whose possession the missing jewel will be found. You didn't think of that, did you? I think you will find, with age and experience, Lord Wimsey, that the appropriate training for the job in hand has a lot to be said for it."'

'You are making this up, Peter!' exclaimed Harriet.

'By our first strange and fatal interview,' he said, 'By all desires which thereof did ensue, By our long starving hopes, etc., etc., I swear I am not.'

'Can he really have been so patronising? How he must squirm at your later successes!'

'I have wondered whether just this very thing is the source of his ill-disguised dislike of me.'

'We can forgive those who injure us, but we never forgive those we have injured?'

'He didn't exactly injure me. Annoy would be a better translation.'

'Well, so Inspector Sugg arrested poor Jeannette, and, I take it, Nandine Osmanthus?' asked Harriet as they stopped to admire a patch of pale blue wood anemones, spreading across the grass like a skylit puddle. 'Did he have a shadow of a reason?'

'He had made a great discovery, which linked the two: the man known to desire the king-stone, and the person who had had the best opportunity to take it. Jeannette it was, and none other than she who had taken Osmanthus his lunch in the little sitting-room.'

'So?'

'So she had an opportunity to conspire with him. Perhaps she had taken the job with the Attenburys specially to await this chance, and indeed had been the one to summon Osmanthus to verify the authenticity of the stone. What do you think of that?'

'I feel a certain shame. If Sugg found it easier to suspect a servant and a foreigner than any member of an upper-class house-party . . .'

'There is no need for either of us to feel implicated in the *bêtise* of Inspector Sugg.'

'But I do so feel, somewhat. I must have read dozen upon dozen detective stories in which the writer evinces such prejudices, and, worse, assumes them in the reader.'

'Popular fiction is of its time. And don't you think, Harriet, that that time is past, or rather passing? I think I can feel the social weather changing as we speak.'

Harriet mused. If Peter was right about that, she thought, the coming world might be hard on him.

'It will be hard on my brother the Duke,' said Peter, as though her thought had been spoken. 'He is already falling into difficulties trying to look after that great house. I'm tired of these anemones; shall we walk on?'

'When you are ready to complete the tale of the Attenbury emeralds . . .'

'By all means. Your powers of endurance are astonishing. Of course Sugg's case collapsed, but with a suddenness and completeness that took our breath away—Bunter's and mine, I mean.

Attenbury's house-party dissolved at once, leaving, I must say, plenty of wrack behind. But everyone dispersed.

'Arresting Osmanthus was a cardinal error. The jewel had not gone missing till after five o'clock at the earliest; Lady Attenbury's maid had taken it from the banker's box and given it to Jeannette at five, and she was unshakeably certain of it. And at the time she did that Osmanthus was on his way back to London, and, it turned out, in company with none other than Mr Whitehead, who had taken the same train, and got so pally with Osmanthus that he provided an indignant alibi. And no emerald of any kind, nor any other jewel than a diamond-studded fountain pen was found in Osmanthus's quarters at the Oriental Club.'

'What about Osmanthus's own king-stone? The Maharaja's, I mean?'

'What indeed? My best guess was that Osmanthus got to hear of the uproar at Fennybrook Hall, and saw at once there was a danger of his own stone being impounded, and got it safely stowed somewhere.'

'Did you take leave of Charles?'

'I'm afraid I didn't linger. Being forbidden to leave somewhere makes it a terrible ordeal to stay there, even if, left to oneself, one would choose to stay and one was having a jolly time. Bunter and I packed up and bolted back to Piccadilly as if the devil were after me.'

'Poor Bunter,' said Harriet with feeling.

'I simply can't imagine why everyone is so censorious about my driving,' said Peter. 'I have never had an accident . . .'

Harriet shuddered at various vivid recollections from the passenger seat, and said nothing. Peter patted the back of her hand where it rested on his forearm, as if he could sympathise. The two walked on in companionable silence for a while. They reached Hyde Park Corner. Peter said, 'Would you like tea at the Ritz? Just because I married you shouldn't put an end to flamboyant assignations.'

'Will there be real Darjeeling tea?' asked Harriet.

'Certainly there will. The world has not yet gone to hell in a handcart. And delectably thin cucumber sandwiches. Do say yes, Harriet, I'm freezing in the open air. Be like Great Anna whom three realms obey.'

'Gladly, my lord,' said Harriet.

'I always think I have been behaving somehow ridiculously when you call me that, my lady,' said Peter.

They ordered tea with cucumber sandwiches, and maids of honour, and settled comfortably at a corner table with a glimpse across the terrace to the trees of the park.

'It almost seems as though the war never happened, here,' said Harriet. 'It's a good place to tell me fairy stories about the world before.'

'Before the war?'

'Before I met you.'

'Where was I?'

'You had unmannerly departed without taking leave of the then Sergeant Parker.'

'I asked him to lunch with me the following week. To talk about Athanasius, you understand. But I learned from him that the person who had shopped me to Inspector Sugg was the wretched girl Jeannette. She had warned him when he tried a second time to bully her into confessing that every word he said was being overheard by his betters. He had the linen room locked immediately, though too late.'

'So Charles kept quiet about you. I'm glad. What happened to Jeannette?'

'Attenbury bailed her on his surety. And my mother found her a job with an elderly cousin, in need of companionship. One of Uncle Paul's many ramificating relations. And in France. Out of the way of English spite.'

'What about her young man?'

'Joined her in France. Don't know how they fared in the war. Must ask my mother. She'll know.'

'So have you been pals with Charles ever since?'

'Pretty much. It was very occasional at first. Then as I got involved in more cases, and he got involved with my sister it took off to the heights at which you see it now.'

'Before we get to more cases, I surmise that there must be more to the famous first one you are telling me about. Because your account so far makes it fall rather short of the sort of thing that makes a man renowned as an apprehender of jewel thieves.'

'Sorry. Lack of refined narrative skills, I fear. Before I left Fennybrook, I told Claire Attenbury that the "paste" necklace in her jewel box was actually the real one. But, alas, the king-stone that had gone missing was also the real one. I have to say that those Attenburys were very offhand about the whole thing. None of them actually liked the king-stone much. The rivière could always be sent to Cartier's and adapted to be worn without it. It was still a spectacular showy thing. And there was insurance money; made me quite cross with them.'

'You wanted to know who had taken it? To be certain. To have cleared it up.'

'Of course. And then a strange thing happened. One evening, about, I suppose, five weeks after the house-party, when everyone but me had stopped worrying about it, I imagine, except poor Sugg whose superiors had presumably given him a flea in his ear, Bunter came up to me in the library, and presented me with a card from Mr Nandine Osmanthus. Might he take up a few minutes of my valuable time? Of course I had him shown up.

'Bunter fetched drinks, but Osmanthus demurred at speaking with Bunter present. He would be grateful for a word with me *privately*. Well, I don't like Bunter left in the dark. It seems to me to be uncivil to imply that a fellow's manservant might not be discreet. We had an arrangement, Bunter and I, in which on a nod from me he would withdraw, and then stand behind the section of the bookcase which was a disguised door through to the drawing-room. He could hear every word from there, and it was useful when I wanted his pin-sharp memory. He was as good as a secretary taking dictation without having to write it down.

'So when the visitor had a drink in his hand and had settled in the best armchair, I gave Bunter the nod. And Osmanthus embarked on his errand. A lot of pleasantries first—wonderful flat, fine show of books, glad to see a good piano—that sort of thing. Take that as read.

'I offered him sympathy over his having been arrested, and on having his premises searched, and hoped it had not been too unpleasant an experience.

' "These things happen," he said, shrugging his shoulders.

' "And Inspector Sugg's men did not find your own jewel and mistake it for the stolen one? I was afraid that might happen."

' "The Maharaja's jewel is in a place of safety," he said.

'I said I was glad of that.

'Then he said, "I had an unexpected visitor

yesterday, Lord Peter. And what he told me has worried me very much. Oh, yes indeed. The short and the long is that I don't know what is to be done. I would like your advice."

' "My advice is free and freely given, old chap," I said, in what I hoped was an encouraging tone.

' "You see, Lord Peter, although I am used to mixing with the highest class of people in my own country, I am not intimately acquainted with the way things are done in English aristocratic families. Not at all. So you see, I am at sea, afraid to put my foot in it as they say. But—" and here he raised his voice, and slapped the arm of his chair emphatically with the hand not holding his port— "it does not seem right to me! That poor young lady!"

' "What poor young lady?" I asked him.

' "The young Lady Charlotte, of course," he said, sounding surprised.

' "Start at the beginning, won't you, Mr Osmanthus," I said. "Who was the visitor who perturbed you so?"

' "It was Mr Reginald Northerby," he said.

' "Aha," said I. "And what did that gentleman want with you, Mr Osmanthus?"

' "He wanted to sell me the king-stone from the Attenbury emeralds!" said Osmanthus.

' "Did he though? And what did you reply to him?"

' "I told him that my master, the Maharaja, wished to acquire not merely the stone itself, but good title to it. He would have nothing to do with trafficking in stolen goods. Not at all; not in any way at all. But, Lord Peter, Mr Northerby replied to me that the stone had not been stolen. It would be his to dispose of as soon as his marriage to Lady Charlotte took place, and he merely wanted to advance by a few weeks the transaction. The stone would be handed over in exchange for a cash-down deposit of a fraction of its value—should we say one-third of the money? The rest to be paid when the sale could be completed. There was a condition however. That was that the arrangement between us must be secret, and must remain so. Any leak of information would result in the sale being aborted, and the stone would then be put beyond our reach. In short, he would make sure that the Maharaja never acquired it.

' "Lord Peter, I was thunderstruck!"

'I was pretty thunderstruck myself.

' "Lord Peter, what am I to do?" he asked me.

' "He gave you to understand that he had the stone?"

' "It was in his pocket, Lord Peter. He showed it to me."

' "I take it you sent him packing?"

' "Oh, yes indeed!"

' "I don't quite see what the problem is. Are you asking me if you should go to the police?"

' "I could go to the police. Then the stone would be returned into the hands of a family who have

96

said they would never sell it to my master. Or I could sit on my hands, as you say, and wait for the marriage to take place, and then attempt to buy the stone. From the new owner. I take it that after the marriage Mr Northerby would be the owner?"

' "I think the emeralds are heirlooms, Mr Osmanthus. Lady Charlotte would still be the owner."

' "But young brides will do what their husbands tell them? As in my country they would . . ."

' "Hmm," I said. "An English woman might not be reliably subservient. But in the early months of a marriage, perhaps . . ." I was thinking aloud.

' "I have come to ask you, Lord Peter, if you think I should tell Lord Attenbury who has got the jewel. Or do you think I should keep quiet while the young lady marries a thief? If I had not been strictly instructed to play above board in every way, I could of course arrange for the jewel to be taken from him by a cut-throat in a back alley. But the matter of the young lady's future happiness and honour would be unresolved."

' "Why are you telling me all this?" I asked. "Since it imperils your chance of buying the jewel from Northerby."

' "There is the young lady to consider. I would like to leave it in your hands," he said. "It is very clear you are a trusted friend of the Attenbury family. You will have the ears of his lordship. You will know best what to do."

'"Thank you," I said. "I will think about it."

'It was tricky one, Harriet. If he went to the police with his story, it would be bound to involve unpleasantness for the family. And I rather agreed with him about young Charlotte marrying a thief. I thanked him for being concerned about Charlotte's honour; and I suggested that he leave Mr Northerby to me. Would you like more tea, or shall we potter off home?'

'I've had enough tea, thank you, Peter. Can we go home via Hatchard's? There's a book I'd like to find.'

'Certainly,' said Peter. 'Who am I to come between an author and a book?'

They wandered along Piccadilly together, and as they went they talked of other things.

7

Harriet took up the subject again as they drank sherry before dinner. 'So what *did* you do about the dishonest Mr Northerby?' she asked Peter.

'I thought a good deal about Sergeant Parker's view of things. And I came to the conclusion, very reluctantly, I am ashamed to remember how reluctantly, Harriet, that I had a bounden duty to tell the police if I knew the whereabouts of stolen goods.'

'Why were you so reluctant?'

'Well, for a start I had come to feel very wary of

Mr Osmanthus. It was touching, and all that, that he should be so concerned about Charlotte's welfare, considering that as far as I knew he had never met her. Of course, I could read his message. People of his class, he was letting me know, would stick up for the reputation of people of class anywhere. And the assumption was that I would do the same. Lord Attenbury's interests would be my main concern; any interest in the wider scene, like the need of society for justice, would be secondary. I would, as he would, wish to preserve Charlotte from marriage to a rogue, but also to preserve her from the shame of having been engaged to a rogue. He expected me to have a quiet word with Northerby, and get the jewel back, and hush everything up. As Charles had so pertinently asked me, whose interests would I act in?'

'Well, Peter?'

'I'm afraid I didn't do anything for a day or two. Paralysis set in. I think, you know, it was the earliest example of that nausea you know all too well. I love the fun of the chase; I had been feeling top-hole all through the uproar about jewels; I had been feeling pretty triumphant at having worked it out. You know that feeling, Harriet—*this* is what I'm good for, *this* is what I can do! But when it comes to someone trapped and suffering, someone going to prison, or, worst of all, someone hanging, then I feel as sick as I ever felt ordering men out of the trenches and over the top. So you see, I didn't fancy doing what I clearly ought to do. I went all pitiful and shaky and went back to bed.'

'For how long,' said Harriet sternly, 'did you go to bed?'

'Two days. On the first day my mother dropped in to see me, and talked and talked about the Attenbury wedding, and how peaky she thought Charlotte was looking, and how oddly Lady Attenbury was behaving, when she should have been delighted, and how she, my mother, would have been delighted had either of her younger children shown any sign of doing their duty and getting married like everybody else's children, and how Gerald had at least got married, even if his choice of wife was somewhat arguable and as I had the whole world to choose from and needn't be bound by the sort of considerations that obtained for eldest sons, she thought I might have been able to find a jolly chorus girl with a heart of gold to gladden her heart by talking vulgarly at table, and shocking Helen; and how she couldn't understand what the fuss was about a stolen gem when the Attenburys were dripping all over with jewellery, and could spare a rock or two better than any family in London; it was of course distressing to lose a jewel, but they should count themselves lucky, when there were families all over London who hadn't got more than one or two jewels, and who *really* couldn't afford to lose one.'

Harriet laughed. And then a shadow crossed her

face as she thought of her adored mother-in-law, now very old and frail, and able to rattle on for only half the time she used to.

'After a bit of this, I managed to get up and sit by the fire in my dressing-gown, and have a bite of supper brought up to me. And the next day, I would have been in bed, only Freddy just happened to call by.'

'Good for Bunter!' said Harriet.

'Yes, indeed. So I dragged myself into a dressing-gown, and staggered through into the library, and there was Freddy waiting for me, stuffing his face with Bunter's excellent cheese straws.

' "What news on the Rialto?" I said.

' "The usual chatter," he told me. "But one little morsel will have you pricking up your ears, Wimsey, and that's that Northerby seems to be in funds. He's been paying off his debts. One pal of mine has been nearly ill with anxiety because Northerby owes him a chunk of money and he was afraid it wouldn't get repaid in time to get him out of some hot water of his own. He's been leaning on Northerby rather desperately, I understand, without result. Then suddenly last week Northerby showed up at his place and paid him off in cash. Dozens of lovely large crisp white fivers. What do you think of that?"

' "I think of pawnbrokers," I said.

' "He could always have had a little help from his

father in Darjeeling," said Freddy doubtfully. "Although as I hear tell the tea traders are having a rather tight time at the moment. Something to do with the weather in the Himalayan foothills."

' "We don't know a thing about the circumstances of Northerby senior," said I.

' "No. Shouldn't jump to conclusions, I suppose."

' "What's a jumped-to conclusion or two between friends?" I said. "But back to pawnbrokers, Freddy. We would be looking for a specialist, I take it? Or a shady one?"

' "Hmm," said Freddy. "Not quite my field. Never needed the friends at the golden balls myself."

' "Of course not," I said. "Didn't mean to imply . . . Let's ask Bunter."

' "Have you been paying your man so little he might be pawning your silver, Wimsey?"

' "That's a very good idea, Freddy," I said. "I'll take you up on that," and I rang for Bunter.'

Matching word to deeds, Peter rang for Bunter as he spoke.

When Bunter appeared, Peter asked him, 'Bunter, do you remember that game of hunt-the-pawnbroker that we played in the summer of '21?'

'I will never forget it, my lord,' said Bunter.

'Explain to Harriet, will you, while you refill our glasses. And a glass for yourself, Bunter, if you feel inclined.'

Harriet noticed with a twinge of affection for

Bunter that he did not feel inclined. She had long given up trying to convince him to behave informally with them, to understand that the age of iron distinctions between servants and family was over, that the war had obliterated that alongside much else. Bunter was more comfortable maintaining a degree of formality, especially, she noticed, in the drawing-room. If one wanted an intimate chat with Bunter, one went to look for him in the butler's pantry, his own ground.

'Pawnbroking is an arcane business, my lady. It's one kind of business pawning a working man's Sunday clothes every Monday to be redeemed on the following Saturday. It's another thing altogether to be taking in a wealthy man's goods for a high sum. For that the broker would need to be very knowledgeable, not to risk paying out more than the goods were worth. Because a person does not have to redeem his goods. He can walk away with the money in his pocket and never be seen again. There are only a few pawnbrokers in London who would be able to take on goods of very high value. And then again, you see, my lady, if the goods were to turn out to be stolen, the broker would just have lost the stake. It would be repossessed without repaying him. So one would have to be very careful, unless what one had in mind was passing the job over to the underworld immediately.'

'Surely a pawnbroker wouldn't like to be a fence

for some famous jewel like that emerald?' Harriet asked.

'People will take risks for large sums of money,' Peter said.

'There are several ships a day from Harwich to the Hook of Holland, my lady,' said Bunter, 'and many expert gem-cutters in Amsterdam.'

'I had rather thought, if I understood it correctly, that the special virtue of that king-stone was the carving; that it would be reduced to nothing special if it were re-cut.'

'It would be reduced,' said Bunter, 'to a handful of small stones, of very fine quality pure green, each of which would be worth a tidy sum. Each of which would make a fine ring, for instance.'

'I see,' said Harriet. 'So Peter despatched you to find a pawnbroker with a guilty secret.'

'We set a sprat to catch a mackerel,' said Peter. 'I reckoned we needed to find a pawnbroker who was willing to take things of very high value. Someone in a position to lend tidy sums of money—none of your two-and-sixpence-till-Saturday people.'

'Although as it turned out,' said Bunter, 'they were not necessarily two establishments working at different levels, but one and the same, depending on who came in. The high-value merchants were discreetly working behind windows full of boots, suits and gewgaws. But Mr Arbuthnot mentioning silver gave his lordship the idea; we zipped up to Bredon Hall and borrowed a Tudor jewel from the Dowager Duchess.'

Peter added, 'She got very excited, Harriet, because she thought that could only mean a girl in prospect to whom I intended to become engaged; she was so disappointed when we returned the thing a couple of weeks later. By then she had run through everything she knew about me in her mind and concluded that it could only be the Sylvester-Quicke girl. She had practically chosen the wedding dress. I hoped fervently that she had been moonshining by herself, and not in collaboration with Amaranth's mother. Sorry, I digress.'

'The idea, my lady,' said Bunter, returning to the subject, 'was to take something comparably exotic and valuable, and find by the experiment which pawnbrokers would consider it. His lordship drove me round, and waited outside each shop in turn while I tried my luck.'

'Why didn't you do it yourself, Peter?' asked Harriet.

'It would have been potentially legit had it been me in person. Bunter took the family bangle into one place after another, with mixed results.'

'It wasn't a question of being offered very poor value, my lady,' said Bunter, 'but of being turned away empty-handed. Not at all the sort of security they liked to have. But at last someone said it was more the sort of thing that Mr Handley in Isleworth might be interested in. So his lordship drove us to Isleworth.

'Mr Handley was not quite what I would have expected in a pawnbroker. He was an English man of a pallid complexion wearing an expensive suit. He offered me a thousand pounds against the family jewel, remarking as he did so what pleasure it gave him to have the guardianship of such a fine piece, and what a pity it was that the scions of great families couldn't take proper care of their wealth.

'So then I told him that I was not actually wanting to pawn the pendant, but was hoping to find a person who might have been willing to take in pawn something even more spectacular.

' "And what would that be?" he asked me.

' "A dark emerald of a squarish sort of shape."

' "I have put out a fair sum on such a jewel as that," he said. "But what is your interest in it, may I ask?'

'I said it had, in a manner of speaking, gone missing from its proper place. I confessed I had not myself seen the jewel, and begged permission to bring in my friend who was waiting outside to identify it.'

'I introduced myself,' Peter continued. 'Mr Handley was very reluctant to show us his pawn. I had to mention that it would be a pity if the police got involved and arrived with search warrants and the like, because if that happened he would almost certainly lose his money.

'Then he took us into a back room, and left us there for a little while. When he reappeared he was holding a square piece of suede. He put it down on the table and carefully unfolded it to reveal—shall we tell Harriet what was revealed, Bunter, or shall we make her guess?'

'It is a difficult guess, my lord,' said Bunter cautiously.

'Oh, come, Bunter. Surely not beyond the powers of the finest mind in detective fiction?'

To her great annoyance, Harriet felt herself blushing slightly. 'I don't compare with Conan Doyle, or Agatha Christie, or Dorothy Sayers,' she said reproachfully. 'Just for a start. And to prove it I cannot guess what Mr Handley had to show you, unless it was simply the Attenbury jewel. Besides, Peter, what I do is fiction. When faced with a difficulty in writing fiction one has always the option of making it up. The real world is much tougher and more resilient.'

'And surprising?' asked Peter.

'Surprise needs careful handling,' Harriet told him. 'The mighty Aristotle himself told us to prefer a likely impossibility to an unconvincing probability. You will have to tell me.'

'*Two* square emeralds. He showed us two, side by side, at first glance identical.'

'Gracious!' said Harriet. 'So much for Aristotle. Wait; let me guess now—the clever Mr Nandine Osmanthus had pawned his jewel to keep it safely hidden from the police. What did you do?'

'I turned them over. They both had inscriptions

on the back. I was mortified that I couldn't read them.'

' "Were these left with you by one gentleman?" I asked.

' "By two different gentlemen, on separate occasions. Both have promised to return and redeem their property."

' "This a very peculiar thing," I said. "Does either of these two know about your custody of the other man's jewel?"

' "I am afraid so," he said. "I don't like this at all. I am out of my depth here and I should not have got into it. The first gentleman was a fellow of about twenty-five or so. Bargained me up a bit about how much I would advance. The second young gentleman was an Indian of some description. Very well-spoken. But when he showed me his pledge I could not conceal my surprise. Such an unusual jewel—and two like it in a week! The gentleman observed my unguarded reaction, and began to ask me most pressing questions. At last I showed him the other man's pledge."

' "Did he attempt to acquire it?" I asked.

' "I told him in no uncertain terms that the period laid down by law during which the pledge had to remain with me was six months."

' "And he went away content with that?"

' "He extracted from me a promise that I would let him know immediately, within the hour be it day or night, when the other man redeemed his jewel."

' "Could I ask you to extend the same courtesy to me?" I said.

' "I really don't think so, Lord Peter. As far as I can see you have no business with either jewel. I have already overstepped the mark in talking to you so frankly."

' "Tell me, then, how are you to tell these stones apart? Can you read the inscriptions?"

' "Indeed not. But the Indian gentleman instructed me. He was very emphatic in telling me that on his jewel the first letter was rounded, and on the other man's jewel the first letter would be pointed.

' "I made a clear mental note of that in case it came in handy." '

8

Dinner in the Wimsey household was not as it had been before the war. The grand dining-room was seldom used. Instead the family ate in the little breakfast-room, at a pretty Victorian oval table, small enough for them to hear each other speak. No longer did a maid serve their food for them; instead it was laid as a buffet on a huge sideboard for them to help themselves. There was still white linen and silver flatware, and even a pair of candlesticks, though they retained the wartime instinct to conserve the candles, which were lit only on an occasional impulse.

Bunter and the cook kept things going with the help of a cheerful daily, who was rather apt to break things. The life of the family had shrunk within the ample grandeur of the London house, and now resembled the easier life they led in the country. Nobody changed for dinner unless there were guests. The formalities—those candlesticks, Bunter's 'Dinner is served,' routine, the announcement of guests, the coffee after dinner in the library—all these continued in a faintly self-mocking manner, a form of affectionate nostalgia for the vanished glory of 'before the war'. During the war and under the rigours of rationing it had been easier to pool resources, and although things were eased quite a bit by now, the Bunters' ration books were still held by the cook, the meals were shared, and now and then both Mr and Mrs Bunter sat down to eat with the family.

The Wimsey boys didn't pick up the nuances, and regarded their parents as incredibly stuffed shirts. Bredon, the eldest, even made a habit of calling Bunter 'Mervyn'. He had yet to grasp that this was unwelcome to Bunter, leave alone why it was, but he was, after all, only sixteen.

Since Bredon and young Peter Bunter were on leave from Eton, dinner that evening was jolly and rowdy, and Peter affected the baffled parent pose all through it. Coherent conversation would have been difficult, and was not attempted.

After dinner, however, Bredon and PB went off to play a game of real tennis at the Queen's Club, and as soon as it was cleared the younger boys began a game of Monopoly on the dining-room table. Lord Peter and Harriet retreated to the drawing-room.

'And then, Peter?' Harriet asked. 'What did you do about the villainous Mr Northerby?'

'I havered a bit. What should I have done, Harriet?'

'You should have gone straight to the police.'

'Arguable. But I suppose I didn't yet see myself as an investigator by trade or choice. I still thought of what I was doing as helping the Attenbury family. Friends of my mother's. I suppose I could have asked them if they wanted young Northerby cast into irons. I'm afraid I didn't. I decided to confront Northerby myself.'

'Entirely by yourself?'

'No; because Bunter would be there. I asked Northerby to call on me.'

'And he declined to come?'

'Yes. How did you know?'

'Because that is what I would have done in his position.'

'Ah. So I had no option but to call on him.'

'And you found him not at home?'

'Once, twice, three times. So I thought, Righty-ho, young fellow-my-lad, it'll have to be the police. And then I thought perhaps the threat of the police would serve as well as Inspector Sugg in person. And it did. It brought Northerby round to my flat within an hour of receiving my note, and in a pretty foul mood.'

' "Wimsey, I'll thank you not to meddle in matters which are none of your business," was his opening shot.

' "I am acting in the interests of my family friends," I said.

' "You are sadly mistaken in your judgement of what they are," he said. "How will harassing me help the Attenburys? Unless you were hoping to marry Charlotte yourself I cannot see what you think you are doing."

' "Recovering stolen property for them," I said. "Perhaps I should tell you at once that I know where the emerald is."

' "I have nothing to say on this subject," he said.

' "I know where the emerald is, and I am minded to tell the police. I do not know what sum of money Attenbury would have to find to redeem his property, but the police can recover it without any cost to him at all. When they have done so I imagine they will want to talk to you."

' "You fool, Wimsey!" he said. "You meddling idiot! What do you mean by referring to the jewel as stolen? Why should I steal from my future wife?"

' "I imagine because your debts were too pressing to wait for the marriage," I said. I was having cold feet, Harriet. I had not yet met the bluster and affected outrage of the crook in the face of his accusers which have become wearily familiar to me in the years between.

' "The gems are Charlotte's," he said. "And Charlotte knows all about this. It is outrageous to talk of theft and threaten me with the police. I demand an apology, Wimsey."

' "Charlotte knows about it?" I was very surprised at that.

' "Of course she does. What do you take me for?"

' "Then I take it you would have no objection to accompanying me now to the Attenburys' London house and asking her to confirm what you say. I think we will find them all at home."

' "Is that really necessary?" he said. He was beginning to falter.

' "Either that or the police. As you wish."

'He blustered a bit more, and made as if to leave, but he found Bunter standing in the drawing-room door, arms folded, legs planted firmly apart. So he caved in, and we all got our coats on and toddled round to Attenbury's.

'And there, Harriet, quite a charade was played out. We got there around six, and the family were assembled in the drawing-room. Northerby did not so much as glance at his lordship or her ladyship, he advanced straight to Charlotte, took her two hands in his, looked her straight in the eyes, and said, "Dearest, I'm afraid there has been a serious muddle. I must ask you to tell Wimsey here that you know all about the supposedly missing emerald. That you gave it to me. Otherwise I am in trouble."

'That girl rose to the occasion magnificently. She turned to me wide-eyed, advanced a pace or two towards me, looked me straight in the eyes, and said, "Yes, Peter, of course I know about the emerald."

'Attenbury positively roared at his daughter: "Charlotte! *What* do you know about the emerald?"

' "I was going to tell you very soon, Father," she said.

'Northerby had regained his composure. "This can be sorted out quickly," he said. "Charlotte, if you will just tell everybody that you knew I was going to pawn it."

' "Yes, Reggie, I knew," she said, and then she burst into tears.

'Well then, as you can imagine, Harriet, the fur flew. Attenbury went pale as ashes, and said in a strangulated sort of voice, "Charlotte! Let me understand you. You gave the king-stone to your fiancé, knowing he was going to pawn it? I suppose he gave you some sob-raiser about being short of cash?"

' "Yes, Father," she said. She was shaking like a leaf.

' "Oh, Charlotte!" cried Lady Attenbury. "What

about Jeannette? You were going to lay the blame on Jeannette?"

' "Only for a while, Mother," she said. "When we got married we would have sorted it out."

' "Because the fellow would then have flogged the whole lot!" cried Attenbury. "Leave us at once, Mr Northerby, if you please, and come and see me first thing tomorrow morning."

' "I think I ought to go too," I said.

' "Stay, please, Wimsey," said Attenbury. Northerby took himself off at once. It was horribly embarrassing. Charlotte was now standing in the middle of the room, weeping her eyes out. But perhaps just because I wasn't family, it was me she spoke to.

' "Oh, Peter!" she said. "I promised to marry Reggie, and everybody knows I did, and now I don't want to, and what am I going to do?"

' "Stop crying if you can, Charlotte," said Lady Attenbury, "and sit down. And tell us the truth. Did you really give the king-stone to Reggie to take to the pawnshop?"

' "Yes; no . . . not exactly . . ."

' "Not exactly!" cried her father. "Well, do you mind telling us what, inexactly, you *did* do? And take a care what you say, my girl, because I won't have any footling about on a matter like this!"

' "Attenbury," said Lady Attenbury, "it really won't help to shout at her. She's beside herself already."

' "Bloody women!" cried his lordship. "You get it out of her, and come and tell me when you have. Come along, Wimsey, come and have a drink."

'So I missed some of the best bit. Lady Attenbury joined us in the smoking-room about half an hour later. It seemed that Charlotte really had known that Reggie was short of money. She had agreed that the emeralds could be pawned, or discreetly sold. She didn't like them much anyway.

' "*Discreetly* sold? The whole of London would have been talking!" cried Attenbury.

' "She seems not to realise that, Arthur. She hasn't much idea of an important jewel."

' "She shan't have them, then."

' "The main thing I have winkled out of her is that she thought the jewels would be pawned after her marriage. She did agree to that. She did not know that Reginald intended to take and pawn the king-stone beforehand. And although she is not very coherent on the subject I really think she suspected he *had* taken the stone. It seems that he entered her room to kiss her just before going off to change for dinner, and she left him there just for long enough to go along the landing and call to Ottalie."

' "It's simple theft, then, Claire. The fellow is a thief. I shall call the police."

'Attenbury got up from his chair, as if he thought to do that at once. Lady Attenbury stopped him.

' "Just wait a moment, Arthur. The police will not

have the benefit of what I have just told you. Charlotte is adamant. She no longer wants to marry Mr Northerby but she will not give evidence against him. If he is prosecuted, she will tell the police, and a court if need be, that she gave the stone to him."

' "She'll damn well do what she's told!" cried Lord Attenbury.

' "I'm not sure that she will, Arthur. And what are you going to do about it? Beat her?"

'I chipped in: "Better not beat a witness, old friend. Suborning witnesses is a serious matter."

' "Suborning her? Getting her to tell the truth? What's wrong with that, may I ask?"

' "Once you start bullying a witness, leave alone beating her, nobody can tell if her evidence is the truth or not."

' "We shall all look like insurance crooks. Is that what she wants?"

' "She wants to break off her engagement and be rid of Mr Northerby without a scandal. Without his going to prison. And, Arthur, that's what I want, too. Can it be managed?"

' "Who would have children," he said, slumping down in an armchair.

' "What can we do, Peter?" Lady Attenbury said, turning to me.

'I was thinking it over. "You can simply 'find' the jewel, and tell the police that it's all a terrible error, and the jewel has been found."

' "To do that we'd have to get it back," Attenbury pointed out.

' "You'd have to get it out of hock, yes. If you leave it where it is, and the marriage doesn't go ahead, I think Northerby won't be able to redeem it. So when the six months are up it will probably get sent off to Amsterdam to be re-cut. And someone is certain to recognise it."

' "You mean I've actually got to *pay* for it?" He almost howled, he was so angry.

' "I think it is in pledge for around a third of its value," I said.

' "That would be still a tidy sum, Wimsey," he said. "Enough to hurt."

' "We can sell my diamonds to cover it, Arthur," Lady Attenbury said.

'His lordship got out of his chair, and went across to his wife, and patted her gently on the back of the hand. "No, no, my dear, wouldn't hear of that," he said. "When I see you wearing those, I remember the first evening I ever saw you . . . I'll manage somehow. Sell a farm or two."

' "I wish you would, Arthur, I would be very grateful."

' "Wimsey, will you see to this matter for me?" Attenbury asked. "I'll get you a banker's draft when we know the exact sum."

' "I'll be glad to, sir," I said.

' "And Peter?" said Claire Attenbury. "Your mother . . . your mother talks a good deal . . ."

' "She does indeed," I said. "But trust me for it—I don't."

'And I didn't, Harriet. I got the bauble back, though not from Mr Handley; I had it from his son. When I went to redeem it I found a timid and uncertain youngster in charge of the shop, and on asking for Handley himself I was told that he was dead. He had been struck down by a hit and run driver when crossing the road outside his house in Chiswick. His son was running the shop and trying to sell it as a going concern. He was still in a shaken state of mind about it, but he was able to find the transaction in his father's records, and do the business with Attenbury's banker's draft. But when I asked him if the other emerald was still in hock he clammed up at once.

'So I did the deed, and I kept my mouth shut. Such juicy gossip—my mother would have adored it! When the end of the engagement was announced in *The Times* the whole of London was seething with rumour and silly talk. Poor Attenbury came in for a good deal of stick, everyone saying he had discovered the Northerby family's slender means, and was too mean himself to support the young couple. I thought it was dreadfully hard on him, when in fact he was being generous to the tune of thousands of quid. In effect, he was meeting Northerby's debts for him. But I kept mum. You are the first person I have ever told about it. After all these years.'

'I think I hear a note of sadness in your voice, Peter?' Harriet looked quizzically at her husband.

'Some faint regret,' he admitted. 'It's not that until then I told my mother everything—what adult male-about-town could do that? But I realised that the tremendous fun I had been having, that wonderful sense of purpose that sleuthing around about emeralds had been giving me, came at a price. Any secret is a burden. It cuts you off, ever so slightly, from the people you are not telling it to.'

'Yes, I suppose it does,' said Harriet thoughtfully. 'And you were just feeling your way . . .'

'And even now, I have to ask you, Harriet, not to mention any of this to anyone, and that is, of course, deeply illogical.'

'You may trust me, Peter. Why do you call it illogical?'

'Of course I trust you. But it's a general principle. If you tell someone a secret, and ask them to keep it secret, you are asking them to display a discretion you are unable to display yourself. Enough of this, now, and so to bed?'

'To bed, certainly. Just one thing—what has become of Charlotte? How is she now?'

'She's very how, I'm glad to say. She abandoned emeralds, diamonds and even pearls, and took her father's affection in the form of racehorses. She runs a stud near Lambourn. She married one of her trainers, rather late—she must have been in her mid-thirties before she tied the knot. He's a common fellow with a terrible accent, a warm heart, a wall eye and a shrewd eye for horses. I've won a few quid at Ascot, now and then, following his tip-offs.'

'Good for Charlotte.'

'She's Charlie, these days,' said Peter. 'Good for her, indeed.'

He stretched out a hand to his wife. 'Come, madam, come,' he said.

9

'Harriet,' said Lord Peter one morning a few days later, 'how's the novel coming along?'

'Not well,' Harriet admitted. 'It got so stuck I decided to take a breather, and revert to the book on Le Fanu for a week or so.'

'I ought to feel jealous of the egregious Sheridan,' said Peter. 'Seeing that you flee to him for comfort, although he is dead. Alas, my love, you do me wrong . . .'

'Don't bother to be jealous, Peter. The brute was no help at all—he immediately got stuck himself. Frankly, I'm stalled until I can get some time in the London Library, or the British Museum. It's a disadvantage of non-fiction that it requires an input of facts. It's like a roaring monster—it gobbles facts as fast as I can discover them, and then refuses to budge until I feed it some more.'

'And last week I kept you away from fact-finding by telling you an interminable tale of old unhappy far-off things. I'm sorry. I won't do it again.'

'I think you'll have to,' said Harriet. 'Because your tale disappointed me. I thought it was going to arrive at the House of Lords, and a blazing public scandal, and it never got there. I shall return from the library at three, and will be glad to hear your explanation over tea. What shall you be doing today? Will tea for two suit you?'

'Oh, I shall idle away the time in vacant or in pensive mood,' said Lord Peter. 'I've to try to match that missing teaspoon in the silver vaults. I'll see you at four.'

Peter returned triumphant and punctual, bearing a silver teaspoon from the right maker, and the right assay office, and only two years off the right date to replace the missing one. Harriet, who felt sure that the lost teaspoon had gone into the rubbish somehow, and felt obscurely responsible, was glad to see it. Whoever was getting careless, it couldn't have been Bunter.

'While I was in Chancery Lane,' said Peter, 'I toddled over the viaduct and had a look at St Paul's. There it is, Harriet, still standing in acres and acres of ruin—tottering walls, propped-up buildings, fields and fields of basements and foundations reduced to ground level and open to the sky. It's a disgrace. Six years after the war, and nothing rebuilt. And yet, you know, it's curiously beautiful. Come June, there will be buddleias and butterflies everywhere. And rampant wild flowers. Rosebay willow herb and goldenrod . . . the most valuable square mile in Europe, one would think, given over to wilderness. Ruin hath taught me thus to ruminate . . .'

'I suppose it won't be left like that for ever,' said Harriet, pouring the tea.

'No, I suppose we shall recover from the war eventually,' said Peter. 'A time will come when there will be no more rationing; when there will be money to rebuild the City; when Coventry shall have a new cathedral, and my brother will have enough money to repair the roof at Bredon Hall.'

'When Jack shall have Jill, Naught shall go ill,' offered Harriet.

'None of this is just round the corner,' said Peter quietly. 'We are on hard times. Our industries are smashed or bankrupt, our own farming has not fed us since the Corn Laws, we are in debt to the Americans to the tune of almost everything we own. We have liquidated all our foreign investments, and we have lost the jewel in the imperial crown, with independence for India.'

'We won the war,' said Harriet.

'So we did. I predict that those who lost it will recover faster.'

'I don't spend much time with thoughts such as

those,' said Harriet. 'Things are so vastly better than they were during the war. We are safe, Peter, and our children are safe, and we have each other, and enough coal for this nice fire we are sitting beside, and enough to eat. Have you forgotten the times when we could not have relied on any of these blessings?'

'I accept rebuke,' said Peter. 'You are right.'

'Before the war is never coming back,' said Harriet. 'It has become the land of lost content, a story-land. And talking of stories, you were going to tell me one. About the House of Lords, if you please.'

'Well, that one is about a different Attenbury daughter. Diana.'

'Did you say she was at finishing school when you were ferreting about in the family's affairs before?'

'She was indeed. I never met that young madam until she got herself into serious trouble.'

'Another teaser. You are getting good at this, Peter.'

'I have an excellent teacher.'

'Thank you, my lord. Toast or muffins?'

'Neither, thank you, Harriet. I was brought up never to talk with my mouth full. Of course, if there happened to be any butter . . .'

'I'm afraid not, Peter. You have already eaten your seven ounces this week, and mine is in the fruit cake poised on that cake-stand.'

'I do like a little bit of butter on my bread,' said Peter ruefully. 'To begin at the beginning. Diana was two years or so younger than Charlotte, and strikingly unlike her. I thought that the finishing school in Switzerland they sent her to had ruined her, but my mother said it was the other way round. They sent her there hoping to tame her a bit.'

'A wild girl, twenties-style? Bobbed hair, sequined dresses, late nights?'

'I don't think her aged parents would have minded any of that. It was gambling and dodgy company that did the damage.'

'Tell me all,' said Harriet, pushing off her shoes, and curling her legs under her in the wide and deep armchair she was sitting in. 'I am prepared to be shocked.'

'The first thing to tell you about Diana is that she was dazzlingly beautiful. Not the tranquil, English rose sort of beauty, but dark and simmering. Lovely figure. Deep, smoky-looking eyes, creamy pale skin. Simply terrific.'

'Your sort of girl?'

'Heavens, no, I was terrified of her. One felt she was greedy—almost unbalanced. That she would snatch at anything, do anything. As indeed, she did.'

'Couldn't her noble parents control her via the purse-strings?' asked Harriet.

'No, in fact, they couldn't. The girl had a wealthy godmother who had left her a chunk of money of her own. And said godmother, having herself been kept out of her inheritance till the age of thirty, had strong feelings about that sort of thing, and the money was in trust only until Diana reached eighteen. Which by December 1921 she had done. What with an allowance of a thousand a year from her father, Diana could do pretty much what she liked.'

'Peter, in this vanished world of long ago, did one normally know this kind of thing about one's friends and acquaintances?' asked Harriet.

'I'm sorry to tell you, Harriet, that one knew that sort of thing about their daughters. It affected their chances on the marriage market. Somehow the financial status and prospects of every debutante got around. Enough beauty might outweigh scant riches if the groom himself was wealthy. Impoverished young men had enough inside knowledge to avoid dancing too often with impoverished girls. The whole thing was rather sick-making really. Can you wonder that I opted out of it, and lay in wait for you?'

'That's another story, Peter. Stick to this one.'

'Very well. During the few months when she was fast and loose on the London scene I heard rumours about Diana. Bumped into her once at a rather dodgy party in someone's house in Chelsea. The rumours came both from talk about town, and from her mother, by way of my mother. The latter rumours were full of parental anxiety and distress.

And veiled requests for help. Didn't I have a friend who might be brave enough to take her on? I did not. It would have been a rotten deal for the friend in question, in spite of the ample funds. Besides, I was living like a hermit, stuck into book-collecting, and playing Bach to myself.

'Talking of my mother, by the way, I've asked her round here for supper tonight, if that's all right. She is sorting out family photographs. I wonder if Mrs Bunter would care to join us, rations permitting. I gather a bit of photographic expertise might be useful.'

'I expect supper will stretch. I've just bought a new book by Elizabeth David, about Mediterranean food, and I found some spaghetti in Fortnum's.'

'I wonder if it can be good for us to think about food so much,' said Peter.

'It won't do us much harm so long as there isn't much food to think *about*,' said Harriet. 'What happened to the glamorous vamp, Diana?'

'She got rescued. The Marquess of Writtle fell for her, lost his head over her, and they got engaged. And then married, within a month or two. Talk of London. He was much older than her, must have been in his fifties, and Diana was twenty-one. Nobody could work out if he knew she was damaged goods, but I think that was part of her charm, don't you know? He had wasted his own youth on being staid and respectable, and he found her thrilling. He wasn't bothered about money, he had stacks of it, and nothing much to spend it on apart from estate management. Don't know if he even asked.

'But the chief point of interest for us is jewels. As you know, Attenbury had that spectacular lot of emeralds that Charlotte had rejected. Writtle had oodles of diamonds. Diana didn't mind being loaded with jewels, but she didn't like the settings, and in particular she didn't like the king-stone in the family emeralds. She said it was a horrid, dark sort of thing. Wouldn't be seen dead in it.

'Hello—I think that might be Mama arriving early. Have you noticed how often she does that these days? Awfully bad form.' But he was smiling.

'Nonsense, Peter,' said Harriet, wriggling her feet back into her shoes, and getting up. 'She can't arrive too soon for me.'

The Dowager Duchess entered the room leaning heavily on Bunter's arm, and audibly short of breath. 'I'm early,' she said. 'I'm sure you have put in more stairs since you first had this house, Peter.' She folded into the nearest chair, and Peter had to stoop over her to kiss her.

Harriet looked at her mother-in-law with concern. For eighty-five, she was tremendous; but she was bird-boned and rather stooped now, and 'not for ever' was her aura these days.

'The tea will be cold, I'm afraid,' said Harriet. 'Shall I order some more?'

'No, thank you, my dear. It's rather late for tea, and a little early for drinks. I shall be quite all right for a while.'

'We were talking about the Attenbury emeralds, Mama,' said Peter, once his redoubtable parent was properly settled on enough cushions.

The Duchess perked up at once. 'Which set?' she enquired. 'Before they were re-cut, or afterwards?'

'Peter has been telling me all about them,' said Harriet, 'but he hasn't mentioned their being re-cut yet. How and when and why was that done?'

'Why do you want to know, dear?' asked the Duchess. 'Is Peter about to buy you some lovely emeralds of your own?' Then she reflected that Harriet had needs-to-know of a rather special and recurring kind, and she said, 'Or are you going to write about them?'

'I might, at any time,' said Harriet, strictly truthfully.

'Attenbury and Writtle got together and pooled their family gems to make a wedding present for Diana. The emeralds and the diamonds were taken out of their settings and redone, all in geometric style,' the Duchess said. 'All square and rectangular stones, and in-line bands. It was a very striking thing. I think Cartier did them—or was it Boucheron? Perhaps I am thinking of the Marchant-Parsons, those friends of Helen's, who spent two months in Paris while the work was being done, and went into the workshop to look at the gems every single day. Helen said, "You can't be too careful," but I think you can, don't you agree, dear? Of course people have other reasons for liking to be in Paris; *she* liked the rue du Faubourg St Honoré, and *he* liked the Folies Bergère, I expect. Denver took me to the Moulin Rouge once, and I was very surprised to find I rather liked it. It was quite tasteful in its way. I disappointed the poor old thing, I think. He must have wanted to shock me.'

'Surely he knew you better than that?' said Peter.

'I don't know, dear. I don't think he knew much about me, really. We were very fond of each other, of course. There now, I don't want to dwell on the past, I want to know why you two are talking about jewellery.'

'I'm telling Harriet about my first case, Mama,' said Peter.

'Mrs Bilt's pearls?' asked the Duchess. 'Or those boots in Sloane Square?'

'Attenbury came before all,' said Peter. 'So at the time we were talking of, Diana had become the Marchioness of Writtle, and off she went to the State Opening of Parliament, decked out in her real knock-you-in-the-eye diamond and emerald necklace. The emeralds had lost a few carats being re-cut, but they were still tremendous. But the king-stone wasn't part of them any more. It would have looked out of place on that sleek remade rivière. I supposed it had been put in the bank vault to await its fate.

'Anyway, all the Lords' ladies trooped into the House of Lords, wearing ermine and red velvet and dripping with jewellery, and somehow, while she was there, Diana contrived to lose her necklace.'

'It can't be easy to lose a necklace in the House of Lords, can it?' asked Harriet. 'Does it contain hideyholes a-plenty?'

'I can't say that I think it does,' said Peter.

'Oh, but things can be lost simply anywhere!' said the Duchess. 'There's such a to-do going on— throngs of people all wearing those enormous great crimson robes, all ermine and gold lace, and leaving cloaks in the cloakroom, and jostling each other. I nearly lost the Denver pearls there once— I suddenly felt a slippery slithery feeling, and the clasp had uncaught itself, and the pearls slid off. I stopped, and held up the whole procession while I looked on the floor for them, and then I spotted them, gliding along ahead of me, lying on the end of the train of Lady Muffleham, who was walking in front of me. I had to move pretty quickly to grab them up before the procession divided left and right and she took them out of reach. She didn't know a thing about it from beginning to end!'

Harriet laughed. 'So the gorgeous baubles disappeared? What then?'

'Oh, but they *were* gorgeous,' said the Duchess

appreciatively. 'They did look so stylish—rather in the fashion of the things the poor Duke of Windsor keeps buying for that awful woman. I rather tend to like the old-fashioned things myself, but you couldn't deny . . . The very next day—when she missed them—Lady Diana started a hue and cry. So the cloakroom ladies and the cleaners were asked to find them, but nothing turned up. Writtle had his Rolls-Royce searched, and his house tooth-combed from the front door up to the boudoir, and all through the jewel caskets and wardrobes, and her personal maid slit the hems of her cloak and train in case anything had slipped inside—nothing! Oh, woe is me, or woe was them, rather. Lost. Both father and husband were fearfully upset. After all, a small fortune, and a lot of trouble had gone into the things. But pretty soon someone murmured the magic words *insurance claim*. That cheered them up no end—the necklace was insured for twenty-five thousand.'

'Good lord!' said Harriet. 'How can it have been worth—'

'I think it was a little on the high side,' said Peter, 'but not much. So they banged in a claim, and the insurers made ready to pay up.'

'I always think,' observed the Duchess, 'that the whole thing was because poor Claire Attenbury was so very ill that summer. She was dead by Christmas. I still rather miss her, after all this time. Everyone in that family went to pieces without her.

And you can't say, well, she was spared knowing what became of the family, because she wasn't spared the trial and the scandal, just unable to do anything about any of it.'

'You're offending the King of Hearts, Mama,' said Peter sternly. 'Running on like that.'

'I haven't an idea what you're talking about, Peter,' said the Duchess. 'I haven't said a thing about playing cards.'

'He is referring to narrative advice in *Alice in Wonderland*,' said Harriet. 'Begin at the beginning, go on till you get to the end, and then stop. It's quite good advice, but it rules out hopping around in a story.'

'Good advice,' said Peter. 'Let's push on then. Talk of insurance didn't console Attenbury much; you remember what I was saying, Harriet, about these ancestral things being a kind of sacred trust. He came hammering on my door a couple of days after the loss asking for my help. A bit of a facer really—if I had found one jewel before, he seemed to think I would be able to find the whole necklace now. He had told "that Johnny at Scotland Yard" which is how he referred to Sugg; but now he was appealing to me.

'I poured him a drink, and promised him that if I could think of anything to do, I would do it. Truth is, I couldn't think of a single useful step I could take. I just tried to cheer him up a bit. Told him that such famous things would be too hot for a thief to handle, and that they would turn up somewhere . . . general sort of blether. Didn't have much effect on him; he trotted away as gloomy as before. Couldn't blame him. But I began to wonder, don't you know, about Diana. She had to be uncommonly careless. So I used my secret weapon—Bunter. I sent him round to Writtle's house to inveigle himself into the servants' hall, and pick up a bit of gossip about their mistress.'

'How does one inveigle Bunter?' asked Harriet.

'Oh, easily. One gives him a nice brace of pheasants from Denver, and sends him round with them and a cock and hen story about having more birds than one can possibly eat, and wondering if they would fancy helping out.'

'Was that brace of pheasants a present from me, you wretched boy?' asked the Duchess.

'I expect so, Mama. Fraudulent conversion. But it made things easy, didn't it, Bunter?'

For Bunter had just arrived bearing a tray of drinks, and with Mrs Bunter in tow.

'It became easier, your ladyship,' said Bunter, 'when I indicated that since Lord Peter knew nothing whatever about the birds in question there was no need for the angel pie, or whatever Cook made with them, to reach the family's table. They could perfectly well be eaten in the servants' kitchen. At that point they sat me down with a nice slice of fruit cake, and became quite talkative.'

'You are very shocking, the pair of you,' said

Harriet. 'Not a scruple to choose between master and man. Sit down, Hope; if you do, perhaps Bunter will and we shall all be comfortable like the old friends we are. We are waiting eagerly to hear about the wicked Lady Diana.'

10

'You would have to remember, my ladies,' said Bunter, 'that the Marquess of Writtle's household was of the old sort. Almost Victorian. Family retainers, man and boy, woman and girl. They had served the Marquess's uneventful father, and the Marquess himself all the remarkably boring years of his majority. Finding themselves with a wild young woman in charge was a severe shock. A ladyship who went out nearly every night without her husband, and came back at all hours! I was told at some length what the Marquess's servants thought of his raising no objection.

'On one occasion the mistress had come home bringing a crowd of noisy, rather intoxicated friends with her, who had put music on the gramophone and danced in the hall. The butler had tried to make them retire to the gallery, where he could shut a door on the uproar, but they had declined—they needed an uncarpeted floor on which to tango. By and by, I was told, the Marquess was roused from sleep by the raucous music, and appeared on the landing in his dressing-gown. The sleepy servants, trying to rustle up drinks and canapés in the middle of the night, expected him to read the Riot Act, and turn all the rowdy visitors out of the house; but he just stood there tapping his foot in time to the tune. In the morning all he had to say about it was, "Girls will be girls."

' "And that was bad enough," Cook told me,' Bunter continued, 'but then she began to go out alone and not come back at all till the following day. "And, you'll never believe this, Mr Bunter, she tried to borrow five pounds from the head footman. Just after we'd had our half-year salaries paid to us. He upped and left us, and I can't blame him." '

'So with her mother ill and her husband doting, there were no brakes on Diana,' said Peter. 'I decided to try to find out who her set were—all these late night party-goers she was hanging out with. I went off for a night on the town myself.'

Harriet looked at her husband interrogatively. She would have liked to ask him if he had recovered from his nerves sufficiently to go gladly partying on the wilder shores of youth, but she was not sure if the question would be kind.

He picked up her glance immediately and said, 'I took Bunter with me as a bodyguard. Lent him one of my flashier ties, and a silk cummerbund to doll up Moss Bros evening wear. I hadn't yet the nerve to go on my own.'

'Wasn't that rather a lot to ask?' said the Duchess.

Bunter said, 'I should have been so concerned about his lordship had I been left at home, my lady, that it was easier for me to accompany him.'

'I think I remember you grumbling about that cummerbund,' said Peter. 'You made a most awful fuss.'

'It was,' said Bunter, 'a rather flamboyant article. I thought it made the wearer somewhat conspicuous.'

'That's the whole idea of cummerbunds,' said Peter. 'Nature of the beast.'

'Wasn't it a bit conspicuous to take a manservant out with you on the tiles?' asked Harriet. 'Was that done?'

'No, it wouldn't have been,' said Peter. 'Escaping the observation of the servants was part of the point of going out. But Bunter didn't come with me as my man. We were not well known as yet anywhere about. People at large wouldn't have recognised either of us. Bunter came with me in the role of a friend. A role he has always played to perfection.'

'It does not require dissimulation, my lord,' said Bunter.

'Thank you,' said Peter.

'Would you listen to them,' said Hope Bunter to Harriet. 'Don't they sound like a script by Noël Coward?'

'Well, they are talking about the past,' said

Harriet. 'Mother, did you want some help with photographs?'

'It would be very kind, Hope,' said the Duchess, 'if you would look at some of these old things for me, and tell me if they can be improved somehow. I heard a talk on the Home Service about being able to get scratches off, and remove dust spots. And some of these ancestors are very dirty indeed . . .'

Hope laughed. 'Let's spread them out on the sofa table,' she suggested, 'and I'll look at them properly.'

'I think this one must be Grace,' the Duchess began. 'It looks High Victorian, don't you think?'

'Was that your first encounter with the rich at play, Bunter?' asked Harriet. 'Was it horribly shocking?'

'It was not worse than talk in the servants' hall had led me to expect, my lady,' said Bunter. 'Perhaps, on reflection, it was not so bad.'

'It was horribly noisy, and horribly stuffy,' said Peter. 'That I do remember. Lots of drink, lots of smoke, dancing and smooching . . . roulette and baccarat being played.'

'How terrible,' said Harriet. 'I am not very shocked, however. Try harder.'

'I would have said, my lady,' said Bunter, 'that the amount of money flowing to the coffers of the club management would have made you draw breath.'

'I suppose one would have needed inside knowledge to be truly, deeply scandalised,' said Peter. 'One would have needed to know who could not afford to be there, who was bringing their father down in ruin and grief, and who should not have been dancing with whom. On the other hand, one didn't need prior knowledge to see who had already had far too much to drink; nor to perceive that the cigarettes going from hand to hand didn't smell of harmless tobacco.

'We were on the trail of Diana, and at the first three places we didn't find her. Then someone tipped us off that she and her party had just left, he thought to go to somewhere called the Hot Potato. He had been asked to go with them, but, he said, as he was on a winning streak here, he was damned if he would. Or if he wouldn't, I thought, but we thanked him and jumped into a cab and asked for the Hot Potato. The cabbie was a bit unwilling. He took the liberty of suggesting two other places, where a pair of young gentlemen might have a good time without picking up trouble, if we knew what he meant . . . But when Bunter told him we were joining friends, he said, "If you say so, gov," with a *gawd help us* look on his face.'

'You see the present line of dukes are of the second creation,' said the Duchess, from across the room. 'That's where the De'ath comes in.'

'Were dukes made on the eighth day, or something?' said Hope in astonishment.

'It's not the *men,*' said the Duchess, 'they're just like anyone else. Or they are if one is lucky. It's when the line fails: when the youngsters don't do their duty, and produce heirs. The Wimsey line faltered when Lord Mortimer thought he was a fish, and went and lived as a hermit on a mudflat. You would have thought he might know that even fishes breed, but he died childless. Came up in a trawl net off Lowestoft. I always think that was so unkind to the trawler men! He should have known better; he must have given them a dreadful fright. There was no one left but cousin Grace, but luckily she married a distant Wimsey from a lesser line, and the Duke of Wellington arranged for the dukedom to go to him.'

'The Duke of Wellington?' asked Hope, sounding bemused.

'Because he had carelessly allowed the real heir to be killed at Waterloo. Although I don't see how the poor man could be expected to bear in mind the descent of titles in English families when the Prussians were so late, and he had the enemy to worry about . . .'

'This picture of Grace is not a photograph, exactly,' Hope said. 'It's a daguerreotype. I will have to re-photograph it, and touch up the negative. It can be done.'

'So how deliciously lubricious was the Hot Potato when you got there?' asked Harriet.

'Surprising. Pretty much the same as the others,

except for that news-hound Salcombe Hardy sitting in a dark corner pretending not to notice anything. We sat down at his table uninvited to assist his disguise. And then the couples on the dance floor parted, and gave space to a pair of rather wild tango dancers—tally ho! They were Lady Diana, and guess who?'

'How could I guess?' protested Harriet. 'Our social spheres having been widely different.'

'Come now,' said Lord Peter, 'you have certainly seen a spade, and more than once. But I grant you the guess was difficult. It was Reggie Northerby.'

'Ho, ho!' said Harriet, seeing that something was expected of her.

'Absolutely ho ho,' said Peter. 'I was flabbergasted. I mean, I thought the fellow would have slunk off back to his family tea-garden with his tail between his legs after what had befallen him. And we knew, or thought we knew, he had been out of funds. Although the pawn money for the emerald would have lasted a normal man some time, this didn't look like the kind of place to practise thrift. I suppose my jaw must have dropped drastically enough to draw attention to me because he spotted us, and at the end of the dance he came swanning over to our table, and said, "Hello, Wimsey! Didn't expect to see you here, of all places. Out for a bit of fun, at last? Shall I introduce you to some lovely girls?"

'I let him do that, since I wanted to know who

they were. Most of the names didn't mean anything to me, but they struck me as a dicey crowd, although one or two of the fellows surprised me later on, in the war. They were pretty quickly bored by me, and Diana in particular was a bit uncomfortable to see me, and she went off to the card table with Angela Shaden almost at once.

'Someone in her party said, "My God, if she loses any more money tonight we won't be welcome here tomorrow."

'And someone else said, "Don't worry about her. She can leave her debts on the ticket with a name like hers."

'So I had a pretty clear picture. Bunter and I extricated ourselves and left.

'I didn't quite know what to do about it, mind. It was none of my business how the Marchioness of Writtle behaved. If Writtle himself wasn't bothered . . .'

'But he ought to have been bothered,' said Harriet.

'A few wastrels can desiccate an estate,' the Duchess was saying to Hope. 'Is that what I mean?'

'Perhaps you meant devastate,' suggested Hope gently.

'Of course, dear. Now that is just what this fellow did to the cadet branch of the Delagardies. He brought a great lineage down to the auction rooms. He has a sneaky face, don't you think?'

'He can't have been more than six or seven in this picture,' protested Hope. 'Surely that's a bit young for a sneaky face?'

'You don't think people can be born sneaky?' said the Duchess. 'Well, perhaps you're right. It's just that I happen to know what the little rat did to his family when he grew up.'

'So did you do anything about the scandalous Diana?' Harriet asked Peter.

'Well, I would have done if my brother Gerald hadn't scolded me so,' said Peter.

'Gerald? Where does Gerald come into it?'

'He invited me to lunch with him in the House of Lords,' said Peter. 'I think it might have been the very next day.'

'To scold you?'

'To implore me to settle down and breed. Spare heir. You know all about that, Harriet. I've done my duty now, with your delectable assistance, but I wasn't ready to do it then. It was much more fun to rile Gerald with hints of a lifetime of celibacy, or alternatively of debauchery being what I thought of. Even so, after the brandy Gerald took me to shake hands with the Lord Chancellor. Courtesy call sort of thing. So I got a close look at their lordships' chamber. I prowled about a bit looking to see if I could spot any hidey-hole sort of place into which a necklace could have fallen, or any sticky-out thingies on which it could have caught; must have done it far too conspicuously, because the Chancellor asked me what I was doing. I told him.

' "Yes, I heard about that," he said. "But you won't find anything, Wimsey. Our cleaners are very thorough, and they've had a good look. The necklace isn't here."

'So I changed the subject. I asked him about the Woolsack. I told him I had heard that it wasn't stuffed with wool, really, but with horse-hair which crackled when the Chancellor sat on it. He said he didn't know; but it did creak a bit if he fidgeted when their lordships were boring. "Not that that happens very often . . ." he said. "Don't quote me." '

'But you are quoting him,' said Harriet.

'What does it matter now?' said Peter. 'It's alarming to think, really, how little the things that loomed at the time still matter years later. Sceptre and crown shall tumble down and all that.

'Well, that very afternoon when the session began, it seems that he began prodding around on it, wondering if I was right. He pushed his fingers down the crack between the seat and the back-rest, and behold and lo! There *was* something stuffed down there—something hard and lumpy. So at the end of the session—it was very late, well after midnight before they called "Who goes home?"— he got up and leaned down and prodded with his fingers again and brought up a paper packet which when opened displayed the wonderful Attenbury emeralds, all set about with fever trees—no, what am I saying?—all set about with Writtle diamonds. Sent round to Writtle's place in Cavendish Square first thing in the morning. Presto! The Chancellor went around for days telling everybody that he would never have prodded his cushion but for a remark by young Wimsey.'

'Very clever of you, Peter. But I thought this case was a source of notoriety for you rather than just fame. Where's the shock, horror element?'

'You are not shocked by this tale of a naughty world? Are you going to tell me that this is just what you expect from my sort of people?'

'Your sort of people? They don't sound at all like your sort of people,' said Harriet, musing. 'Except in being rich enough to pay for their vices. Having unthinkably more money than my sort of people rather exposes their taste, I suppose. You spent your money on incunabula, rather than on vice. But if you had been born poor and could have afforded neither books nor debauchery it couldn't have been known which you would have preferred given a chance. I don't think poorer people are more virtuous than richer ones; they just have a narrower choice of vices.'

'Except gambling,' said Peter. 'Rich and poor alike, each in their own way, succumb to that.'

'And that is how the deplorable Diana got into trouble.'

'Exactly. And unfortunately simply retrieving

the emeralds from the Woolsack didn't put all to rest, because of that insurance claim. Writtle had made the claim a whole fortnight before the recovery of the jewels, and the assessor had trotted along and interviewed the Marchioness, and heard her artless story. The Marquess withdrew the claim, but not before the insurers had called the police. The whole thing landed up in the courts with the Marchioness on trial for fraud. And *there's* your scandal.'

'It certainly was fraud,' said Harriet severely. 'One of my sort of people would have gone to jail for it.'

11

'Diana didn't go to jail,' said Peter. 'She had Sir Impey Biggs defending, and he hoodwinked and beguiled the jury as only he can do. She had a desperate time in the witness box. Prosecuting counsel dragged out of her, morsel by morsel, what she had done. She had squandered her entire inheritance from her godmother, and completely failed to live on her allowance from her father. She was deeply in debt. And she hadn't wanted to admit as much to her fiancé. In view of the attitude he took after her marriage she probably could have done so, and he would just have thought, Well, girls will be girls. But I suppose she didn't know him well enough to rely on that.

And she was terrified of confessing to her father.

'You would have enjoyed seeing Impey Biggs at work, Harriet, because at first you would have thought he was doing the prosecution's work for them. He teased out of the wretched girl a picture of her lifestyle, and got her to admit that although she had lost thousands at cards, she had also been lending money to friends, and paying their debts for them. I wondered what the devil he was up to as he extracted accounts of those friends—spendthrift hangers-on with a liking for expensive things like gambling and cocaine. He had already extracted from the Marquess, who at first claimed to know all his wife's friends, that what he actually meant was that he had been at school with their fathers. I was fascinated—it's a funny way of defending someone to drag their name through the mud.'

'Were you allowed to listen to him, Peter, being yourself a witness?'

'Oh, he finished with me early on. I gave them my halfpence worth, and then retired to the public gallery to squeeze in beside Mother, who was having the time of her life. I got there just in time to hear the evidence of the accomplice, one Mrs Prout.'

'Enlighten me. What was the scandal of your evidence that famously so upset your elder brother?'

'There was nothing to it. Just the mere fact that I

had been doing a spot of sleuthing while possessed of a title was enough. But you can imagine, Harriet, what the gutter press was making of all that stuff. Gerald just hated the fact that the family name was coming up in connection with the trial. The words "noble sleuth" simply maddened him.'

'You can't really blame him for that, dear,' contributed the Duchess. 'You must remember that he was brought up Edwardian. Your grandfather was very severe upon Gerald, in case he took after any of these crocodiles . . .' She waved her hands across the table of family photographs. Everyone laughed. 'I expect that's not what I mean,' said the Duchess, joining in the laughter. 'What do I mean, Peter?'

'I haven't the faintest idea, Mama,' said Peter serenely. 'I'm telling Harriet about the Writtle trial. And you were there, I remember.'

'Wouldn't have missed a minute of it!' said the Duchess. 'I was so proud of you!'

'Were you?' said Peter, sounding astonished.

'Gerald was wittering on and on about the family name, as if the family name hadn't got a lot of blotches already, what with all these wicked ancestors, and in any case what does all that matter nowadays—well, I suppose 1923 isn't nowadays now even if we thought it was then, although we of all people ought to be able to imagine how times change, what with the family habit of lasting through everything—why isn't 1923 called thenadays, do you know, Harriet, dear? And all I could think about was worrying whether Peter would be able to manage the witness box, or whether it would remind him of being under fire, and send him into a jellyfish again; and he spoke up so well and sensibly, it would warm the molluscs of any mother's heart to see him, although if my heart has molluscs I'm not quite sure what they actually are . . .'

'I think you mean cockles, Mother,' said Harriet. 'And I don't know what they are except on beaches. If you please, Bunter, will you go and look them up for us?'

'The curse of the Wimseys strikes again,' said Peter.

'What is that, dear?' asked his mother. 'Have I heard of it?'

'You are a prime example of it, Mother,' said Peter. 'It is a congenital inability to stick to the point.'

'Pray silence for his lordship,' said Harriet. 'He would like to resume his tale. Although you were doing only slightly worse than the Ancient Mariner, Peter.'

'Stopping one of three?'

'I was listening. So you had one of four.'

'Two of four. Bunter always listens to me.'

'Bunter has left us to consult the *OED*. As you were saying, Peter . . .'

'I was, I think, about to tell you how cunningly

Sir Impey Biggs had managed things. I thought he was ruining the egregious Marchioness Diana. He had succeeded in showing her to the jury as spendthrift, louche—well, I just said all that. He got her to admit that some huge sum of money had been spent over just a few months on dope, mostly heroin. But then he asked her how much of the stuff she had sniffed or smoked herself; and she said she had tried it once when somebody pressed her hard, and it made her sick, so she didn't do it again. Then he asked her to estimate how much of the champagne she had paid for she had drunk herself. "Oh, quite a bit," she said. "I like champagne."

'And he produced with a flourish a bill from the Hot Potato, and waved it round the courtroom. "Twenty-seven bottles of Moët et Chandon in the course of a week?" he asked. "Surely you don't like it that much?"

' "I like to treat my friends," she said.

' "Indeed you do," said he. "I suppose some of the roulette chips on this bill may have been staked and lost by you in person, if you spent a lot of time at the wheel."

'And then his *coup de théâtre*. "But I suppose also that the items on this bill which cover the use of prostitutes are not down to you personally? You were often picking up the tabs for other people, weren't you? Would you tell the court the name of the person for whom you paid the price of Lulu, Francine and Ziggy?"

'She raised her head, so you could see the tears in her wicked eyes, and clutched the rail of the witness box, and said, "No, I won't. You can't make me."

'The judge warned her that he could make her—he could send her to prison for contempt. Still she said no. Impey said, "Your loyalty is misguided, your ladyship. And it is all in vain. The name of the client entertained by these ladies is on the bill. It is Mr Northerby." So you see, Harriet, Charlotte had a narrow escape, all told.

'There was uproar in court. Hooting and cat-calling from the spectators' gallery . . .

'The judge suspended the session.

'When the session resumed Biggy suddenly asked his witness whose idea it was to fix up that fraudulent claim. "It wasn't your idea, was it?" he asked. She shook her head. This is what he got out of her. She had pledged the necklace as security against a loan to tide her over till the next instalment of her allowance was due. Then she learned that her father was stopping the allowance, now that the marriage settlement with the Marquess of Writtle was providing for her. She was terrified of losing the necklace, on which both families set such store. A friend suggested that she had better "lose" it in a place of safety, and hold off her creditor for a while with that story. So she recruited a girl she knew from the club scene, whose day job was as a cloakroom attendant and cleaner in the House of Lords. Diana slipped the necklace to her as she collected her cloak at the end of the ceremony, and the girl hid it in the fold in the Woolsack. A Mrs Prout who confirmed all this when called as a witness, said that she was to be paid when she was asked to retrieve it.

'All would have been well had Writtle not wanted to show the jewels to a visiting friend, and asked to see them. Then she had to tell him they were lost.

'And whose idea had it been, asked Sir Impey Biggs, to make an insurance claim? Was it her idea? No, it had been her husband's idea. Had the Marquess consulted her about the claim? Or even told her he was about to make it? No, he had acted without telling her.

' "So you were trapped in your lie?"

' "Yes," she said, so softly the court could hardly hear her.

' "How did you feel," he asked her, "when at Lord Peter Wimsey's suggestion the Lord Chancellor recovered the jewels? Were you relieved?"

' "Immensely relieved."

' "What about the debt against which they were pledged?"

' "In the meantime I had made a clean breast of the matter to my husband, and he paid the debt for me."

' "Your husband must love you very much."

' "Yes," she said, blushing deeply, "I believe he does." '

'Well, you can now imagine, Harriet, Biggy's summing-up. Young, trusting, gullible and beautiful girl; secluded childhood with nannies and chaperones, and schooling in Switzerland, where by common consent nothing ever happens to stain the pure white snow . . . let loose with money in a tranche of London society deeply corrupted by the wastrel hangers-on of the rich . . . after some fun, as it's natural young people should be . . . too good-hearted to suspect that friendship offered her was two-faced exploitation . . . Misled—and here he paused for effect—by supposing that the friends and associates of her family and her prospective husband were "good society" when in fact some of them were deeply wicked, and using their status and titles as no more than a means to escape paying their debts . . . He actually used her folly and stupidity to gain sympathy for her. Brilliant, simply brilliant!'

'Yes, Peter, but fraud.'

'Of course he emphasised that Diana had not herself made the insurance claim, which would have been fraud. She had just got herself into a terrible tangle in which it took time for her to face up to the need to confess to her husband. *But, members of the jury, if this husband can find it in his heart to forgive the peccadilloes of his young wife, surely you, too* . . . You could write it yourself, I'll bet.'

'And what happened?'

'Not guilty.'

'But she was guilty,' said Harriet firmly.

'Oh, I expect so,' said Lord Peter breezily. 'I expect she thought she could pay off her debts with the insurance money, and get the jewels back too. But she didn't make out and sign the claim form herself. Writtle did. So the judge told the jury she was entitled to the benefit of the doubt.'

'Cockles, my lord, your ladyships,' said Bunter, who had returned some minutes since, and was waiting for a pause in the talk, 'are so called in reference to hearts because of the likeness of a heart to a cockleshell; the base of the former being compared to the hinge of the latter.'

'A pilgrim heart is mine,' said Peter. 'Give me my cockle-shell of quiet . . .'

'Wrong shellfish again,' said Harriet. 'Shall we go to dinner?'

Only as they were on their way to bed, much later, did Harriet say to Peter: 'You know, Peter, when your mother described Diana's necklace in such glowing terms, she didn't mention the king-stone. It had made a deep impression upon you . . .'

'Remember, it got left out of the remake and shoved away in the bank,' said Peter, yawning, and turning out the light. The room filled with moonlight, and on the walls fell faint moon-shadows of the leafy trees in the London square outside. It was a high window, and they never drew the curtains across the mysterious night.

12

It was just after breakfast two days later that Bunter reappeared after clearing the coffee, and said, 'Lord Attenbury to see you, my lord.'

Harriet looked very startled, but Peter said, 'The king is dead, long live the king! Show him up, Bunter, show him up. We'll see him in the library, I think.'

To Harriet he said, 'Are you working this morning, or would you like to join in this encounter?'

'I'd like to join, if I may, Peter.'

'This will be Edward, the old man's grandson,' Peter told her as they crossed the landing to the library. 'The Abcock whose name you know from the story was Roland, killed at Dunkirk.'

'I'm sorry,' said Harriet. 'Didn't I meet him once? Just briefly, at Denver?'

'Oh, you could have. But the new Lord Attenbury is unknown, I think, to both of us.'

They had reached the library doors, and Peter stood back to let Harriet precede him.

The young man who awaited them was striding about the room in very obvious agitation. He looked as if he had slept in his suit, and not taken the time to do up his tie properly.

'Oh, look here, Lord Peter,' he exclaimed as soon as they entered the room, 'I'm in a hell of a fix!'

'Sit down, won't you?' said Peter. 'But first, let me introduce Harriet, my wife.'

The visitor was so agitated he could barely manage the minimum courtesy of a handshake, and no sooner had he sat down than he jumped up again and resumed pacing about the room.

'You're going to need to calm down a bit, old chap, aren't you,' said Peter, taking young Attenbury by the arm, and firmly leading him back to a chair, 'if you're going to be able to tell us what this is about.'

Harriet rang the bell, and when Bunter appeared, asked him to bring brandy and water.

This was one of the occasions when Peter nodded discreetly to Bunter, who, having set down his tray, quietly retreated to the far end of the room, out of the eye-line of the visitor, and took a seat behind an elaborate Japanese lacquer screen.

'I suppose you know about those damned emeralds,' Attenbury said at last. 'Since you famously found the things for my grandfather.'

'Haven't seen any of them since, though,' said Peter. 'Except from afar, once or twice. And I rather think they weren't complete when they were re-mounted.'

'No, they weren't,' said Attenbury. 'Aunt Diana

didn't like the big dark chunky stone. She said it was inscribed with a curse. So Grandfather just took it back and put it in the bank. He set great store by it. When my father died he transferred ownership to me. He thought it would cover nearly half the estate duty, if it wasn't liable to duty itself.'

'I expect it would help with it if you didn't mind selling,' said Peter.

'*Mind* selling?' cried Attenbury in distress. 'If only I could! But now I'm in terrible trouble!'

'It wasn't with Spink, was it?' asked Peter. 'Spink has a vault for its customers' treasure, and it took a direct hit in the Blitz, you remember,' he added for Harriet's benefit.

'No, no, it was still with Cavenor's Bank,' said Attenbury.

'Well, has it gone missing?' asked Harriet.

'Or found to be a paste copy?' asked Peter.

Suddenly the young man in front of them slumped in his chair. He took a gulp of brandy and said, quite levelly and calmly, 'Not the one nor the other. It's there. I don't think it's paste. But someone else has shown up who says it isn't mine and he can prove it.'

'Good lord!' said Peter. Then after a minute or so he said, 'I don't suppose this person is an Indian gentleman of about my age called Nandine Osmanthus?'

'I don't know who he is,' said Attenbury. 'I haven't clapped eyes on him. The bank won't release the stone to me because they say there is a problem with ownership. And that's about all I know. But what am I to do, Wimsey? The blasted pompous ass in the bank vault said I couldn't sell the jewel anyway, because the auction houses wouldn't touch it with a bad provenance. But I really must sell it. Without a bit of cash I might have to sell not just the land from the estate right up to the front door, I'll have to sell the house itself. I'm having to let most of the pictures and the London house go, as it is. My mother can't stop crying . . .' He looked as if he was having difficulty not crying himself.

'How can this possibly have happened?' he asked.

'Well, I think, Attenbury,' said Peter, 'the first thing to be done is to make sure that it really *has* happened. There was a very similar jewel; I once saw two side by side. I think I might be able to tell yours from the other one, with a bit of luck. Write me a letter authorising me to act on your behalf, and I'll see if I can sort this out.'

'Oh, would you really? That's exceptionally kind of you. I'd be for ever in your debt.'

'Hold on, hold on. I said I'd try. I might not succeed. I have a feeling this will be difficult.'

'I suppose it's a bit much of me even to ask . . .'

'Of course not. I was a friend of your father's from schooldays. I really will do my best. Now your part is to write that letter.'

Bunter appeared as if by magic, lowered the flap of the little writing desk that stood between the tall windows of the room, and laid out a sheet of writing paper and a pen on the blotter.

As Attenbury sat down to write, Peter said, 'Tell me, if you can, when the king-stone was deposited in the bank.'

'I do know that,' said Attenbury. 'It was when the rest of the emeralds were re-set, just before Aunt Diana got married.'

'March 1923, then. That's a start. Then I'd like to know exactly when and for how long it has been taken out of the vault, in the years between then and now.'

'I can ask my mother and aunts. I suppose they might know.'

'I expect the bank can supply the bare dates,' said Peter. 'But I might have to nose round your family a bit, asking questions.'

'They won't mind,' the young man said, adding, suddenly authoritative, 'They'd better not!'

'Have you told the insurance company?'

'What can I tell them when I don't know what has happened? And look, Wimsey, the family lawyer says not to tell anybody that there is a problem with the jewel, as that might make it harder to sell. I'd be helping to create a dicey provenance, was what he said.'

When he had gone, Peter was thoughtful. 'Are you working this morning, Harriet?' he asked.

'I ought to, yes,' she said.

'Then I think Bunter and I will tool along to Messrs Cavenor and report to you later,' his lordship said.

As Bunter brought him his coat and gloves he said, 'You know, Bunter, I think the stones were identically carved in front. So our only hope would lie in the inscription. I think that I remember Mr Handley telling me that the Maharaja's stone was inscribed with a rounded first letter.'

'That is what I recollect our being told at the time, my lord,' said Bunter.

'What a man in a million you are, Bunter!' said Peter, taking the steps down from his front door two at a time like a rash young boy.

'Whatever has got into Father?' said his son in astonishment, seeing him from the corner of the square.

Bankers are not much given to the expression of emotion; not when on duty, anyway. But obviously the Attenbury emerald had become a hot topic. There were pursed lips, and references to more senior people the moment Peter raised the subject. By and by he and Bunter were admitted to a large oak-panelled office with a high acreage desk, a fire laid but unlit in a marble surround, fine carpets and large windows, where, palatially ensconced and expensively suited, sat one of the bank's directors. Wimsey passed his letter of authority from

Attenbury across the desk. Mr Snader picked it up and read it with a flash of consternation, quickly suppressed, crossing his face.

'You do seem to be in a spot of bother over this,' Wimsey remarked pleasantly. 'I hope I shall be able to help.'

Mr Snader reacted sharply. '*We* are not in difficulties,' he said. 'Your client may well be.'

'Oh, I don't know,' said Wimsey languidly. He stared at his opponent, for opponent Mr Snader undoubtedly was. 'I don't suppose it would improve the standing of your bank if it got around that your safe deposits were not very safe, don't you know.'

'Our safe deposits are for the use of honest clients,' replied Mr Snader, with a note of indignation in his voice. 'We have never been touched by a breath of scandal in more than a hundred years of business.'

'I should be careful what you imply about my client,' said Wimsey. 'He is entitled to the presumption of innocence, and there are the libel laws—God bless them!—to consider. As I understand it all he has done is to request the return of his property.'

'If he imagines that we will hand over to you what we have declined to hand over to him in person, he is mistaken,' said Mr Snader. 'We are not sure that he is entitled to ask for the gem in question.'

161

'If he is not entitled to ask for it,' said Wimsey, 'then you are indeed in a spot of bother. For the family can produce a sequence of receipts for the very famous jewel, famously belonging to them, each time it has been deposited with you.' As he spoke Wimsey silently hoped that this was the case. 'If there has been some hanky-panky, then the very least that has happened on your side is carelessness in writing receipts for the property handed in to your care.'

He let a silence develop in the room, before continuing. 'You have perhaps mistaken my standing in this matter. It is true that I am a private detective, although professionally I prefer murder to fraud.' He smiled softly as he saw the shudder of revulsion cross Mr Snader's face. It was uncertain whether the word murder or the word fraud had most affronted him. 'But it is as a friend of the family that I am here today. I have seen both the Attenbury jewel, and one very like it in the past. Admittedly rather long ago. It is possible I may be able to tell you whether you do or do not have the Attenbury gem in your deposit box.'

Mr Snader silently fiddled with his gold pen, taking the cap on and off.

'This matter will have to be taken further, one way or another,' said Wimsey. 'You can hardly suppose that young Attenbury will simply walk away from his heirloom on the say-so of a bank employee, and keep his mouth shut about it. He will raise an awful stink, and who could blame him?'

'You say you can identify the Attenbury jewel?'

'I say that I might be able to.'

Mr Snader rang a discreet silver bell on his vast desk. An employee appeared, and was asked to bring a numbered strongbox. All this time Bunter was standing well back, seeming to be absorbed in the view from the window. Minutes passed.

The porter appeared with the box, and set it down on the desk. Mr Snader went to a locked cabinet, and produced a numbered key. He opened the box and removed a leather case about six inches square, which he opened, and pushed across the desk towards Wimsey. Wimsey leaned forward, and picked up the jewel. He looked closely at it, removing his eye glass, and using it like a jeweller's loupe. Then he turned the gem over, laid it back on the velvet lining of the box, and stared long and hard at the inscription on the back. What had Mr Handley told him, all those years ago? That the Indian gentleman had said one jewel had an inscription beginning with a spiky letter, the other with a round one . . .

'Well, sir, what do you say?' demanded Mr Snader.

'Ah. I cannot read this inscription myself, so I am relying on my recollection of the letter shapes in the first line. Will you permit my man to take a photograph of this inscription so that I can consult someone who can read it?'

Mr Snader looked distinctly unwilling.

'All that I require,' said Bunter, 'is that you will lay the jewel on the windowsill for several seconds.'

'You can take a snap at once, without fuss or extra equipment? In that case I cannot object. As far as I can see it is in the best interest of everyone to establish the identity of this jewel.'

Almost before the sentence was out of his mouth Bunter had placed the jewel on the windowsill. The cloudy, shadowless light of an overcast London day, and his Leica did the job. Peter heard the shutter click three times with the jewel lying face down, three times with it lying face up, and then Bunter returned the box to Snader's desk.

Snader had not taken his eyes off the jewel for a split second during this procedure.

'May I ask you what is your opinion, Lord Peter?' he asked.

'I would like to be able to tell you that I am certain that the jewel you have is Attenbury's,' said Peter. 'So much less trouble all round. But I am afraid that it is not. And yet you *are* in possession of Attenbury's jewel, for he has your receipt for it. He could go to the police.'

Mr Snader appeared to have lost an inch or so in height, and a good deal of confidence along with it. 'Is there any way of avoiding the involvement of the police?' he asked.

'We could try where whole-hearted co-operation might get us,' said Wimsey drily.

'What do you need me to do?' asked Snader.

'I take it you have carried out a thorough search of all your deposit boxes, to be sure that you have not got custody of two nearly identical stones, and all that is amiss is that the wrong one is in the Attenbury box?'

'We did that as soon as we understood that there were two stones. No other was found to be here.'

'Then there has been a substitution. But I am naturally deeply curious to know *who* told you that there were two stones.'

'A Mr Tipotenios,' said Snader.

'But, my dear fellow, that is just Greek for nobody!' said Wimsey. 'Did you see Mr Nobody in person? He wasn't an Indian gentleman, was he?'

'Oh, no, he was a white man,' said Snader. 'He called here in person.'

'To do what, exactly?' asked Wimsey.

'To tell me that he acted for somebody who claimed ownership of the emerald in the Attenbury strongbox, and to threaten me with all sorts of legal reprisals if the stone were released to the Attenbury family. He was very definite that he could prove the ownership of the stone that he claimed the Attenburys were passing off as theirs.'

'He did not ask you to give the stone to him?'

'We would not have done that. We told him we would require to see his proof of ownership, and he went off to get it, saying that it would take some time as the documents were not in England.'

'How long ago was this?'

'It was a week ago. It is very unfortunate that Lord Attenbury did not appear first.'

'Who interviewed Mr Tipotenios?' asked Wimsey.

'Orson, my second-in-command. I was out of the office myself that day.'

'Could you instruct Mr Orson to give a full description of the man to Bunter?'

Mr Snader rang the bell again, and Bunter departed, notebook in hand.

'It looks very likely that there has been a substitution,' Wimsey said once more. 'It's a clever manoeuvre; a version of the three-card trick. The thing to do is to work out when and how the substitution was made. Can you give me a list of all the occasions since 1923 when the jewel has been out of the strongbox, and in the hands of the family?'

'You mean the substitution might not have been made by tampering with our strongboxes?' said Mr Snader, brightening visibly.

'I would be deeply obliged to you if you can find me those dates and receipts,' said Wimsey. 'Then I can begin to find out.'

'If there is one thing we are meticulous about,' said Mr Snader, 'it is record-keeping. We can tell you what has come in and out of our boxes going back to the 1880s. Except the secret boxes. Only the client knows what is in those.'

'But the Attenbury box is not one of those?'

'No. So we shall be able to provide you with what you ask for. With a bit of burrowing around in the files.'

'I'll send Bunter round tomorrow morning to collect what you can find for me,' said Wimsey.

'Oh, Lord Peter,' said Mr Snader, recovering poise, 'if any rumours were to start to circulate about the security of the bank, it would be as well for you to remember that we too have lawyers.'

'Good heavens, man, what do you take me for?' said Wimsey, getting up to leave. 'Some of my best friends are lawyers.'

13

Late the following morning found Lord Peter, Harriet and Bunter sitting in conference round the library table. 'This is what we have,' said Peter. The papers Bunter had fetched from Mr Snader's office were spread out on the table in front of him.

'Seems that the jewel has been delivered to the family, or fetched by them on only four occasions in the last thirty years. It was taken out of the bank for Charlotte's engagement party, as we all know, and returned with the whole parure on 20th April 1921. The king-stone was left in the bank when the other stones were taken to be re-set for Diana. So at that stage the king-stone on its own belonged to the Attenburys and the rest of the emeralds had become combined with Writtle diamonds, and were now owned by the Writtle family. The king-stone was removed from the bank in 1929, and returned a month later. And again it was borrowed from the bank in 1941, and returned twelve days later. Finally it was lent to one Miss Pevenor to assist her in writing a history of jewellery, and returned to the bank in November 1949. And there it should still be.

'Here we have it lying all before us—pairs of receipts, signed by a family member who took the jewel out of the strongbox, and by a bank employee when the jewel was returned. We are fully briefed, and can begin.'

Harriet said, 'Peter, the first of these occasions is the one in the tale you have been telling me, which includes the two stones side by side in a pawnbroker's shop. Are we sure the exchange didn't happen then?'

'Well, Osmanthus is the only person in the tale so far who could tell the stones apart. He could read the inscriptions.'

'Could he have been less honest and fair-dealing than he represented himself as being?'

'Could he deliberately have taken the wrong stone? Was the jumpy Mr Handley careless enough to let him? Somehow I don't think the man I encountered was a likely scoundrel. But I can't rule it out. Meanwhile, we must see what we can find out about more recent occasions.'

'How do we begin exactly, Peter? All these trails are by now stone-cold.'

'Cold, cold, my girl, no doubt,' said Peter. 'But we must try to warm them up a bit. We'll walk around and talk to people. Would you like to be my woman's-eye view, Harriet? After all, jewels are women's stuff.'

'Won't a deputation of three of us rather seem alarming? Are we declaring our purpose?'

'Talking to the family I think we can. And we shall talk first, I think, to Sylvia Abcock, Roland's widow, and mother of young Edward who has appealed to us. You and I shall call on her ladyship, and Bunter will be offered a cup of tea in the kitchen, just like the old days, and we'll find out what we all can.'

The Wimseys were welcomed in Lady Sylvia Abcock's establishment, which was a mansion flat in Victoria. There was a servant to open the door to them, and offer tea to Bunter, but the flat was very modest compared to the glories of the past, even of the recent past. The rooms were filled with furniture clearly intended for much larger spaces. Lady Abcock invited them to sit in her capacious sofas and asked for coffee to be brought to them.

'I know that my son has asked for your help, Lord Peter. I will obviously do all I can, though I cannot imagine what that might be. I am astonished at this whole affair. How can the jewel in the box at the bank not be our jewel?'

'I thought it might be useful to find out what we can about every movement of the jewel. Brought Harriet along because she's heard me talk about your family till the cows come home, though it must be a while since there were homing cows in Piccadilly . . .'

'You are very welcome, Lady Peter. I would be grateful if you would sign your latest book for me. If I can find it, that is . . .'

'Gladly,' said Harriet. She got up and moved to the window, contemplating the view of the fake Byzantine cathedral, and then returned and sat down on a chair out of her hostess's eye-line, leaving the field clear for Peter.

'Would you like to start by describing to us what was left with your family when the stones were re-mounted for Lady Diana?' Peter asked.

'Oh, just the big dull emerald all by itself, and the golden wire thing that let you wear it as a tiara or a necklace. I can't imagine anybody wanting to wear it without the other stones. They had all the sparkle. So it was just kept in the bank.'

'Do you by any chance remember why it was taken out in 1929?' Peter asked.

'I certainly do!' said Lady Sylvia, suddenly animated. 'We were short of cash. Without warning, all the family's shares were melting away

170

to nothing, and Roland couldn't use them as security for a certain debt. The stone was taken out to serve as collateral, and buy a bit of time from a creditor. Troubled times, Lord Peter, troubled times.'

'Indeed they were,' Peter said. 'Would you know who the creditor was? And if he retained the stone in his possession for any part of the time it was out of the bank?'

'It was about a horse,' she said. 'Was it a racehorse, or a polo pony? I can't remember. I'm afraid I have rather a blank spot about horses. I think the story was that Roland promised to buy it as a result of a bet of some kind. Then when he came to sell some shares to find the money, the stock market was falling like a stone. He sold a parcel of shares that should have been enough, but they raised only half of what was needed, and time was running out. Poor Roland, he isn't here to tell you about it himself. And I'm afraid I'm very cloudy about the details, Peter; I didn't take much notice at the time, because I was so cross about it.'

'May I ask you why you were cross?' asked Peter.

Lady Sylvia paused. Then she said, 'It was a terrible time to buy a horse; or any other luxury. The world was falling about our ears. If my husband had taken the time to read the newspapers he would have realised. Well, of course he realised, but he somehow contrived to think it couldn't have anything to do with a family like his. Ours.' She paused again. 'Just a few weeks earlier he had told our estate manager that he couldn't afford to re-roof some of the tenants' houses. I was angry with him. When I heard about the horse I wasn't speaking to him for quite a few days. That makes me pretty useless to you now, I'm afraid.'

'You are putting us in the picture, Lady Sylvia,' said Peter.

'Of course, for Roland it was a question of honour,' she said. 'If he had promised to buy the horse for a certain sum he had to buy it, whoever the fellow was. He never could get the hang of thrift. He actually told me how cheap it would be to have it, because Charlotte would stable it for him.'

'Then perhaps Charlotte will be able to tell us some more,' said Peter brightly. 'Sign that book, Harriet, and we will leave Lady Sylvia in peace.'

'Do let me know if there's anything else I can do,' Lady Sylvia said.

'I will, certainly,' said Peter.

Halfway down the stairs Harriet said, 'You shouldn't have reminded me to sign that book, Peter.'

'Why ever not? Have you suddenly become bashful about your hard-earned glories?'

'Because it wasn't hers,' said Harriet. 'It was a library copy.'

'Stroke of luck for the ratepayers of the City of Westminster,' he said, grinning. 'Now, when can we go and see Charlie?'

The A4 is a grand road, connecting the glories of London with the glories of Bath. It passes the Royal Courts of Justice, St Martin-in-the-Fields, Nelson's Column, the National Gallery, the Royal Academy, the Ritz, Harrods, the Victoria and Albert Museum, the Natural History Museum before descending through South Kensington to Chiswick and Hounslow. It passed what Peter still called the Great Western Aerodrome and headed out into open country going to Newbury and points beyond, sweeping through the oldest landscape in England, West Kennett and Avebury, before arriving in triumph in the Roman glories of Bath. At Hungerford, however, Peter turned off towards Chilton Foliat, and then towards Lambourn Downs.

Charlotte's establishment was approached down a long and splendid avenue of mature trees. The carriageway was gravel, heavily grown into by grass and weeds, with two tracks down it made by the wheels of visitors. It mounted a small rise, and offered a sudden prospect of a grandiose and dilapidated Georgian mansion. The frontage was covered with a grey render, now badly cracked, and partly covered with ivy which was beginning to creep on to the window glass. At this point there was a fork in the driveway. The broad way straight ahead towards the house, on which not a pebble of gravel could now be seen for weeds, was marked 'Horlus Hall'. The turnoff to the right was marked 'Attenbury Stud Farm'. This led to a fine building in tip-top repair, adjacent to the main house, but which had at first been screened from view by a stand of trees.

It was a very grand stable block, brick-built in lavish style, with a clock tower above the gate to the courtyard. All around the stable, away to the right as far as the eye could see, the landscape was laid out as paddocks between smart painted white rail fences. Harriet had no particular eye for bloodstock but she could see that the animals in the nearer paddocks were handsome creatures with glossy coats, and a delicate way of stepping. They came towards the edge of their grazing area as though expecting carrots.

Peter stopped the car just outside the gate, and tootled the horn. A man appeared in jodhpurs, riding boots and a flat cap, who stared for a moment and then roared, 'Lord Peter! Damn you, Peter, it's good to see you! And this will be your lady wife? All these years and you haven't brought her to see us. Come on, come on, I'll raise Charlie.'

'This is Frank Morney, Harriet,' said Peter. 'Best trainer in Berkshire.'

'Not any more,' said Frank. 'We raise them for others to train these days.'

Within the stable yard the cobbles were covered

with a drift of straw. Horses looked over their half-gates from the stables with long, intelligent faces, making Harriet think simultaneously of Houyhnhnms and Virginia Woolf. There was a smell of straw and manure and leather mingled with the smell of the horses themselves, a pleasant pungency.

Frank led the way across the yard to a door in the corner, behind which was the tack-room, with Charlotte sitting at a desk, grumbling over paperwork.

'Good God!' she said, on seeing Peter. 'However long is it?'

'Don't count,' he said. She got up from her chair, and rated, Harriet noticed, a peck on both cheeks before Peter introduced her.

'I don't suppose you've come to ride, or to buy,' she said, having shaken Harriet's hand. 'You'd better come through.'

She led the way through a door from the tack-room which led into a sitting-room, with a Victorian cast-iron fireplace, and large chintzy sofas, rather sagging and bulging. There were hunting prints on the walls, and the mantelpiece was lavishly adorned with rosettes of coloured ribbon, and a row of silver cups either side of an elaborate carriage clock. At the far end of the room a grand piano was wedged into the corner, with rows of family faces in silver frames standing on it.

'I see you've got your mother's piano, Charlie,' said Peter.

'And not much else, you mean,' she said drily. 'And before you ask, the pile next door isn't ours. Not our responsibility at all, thank God. Owners ran into trouble and had to sell the land. We bought all the paddocks and the stable block, and this cottage. Quite enough for Frank and me. Who wants a stately pile these days?'

'Not me, certainly,' said Peter.

Harriet was studying Charlotte during this exchange. She was a tall woman in middle age, with a somewhat manly deportment. Her hair was streaked with grey, and cropped rather short. She was actually wearing a pale pink twin-set, and she certainly still looked more like a girl for pearls than one for emeralds. There was a faint, fleeting likeness to the newly ennobled young Lord Attenbury, so recently seen in the Wimseys' drawing-room in London.

Ignoring Peter's placatory remark she went on, 'I enjoy being a traitor to my class, as you see.'

'Get off your mounting block, woman, and offer our guests a cup of tea or a tot of something,' said Frank suddenly. Tea was opted for, and brought out in pretty china, and they all subsided into the saggy sofas, which proved remarkably comfortable despite appearances.

'So what's this about, Peter?' asked Charlie when the tea was poured. 'Are you after one of Frankie's hot tips?'

'I wouldn't say no,' said Peter.

'But actually my nephew has been after you, I suppose.'

'Yes, he has,' said Peter. 'And there is some sort of story about Roland and a horse, and how you were going to stable it for him.'

'What does it matter now? Roland is dead.'

'It seems he used the great emerald as collateral on a loan to buy the horse. I just wondered if you knew anything about it. As in who the seller was?'

'I can tell you his name,' Charlotte said. 'But that's practically all I know about him. Do you want the full story?'

'Yes please,' said Peter quietly.

'Well, Roland used to stable a racehorse here in those days. We kept it in good fettle for him. Decent sort of horse, but not as good as Roland thought it was. He was down here one day with some friends, playing about, riding round our practice track. It was quite a party, because it was my birthday. Ada had brought a cake. All very jolly. And we had some customers there that day too. Including this fellow who had a horse at livery here; a nice little Arab filly called Red Fort who had won some local races for her owner. He was trying to sell her, but he couldn't get the price he was asking. There was a good deal of ribbing and boasting going on. They had the stable lads all leading the horses out to be looked over, and a couple of our jockeys riding them round the track. Lots of mouth; although Frankie said to me on the side that they didn't know the shit end from the bridle end. Anyway, Roland got into a tussle with Rannerson over who had the best horse, and offered to lay a bet on his horse against Red Fort. Rannerson said he didn't believe in betting money, and some of the silly crowd around them were saying that he was just chicken about taking Roland's bet because he thought he'd lose.

'Then Roland said, "Tell you what—if your horse beats my horse I'll buy it from you at your asking price." He got it out before I could stop him; I thought it was a bad bargain and a damn silly way to buy a horse.'

'Harriet's on unfamiliar ground here,' said Peter. 'Would you mind explaining why it was a bad bargain, and moreover a silly way to buy a horse?'

'A bad bargain because Red Fort was too nervy and unpredictable to make a good racehorse. Lots of style, but too much temperament. A silly way to buy a horse'—here she looked directly at Harriet—'because people ought not to buy horses as though they were fast cars or just valuables. They're not simply horse-flesh, if you see what I mean, Lady Peter; they deserve to be owned by people who can tell them apart and see their virtues. Peter says you don't know much about horses, but admitting that you don't is offering them a kind of respect, like admitting that you don't know much about some human being.'

'I understand *that!*' said Harriet. 'I can see in that

178

case that you must have been outraged at buying a horse on a bet.'

'Of course,' said Charlotte, 'Roland didn't mean to buy the horse; he was fool enough to think that his horse would win. Red Fort was standing there, fretting and stamping and bucking a bit, and Little Jim who was in the saddle was having trouble keeping her behind the starting line. When Frank popped the starting pistol she was off. She didn't so much run as bolt round the course, and Jim was lucky to stay mounted. But she finished first by about three lengths.'

'Whose horse did you say she was?' asked Peter.

'An army chap called Rannerson. Captain Rannerson, and no, Peter, I don't know what regiment. Pleasant enough fellow, but Frankie didn't like him.'

'Why not, Frank?' asked Peter.

'Never looked me in the eye,' said Frank. 'Makes you feel like a bloody footman when someone does that. You don't get to be muck by mucking out, Lord Peter.'

'Of course not,' said Peter. 'Is there more to this story of the Captain with the averted gaze?'

'Well, both horses stayed with us,' said Charlotte. 'But then there was huge bother about finding the price for Red Fort. Rannerson had asked a thousand guineas, and Roland went off looking rather glum to raise it. And then the punch line—it was 24th October.'

'That was dreadful bad luck,' said Peter. 'As far as I remember nobody saw the Great Crash coming till it came. Look, Charlotte, I know that Roland used the family emerald as collateral while he tried—'

'It was awful, Peter. He simply couldn't bear the disgrace if he hadn't stood by his word and paid for the horse. He'd made his offer in front of all those friends. And you know what Roland's fancy friends were; some of them are smooth as cream to your face, and can't wait to spread bad news about you if they get the chance. Anyway, the stockbrokers couldn't sell the shares fast enough; all Roland's money was melting away. In the end he had to ask Rannerson for more time, and Rannerson said he would agree to that if he could have the emerald as a pledge. It took Roland nearly a month to find the cash and get the blasted thing back. And it was ruinous. Most expensive horse in the history of England, I should think. And she never did win a major race. His wife wasn't very sympathetic. Neither was I. Daddy washed his hands of the whole thing; said Abcock was old enough to get himself out of a scrape he had got himself into.'

'The thing is,' said Peter, 'it would be good to know exactly how the emerald was used. Was it actually handed over to Rannerson?'

'Oh, yes,' said Charlotte. 'I'm sure it was. I remember a furious family conference in which we were contemplating disaster on another front, if Roland couldn't get it back, and Rannerson sold it. Scandal; disgrace! You couldn't sell such a thing in secret. If it had been up to me, mind, I would just have let the damn thing go. It's been trouble all my life, and none of us likes it. But that was too sensible for my brother. And in the end he did get it back.'

'What became of Captain Rannerson?' asked Peter.

'Search me. He never showed up here again once he no longer owned a horse here. Never met him at a race meeting, or a hunt. Simply vanished. Some of his friends were around for a bit.'

'Well, I have to ask you, who were they? Anybody special?'

'Not unless you count that friend of yours— Freddy, Freddy Arbuthnot as special.'

'Indeed I do! I'll trot off and talk to Freddy.'

'Do you want a bit of a canter before you go?' asked Charlotte. 'I take it Lady Peter doesn't ride?'

'I'd love to,' said Peter.

'I'll watch,' said Harriet in the same breath.

So for the next half hour she watched Peter riding a very frisky chestnut mare round the circuit, and although he looked at ease on horseback and she admired him very greatly, she perhaps didn't sufficiently appreciate his ram-rod back in the saddle, and the slack and easy way in which he managed the reins.

14

The moment Peter mentioned Captain Rannerson, Freddy lost his usual urbane and confident manner, and began to look a bit uneasy. 'What about him?' he asked.

'About him and a horse called Red Fort,' said Peter. They were sitting comfortably in the library of the London house, with coffee and buns on a table before them.

'Well, I remember the horse all right,' said Freddy. 'Your friend Lord Abcock bought it.'

'And offered the famous emerald as security?'

'That's right,' said Freddy. 'I know about that because Rannerson asked me to give the thing a look-over to make sure it was kosher. What's this about, Peter? Whole deal was made and paid long ago.'

'What was Rannerson like?'

'Decent enough chap. Well mannered, well dressed. Anyway, I took him round to Hatton Garden to show his booty to a fellow I know. Thing was quite all right.'

'Had your friend seen it before?'

'Don't believe he had, no. But he could tell a fine old emerald from a newer one all right. Anyway, as you know, Peter, Abcock found the money and took his stone back.'

'Leaving Rannerson with a wad of cash.'

'I believe so. Poor fellow didn't enjoy it long enough to spend it, though.'

'How so?'

'He got murdered by a pick-pocket the very next day. Just sitting looking at the ducks in St James's Park. Someone came up behind him and throttled him. I read all about it in the *Evening Star*. Didn't you happen to see it, Peter?'

'Well, I only heard the name Rannerson two days ago, so it wouldn't have meant a thing to me if I had. But if the emerald got into the stories I'd have pricked up my ears. Must have been abroad when it happened. Tell me all you can remember about it, Freddy.'

'There's not much more. Rather an odd thing; his wallet wasn't taken. But the next day a gardener found a jeweller's box thrown away in one of the flower-beds.'

'It sounds as though someone thought they were killing him for that emerald. Who would have known about it, Freddy?'

'Oh, half the world knew he had got it off Abcock. Talk of the town. And then quite a few people in the City would have known that Abcock was raising funds to get it back.'

'And quite a few people would have known when he succeeded?'

'Yes. But news takes a day or two to get right round the gossip channels.'

'So someone might have thought he still had the emerald?'

'I suppose so. Rather more your sort of thing than mine. Though I think you'd have had to be batty to think a fellow would carry the emerald around with him in his pocket.'

'I suppose most throttlers could be described as batty,' said Lord Peter, thoughtfully. 'Considering that they risk a punishment that perfectly fits the crime.'

'Must think they can get away with it. And he has got away with it; can't remember reading about an arrest in that connection.'

The following morning Lord Peter called on his brother-in-law at Scotland Yard.

Commander Parker had a comfortable office these days, with a sideways view of the river through his windows, and when Peter asked about the murder of Captain Rannerson all those years ago he simply rang a bell on his desk, and asked the WPC who appeared to find the files for him.

'What's my little sister up to?' Peter asked him while they waited. 'She seems never to be at home now all the young are grown and flown. Whenever Harriet or I drop by we find that she's out.'

'She's doing social work, mainly,' Charles told him. 'For the Prisoners' Aid Association. She turns out to be very good at fund-raising.'

'Yes, I imagine she would be. Still calming her conscience, then?'

'There's not a blot on her conscience, as far as I know, Peter. She's working because she wants to work.'

'Still expiating the abominable crime of having been born aristocratic and wealthy,' said Peter.

'Well, you would know more about that than I do,' said Charles. 'But there are plenty of discharged prisoners getting a helping hand just when it hangs in the balance whether they go straight or go wrong again.'

'I didn't mean to cast nasturtiums at her work, Charles. It's an excellent thing to do.'

'Well, I don't suppose any of the men and women she has been helping give a damn why she does it,' said Charles. 'You should stop psychologising and get out more.'

Peter leaned back in his chair, and regarded his brother-in-law with affection. After all these years of marriage he was still Mary's ready champion, springing to her defence against the least breath of criticism. And about the crime of being born aristocratic, Charles after all didn't know where the shoe pinches.

'Pax, Charles,' he said softly. 'Pax.'

And at that moment the WPC reappeared with a thick, dog-eared, rather dusty file, and they could cut to the chase.

They spread out the papers in the folder all over

185

a table under Charles's office window, and began to read.

There was quite a lot about Captain Rannerson. He was a captain in the Indian Army, who had been home on extended leave. Compassionate leave on account of his father's illness. Rannerson senior had in fact died a few months before his son was murdered.

'Better than the other way round,' said Peter.

There had been no witnesses to the assault, although people were passing along the path beside the lake; the bench on which Captain Rannerson had been seated was, however, in a niche formed by a herbaceous border which had been in full bloom, including foxgloves and delphiniums and other tall flowers which the scene of crime officer had not been able to identify. The detective in charge of the case had quickly decided that the motive was theft, and the object of the theft was to have been the emerald. Batty though it had seemed to Freddy for anyone to think that Rannerson would be carrying the emerald around in his pocket, it seemed that during his brief possession of the jewel he had indeed been doing just that, and whipping it out to show it off to all and sundry in his club, and at cocktail parties. There were several witness statements to that effect.

'So the murderer was in Rannerson's social circle,' said Charles.

'Oh, maybe. But people talk, especially about a thing like that confounded emerald,' said Peter.

The jeweller's box recovered from the flower-bed, and supposed to have been thrown away in disgust by the murderer when it was found to be empty, was gold, embossed with a Fabergé label, but the police had also quickly discovered that the box did not really belong to the jewel. Abcock had borrowed it from his wife for the purpose of consigning the emerald to Rannerson.

A matter of some interest was what the police had discovered about Rannerson's financial affairs. His need to sell his horse was all too evident; he had a long list of unpaid bills, and he was living far beyond what his captain's salary could sustain. His father had been supporting him generously, but his father's money was, like so many other people's, melting like snow in June as the Stock Exchange staggered to its knees under the blow of the Great Crash.

'Nothing of much use here, I'm afraid,' said Charles, beginning to gather up the papers to replace them in the file.

'Except this, perhaps,' said Peter, picking up the postmortem report. He had never heard of the doctor who had carried it out, but it was very thorough. There was no doubt of the cause of death, nor any contributory cause; Rannerson had been a well-built, well-muscled man in robust health. He could probably have fought off an assailant who used a scarf or a garrotte. But the assailant had applied pressure simultaneously to the left and right carotid artery, an expert and swiftly effective method.

Charles read over the paper which Peter handed to him.

'This is very odd, Charles, isn't it?' said Peter.

'Not unheard of,' said Charles.

'But the attack was supposedly made from behind,' said Peter.

'So it seems; there were depression footprints in the grass behind the bench, where the assailant's feet had sunk in a bit with the strain of pulling against the victim's weight.'

'Well, the famous swift death attack is carried out by putting one's thumbs on the pressure points of the neck. Fingers and thumbs work as pincers. Can that be done from behind?'

'Turn around, Peter, and I'll try,' said Charles.

Peter spun his chair round, and obediently offered himself as a sacrificial lamb in the name of science. Charles put his thumbs on the nape of Peter's neck, and pressed lightly with his index fingers on the softly pulsing arteries. 'It's not as easy,' he said.

'One would need strong hands,' Peter said, gently removing Charles's grasp from his neck.

'Perhaps that would have left the bruises of two fingers each side,' said Charles.

'But the report in front of us just says "Bilateral

bruising to the neck." Exact kind and extent of bruising unspecified.'

'Yes. Peter, I don't know that anything could be done about any of this now, after so much time.'

'I imagine this case is on the unsolved murder shelf? I thought you people never gave up on a murder case.'

'We certainly don't!' said Charles emphatically. 'But that doesn't mean that we can think of any further measures to be taken. We are just lurking like a cat at a mouse-hole, waiting for something to come out.'

'And ready to pounce if and when . . .'

'Certainly ready to pounce.'

'Well, in the meantime, can you corral Mary and bring her round to dinner with us? We could have a pleasant evening *à six*.'

'Wouldn't there be four of us?' asked Charles.

'And the Bunters,' said Lord Peter, rising to go. 'There are always Mr and Mrs Bunter.'

'Another coincidence for you,' said Lord Peter to his wife, on reaching home. 'A man is murdered in full daylight in St James's Park only a day after he has relinquished ownership of the king-stone emerald. The circumstances are curious.'

When Peter had finished an account of them Harriet agreed that they were indeed curious. 'What's more, Peter, that's the second coincidental death, I think. Wasn't the pawnbroker who had staked for both emeralds in 1921 mown down by a motor car before you appeared to redeem Lord Attenbury's jewel?'

'Odd, that,' Peter agreed.

'Perhaps more than odd,' said Harriet. 'Do you suppose that we shall find another fatality just about the time the emerald was next taken out of the bank?'

'I am beginning to think that we might,' said Peter grimly. 'Time to discover what we can about the 1941 escapade. I think Bunter has charge of all those chits from the bank.' Peter rang for Bunter, and asked him to produce the papers.

'It would seem, my lord,' said Bunter, spreading the documents out on the console table, 'that Lady Sylvia signed the request to the bank to release the jewel. It was to be handed over to Verity Abcock. And here is that lady's signature.'

'Who is Verity?' asked Harriet.

'Was,' said Bunter. 'Now dead. Here is her signed receipt. You will notice, my lord, my lady, the significance of the date.'

'I think she was young Abcock's sister,' said Peter.

'I have taken the precaution of consulting *Debrett's* for you, my lord,' said Bunter, fetching the stout volume from a side table, and bringing it with a bookmark already in it.

'Oh, Lord,' said Peter.

'What is it?' asked Harriet, coming to lean over his shoulder at the closely printed page.

But she saw at once. 'Verity Abcock, b. Dec. 1924, d. 8 March 1941 . . . Daughter of Roland and Sylvia Abcock . . . educ. Ascot . . .'

'So she withdrew the jewel on Wednesday, and died on Saturday of the same week,' said Harriet.

'And the jewel was not returned to the bank for a month afterwards,' said Peter.

'But the oddest thing of all—doesn't it strike you, Peter?—is that Lady Sylvia, talking to us about the brouhaha over the purchase of that horse, didn't mention this at all. Not a word.'

'I do find that curious, yes,' said Peter.

Bunter cleared his throat discreetly. 'Perhaps the whole subject was too painful for her,' he said.

'You could be right, Bunter,' said Peter. 'She had lost her husband the year before. The loss of her daughter must have been a terrible blow.'

'She did offer further help if we needed it,' said Harriet. 'And we do need her to help, don't we?'

'Will you obtain an invitation for us, Bunter?' said Peter.

Lady Sylvia's distress was evident immediately Peter asked her about Verity. She went very white, and took a few moments to collect herself to reply. 'I feel the lack of a daughter every day of my life,' she said. 'Of course, I have a dutiful son; but for a woman, to have a daughter . . . I wish I had had more children, although no child can substitute for another . . .'

Peter glanced anxiously at Harriet, also a woman without a daughter. Their eyes met, and he saw her tranquil.

'Could you tell us why she wanted to wear the emerald?' Harriet asked gently.

'Oh, it was for a fancy dress party,' said Lady Sylvia. 'No, wait, I must tell you more. That girl was having such a dismal time. I thought the war was terrible for young women. No nice dresses, clothing coupons even to buy underwear, all the men away and in danger, nothing nice to eat, blackout all evening every evening; when I compared her life with mine at a similar age, balls and court occasions and lavish dresses, and eager young men paying attention—so deprived. So deprived. But you remember all that. It's just that when the war started you were already married, I think. Of course she was doing war work. She was with another young woman, a green-grocer's daughter if you would believe it, but Verity kept telling me the war was a great leveller and a good thing too; and they were driving a van with showers in it, to help bomb victims and rescue workers clean up. Going wherever the trouble had been worst the night before. Once they were nearly blown up themselves when they parked their van next to a collapsed house where the Home Guard were digging people out, and there was an unexploded bomb that went off within yards of them. I asked her over and over to stop; she was looking so drawn and tired. I saw all her young beauty fading before she had a chance . . . She simply told me she was needed doing a useful job.

'Well, I mustn't run on. But you see, when her aunt, my sister-in-law Diana, invited her to a ball, I implored her to go. I have to live with that; she was reluctant, and I implored her to go. First she said she couldn't because it was fancy dress, and where could we get a costume with a war on? Diana's friends had wardrobes full of fancy clothes from before the war no doubt, but we hadn't anything. Then I had a brilliant idea: if she went as an Indian princess, she could wear a sari; and we could easily make her a sari, because I had a bale of a light green silk that had been meant for curtains, and had never been used. She would look lovely in a sari, just lovely, though we had a bit of trouble working out how it should be worn.

'But I had a friend, Susan, who had been brought up in Bombay, and who had brought her ayah home with her as a family servant, and so we asked advice. And the ayah was so helpful. She showed us how to wear the sari, and she lent Verity a dozen glass bangles for bracelets and showed her how to make a caste mark on her forehead with a dark red lipstick; we were all so happy playing dressing-up together, and forgetting our troubles.

'But then the next day Diana called on us; she's

the Marchioness of Writtle, you know. And she asked what Verity would do for a costume, and when we told her she looked rather put out and said her friend Helen was coming as a maharani. Then she saw Verity look a bit crestfallen, and she said it wouldn't matter if there were two Indian ladies in the party.'

'It sounds like twice the fun, to me,' said Harriet.

'You will perhaps think badly of me, Harriet,' Lady Sylvia resumed. 'But I was so cross! I was sure that Diana's wealthy friend would have a real sari, and all sorts of authentic stuff, and it would put my beloved Verity in a curtain in the shade. And then I remembered that emerald. I thought I remembered that you could wear it as a necklace or as a tiara, and I sent Verity round to the bank to get it and see.'

'For such a purpose you could have used the paste copy,' said Peter.

'Was there a copy? I didn't know that,' she said. 'I knew only about the real one. And we asked the ayah to advise us how to wear it. She came round right away, and looked at the emerald, and was very impressed by it. She looked at it and turned it over, and looked again. Then she said to wear it as a necklace. I must say, it looked stunning against the pale green silk. It drew your eyes at once. And it looked, well, authentic. It didn't look gloomy or out of place at all, as I had heard Roland's sisters say.

'Lily—did I mention the ayah was called Lily?—was all over smiles, and almost reverent about the emerald. She told us it was really something special—well, we knew that—and she said it would bring good luck in love, because there was a love-spell written on the back. Verity said that would be nice, and we gave Lily a discreet present for her trouble—half a dozen eggs, as I remember, which we had from the chickens at Fennybrook Hall.

'So on the night of the party Verity got herself dressed up, and put on the emerald, and she stood in the hall of the London house looking so lovely, and so confident. My son happened to be there, on his way back to his regiment, and he said, "My God, you look beautiful!" just like that. And he went out into the street and called her a taxi, because it was a bit wet, and she was wearing little gold sandals that just slip on between your toes. And she waved at me from the foot of the steps, and got into the taxi, and I never saw her again.'

At this point Harriet realised that tears were running down Lady Sylvia's face.

'I'm sorry we have brought such sadness to mind,' she said.

'Oh, no—I quite understand,' said Lady Sylvia. 'You are only trying to help my son. But I think I had better ask you now to go and talk to Diana about what happened. After all, she was there, and I was not.'

Peter got to his feet. 'I shall try to make sure that the distress we have caused you in asking you to recall such a painful affair is not wasted,' he said. 'I hope we shall get to the bottom of what has happened to the family jewel, once and for all.'

'I wish you luck, Peter,' she said. 'Naturally I do.'

15

'So are you game to encounter the notorious Marchioness of Writtle?' Lord Peter asked his wife the following morning.

'Certainly,' said Harriet. 'But put me in the picture first. I take it the Marquess is dead by now?'

'Oh, long ago. Somewhere around 1935, I think. Leaving no children and a great deal of money.'

'But if you are still calling her the Marchioness, she has not remarried?'

'No.'

'I suppose she had a slightly toxic reputation?'

'Well, after the notorious trial Writtle kept a firmer hand on her, I gather. Perhaps she didn't want to risk a second husband who might cramp her style.'

'No triumph of hope for her?'

'Well, most husbands would expect to rule the roost. Would expect obedience, submissive charm and co-operation. You have an unduly rosy view of marriage, Harriet, because I myself am so exceptionally permissive and undemanding.'

But this squib failed to flare, because Harriet simply looked at her husband and said, 'Indeed you are.'

The conversation was interrupted, as their conversations sometimes were these days, by a long, steady, slightly smiling mutual contemplation. Then Harriet said, 'So what was this lifestyle that a normally repressive husband would have impaired?'

'Oh, house-parties; moving around with a great cluster of satellite friends between Chamonix, the Riviera, New York and Madeira. Always in the *Tatler* for this or that grand do.'

'I wonder how such a person got on in the war?' asked Harriet.

'So do I,' said Peter. 'Shall we call on her and see what we shall see?'

Lady Diana opened her front door herself. She was wearing a caftan of Liberty silk spattered with sequins which might have been an evening dress, and might have been a dressing-gown. She was smoking a Balkan Sobranie in a long black cigarette-holder. She stared at Peter and then said, 'Oh, it's you. Come in. Place is a bit of a mess, I'm afraid. Can't get servants these days. I suppose you've still got that creepy manservant of yours?'

'No,' said Peter firmly. 'I can't stand creepy servants. I've got rid of any I ever had.'

'You must be Harriet,' said Diana. 'Don't you do something rather odd? Writing or something?'

'I write detective stories,' said Harriet.

'Quite a family quirk, then,' said Diana, leading the way into her drawing-room.

The lack of servants, creepy or otherwise, was immediately apparent. There were dozens of ashtrays full of cigarette butts lying around, and fashion magazines lying everywhere, on sofas and on the floor. A dead fire in the fireplace had probably not expired recently, since the ash pile was sprinkled with cigarette butts and sweet papers. Unwashed glasses and empty wine bottles stood around. The curtains had been roughly and unsymmetrically partly drawn. There was only one chair in the room uncluttered enough to sit in, and Diana sat down in it, and said, 'Sit down,' to her visitors.

Without comment Harriet and Peter picked up piles of papers, moved them from a sofa to a side table, and sat side by side.

Harriet reflected, looking at Diana, on the advantages of having been a striking rather than a beautiful woman in youth. Diana, now in her mid-fifties, still looked striking. Any grey in her dark, short-cropped hair had been dealt with. She was boldly and skilfully made-up, and had arranged herself gracefully in her chair. There was a curious, bright, hard glitter about her dark eyes. No fading for her, unlike her unfortunate niece Verity.

'If you expected a drink you should have let me know you were coming,' Diana now observed. 'What do you want?'

Harriet wondered how Peter would start. 'I suppose you know about the strange claim that the family emerald has been swapped for another, and the one in the Attenbury strongbox is not the right one?' Peter asked.

'No, I don't,' Diana said. 'Nobody tells me anything. That will have put the wind up Edward, I'll bet. What fun!'

'What I need to ask you might not be fun,' said Peter. 'I am trying to track the emerald on every occasion when it has been out of the bank. As, for example, it was when you took your niece Verity to a ball at the Café de Paris the night it was bombed.'

'And you've brought *her* along so that she can make a bob or two out of putting it in one of her paperback shockers, I suppose?' said Diana, waving her cigarette-holder at Harriet.

Peter put a hand on Harriet's arm.

'If this were a social occasion, Lady Diana,' he said, 'we would leave at once and make sure that we never encountered you again. But I have a professional obligation to your nephew which I shall discharge as faithfully as I can.'

Lady Diana turned her face away from them and

answered in a very different tone from her previous brittle light voice: 'It was absolutely bloody, if you want to know. Bloody, bloody bloody.'

'It would be helpful if you could tell us as best you can remember what happened that night,' said Peter.

'I don't want to,' said Diana. 'The whole thing gives me nightmares every time I think of it. And don't tell me it would help Edward, because I don't give a toss about Edward. He's a pompous, disapproving young shit.'

Harriet said, 'There have been some deaths in the penumbra of that jewel. Not helping Peter might amount to helping a murderer. How would you feel about that?'

'You know something?' Diana said. 'I could believe that. I really could believe it. I always hated that thing.'

'What did you hate about it?' asked Harriet.

'It was dark. It didn't look right with the other stones. It seemed somehow jinxed. It wanted to be picked up . . . Oh, I don't know, I just didn't like it. More fool me if we were just thinking of the price it could be flogged for.'

'Murders have happened for less,' said Harriet. 'Please help. Tell us what happened at that party.'

'I need a drink,' said Diana.

Peter looked around the room, spotted something that looked like a cocktail cabinet, and went over to open it. He found some tumblers and a bottle of malt whisky.

'Don't worry about water,' Diana called over to him. 'And there isn't any ice. I'll have it neat.'

Peter brought the drink across to her, and sat down again.

She downed the whisky with remarkable speed and then said, 'Right. Well, I thought Verity was looking a bit peaky, so I asked her to join a mob of friends I was getting together to go out for the night. It was a fancy dress affair—we used to have such fun with those before the war—there were ten of us, enough for one table in the ballroom. A day or so before, I asked what costume she had dreamed up, because I thought with that boring mother of hers there might not be too much French lingerie or harlequin coats around in the wardrobes. I meant to help. When she said she was going in a sari I was a bit bothered, because the Honourable Helen Harrison had said she was going as an Indian girl, and I thought Verity would be shown up. Helen was so good at costumes . . . anyway, you don't really want two the same in the same party. So I asked Helen to think of something else, and she came dolled up as Marie Antoinette. Funny, that, when you think what happened to her.'

'What did happen to her?' asked Peter.

'She was decapitated by a sheet of flying glass,' said Diana. 'I need another drink.'

Peter got up and refilled her glass.

'I ought to offer you one,' she said.

'It's a bit early in the day for us, thank you,' said Harriet. She was beginning to look at Lady Diana with concern.

'We all met in the foyer,' Diana continued. 'And pretty damn good we looked too. A bit of glamour and fun about every one of us. That basement ballroom was supposed to be safe!' she added indignantly. 'There was a big crowd milling about, and I saw there was another party in fancy dress, including, would you believe it, another girl in a sari. Someone said she must be a silly cow because she was wearing a turban fixed with a brooch in front, and it wasn't right to have a turban with a sari. I can't think why, but he seemed very sure of it. I looked across at this annoying woman. She had a red turban fixed with a big green brooch. Anyway, we all went in and sat at the corner table I had booked, and ordered some champagne. Well, it was supposed to cheer us up. And people got up from time to time and danced; it was Snakehips Johnson and his band. Jolly good.

'Then there was a rumble, and a terrific bang, and all the lights went out, and stuff started falling on our heads. People were screaming . . . I reached out for Helen, and her arm was all wet and dusty, and she fell over as I touched her. My ears were hurting, and there was something trickling down my forehead. I called to everyone, "Get out! We must get out of here!" and we began to struggle out into the foyer. Someone had a torch, and was playing the beam around the floor, and there were terribly injured people all over the floor, half buried in rubble, some of them, and I didn't want to see. I'd give anything not to have seen . . .

'Anyway, we were holding hands and struggling to get out into the foyer, and walking all over dead people and stuff, and it was very cold. I looked up and the place was open to the sky. Stars. There were stars, and such awful screams and groans . . . and the foyer was still there. It even had lights on. People were milling about in it covered with dust, and scratched and bleeding. And the emergency services were there, helping people out into the street, and I looked around and saw at once that we weren't all there. Helen was missing, and Verity and Jamie. So I started trying to get an ambulance man to go back and look for them, and he wouldn't. They didn't seem to realise that they were helping people who were still on their feet, and there was all that mayhem in the ballroom. So Donald wrestled a torch off one of the ambulance men, and we went back ourselves.

'I thought she was all right at first—Verity, I mean, because she was sitting with her back to the wall, and there was no blood on her, only dust on her hair, and her drink was on the table in front of her. I began to shout at her to come out. Then Donald's torch picked up Helen's head on the floor, and I threw up. And when I straightened up Donald had got across to Verity and he said she was dead. And then the rescue services arrived, and crowded in and told all the walking wounded to get out quick, and someone carried me out of there. They put me in an ambulance and drove me to Bart's. It was full of frantic people, and terribly injured people being carried in. Someone gave me a cup of tea, and I realised that I only had a cut forehead, I wasn't injured and I was getting in the way of people who were. So I staggered out of there and walked home.

'I can't have been thinking clearly because the way home was down Coventry Street, past the Café de Paris. There was still a line of ambulances, and there were all these bodies lying lined up on the pavement. All dressed up. Like beautiful broken dolls. I thought of looking for Verity but I couldn't manage it. I only just managed to get home.'

'How dreadful for you,' said Harriet softly.

'I'll get over it,' said Diana. 'I don't think of it so often now.'

Peter said, 'We don't need to ask you much more, Lady Diana. But can you tell us how it is that the jewel Verity was wearing came back to the family?'

'The rescue people found it. They sent for me because they were able to find that the table had been booked in my name.'

'That was lucky, in a way,' said Peter.

'Lucky for the Attenburys,' she said, recovering the sharpness in her tone. 'Not for me. I had to identify the body. Roland was dead, Edward was in some awful military training camp in Yorkshire, Sylvia was in a state of collapse. I had to do it.'

'I'm so sorry,' said Peter. What else could be said?

'And while I was in the mortuary they gave me this pathetic bundle of her things. One sandal with bloodstains. A few glass bangles. How could the bangles not be broken when the wearer was dead? And the emerald in its gold clip. Undamaged. But you know, now I come to think of it, they did ask me a queer question. They asked me if it was the right one. I picked it up and looked at it and said I should jolly well think so, and I brought it back to Sylvia. God, that was a difficult visit. If I had a five pound note for every time she said she didn't blame me . . .'

'Well, nobody in their right mind could blame you,' Peter said.

'If you really don't blame someone you don't keep on saying so,' said Diana. And then, abruptly, 'Tell me, Lady Peter, do you have to go somewhere by yourself to write?'

'Yes. I have a pleasant study with my books and papers round me. And no telephone within earshot.'

'I wouldn't like that,' said Diana. 'I hate being

alone. I'm afraid of being alone. And people don't come as much as they did when I was younger. When I was more fun, I suppose. I have to rustle up friends to get company. Hell for me is an evening like this evening when I shall be alone in the house.'

'Come to the cinema with me,' said Harriet. 'We could see *Strangers on a Train*.'

'That's meant well,' said Diana. 'But I'm not your sort of person, am I? And I'm not Peter's sort either. Never was. And I saw *Strangers on a Train* the day before yesterday. Pour me another drink, and then push off.'

Once out in the street again, Peter and Harriet instinctively walked briskly and silently away. There was a grey persistent drizzle outside, which had started while they were indoors. Since they had come out in fine weather they neither of them had an umbrella. Harriet was bareheaded, and Peter offered her his trilby. 'You have a rakish charm in a man's hat,' he observed.

Two corners down the street Harriet said, 'It will be easier to rebuild and reopen the Café de Paris than to mend the damage there.'

Peter said, 'You were kind to her, Harriet.'

'I was trying to be, but it didn't work, did it? Did we get any further, do you think?'

'There was that tantalising detail about her being asked if the emerald was the right one.'

'Could the other person in Indian dress have been wearing the Maharaja's jewel?'

'I was wondering that.'

'Baleful coincidence again,' said Harriet.

'Because if so, and if both wearers were dead it would have been very easy to muddle the stones.'

'They had successfully connected Verity with a sandal and those borrowed bangles, as well as the jewel, or perhaps one of the jewels. And there were dozens of the dead and their accoutrements to deal with. I wonder how that was done?'

'We don't wonder, we ask,' said Peter firmly.

'But whoever do we ask?'

'Charles, of course. What's the point of having a policeman as a brother-in-law if one cannot pester him with trivial queries?'

'If we really think those deaths are connected, it isn't trivial,' said Harriet.

'Of course it's not. Murder most foul, as in the best it is. And yet . . .'

'*And yet,* Peter?'

'I suppose at a time when all over the world people were being massacred in their hundreds of thousands one should keep a sense of proportion about a few gadflies in a ballroom.'

They had reached their own front door.

'You are wrong, my lord,' said Harriet. 'Let's get indoors, and I shall rebuke you severely.'

Peter helped Harriet out of her coat, and hung it over the banister post with his own. To Harriet's raised eyebrows he said quietly, 'I shall bare my head, and my breast if need be, to your rebuke, Harriet; but it is too much to ask of me to summon Bunter to witness it. The worst of Job's tribulations was the complacency of his friends in his abasement.'

They went tiptoe up the stairs to the library, where a bright fire had been lit, but for all their care Bunter heard them and appeared, asking if there was anything he could do.

'Would you bring me a dry towel, Bunter, please?' said Harriet. 'His lordship is rather damp.'

Bunter looked for a minute as if he was going to offer to dry Peter down himself, but then he thought better of it. He brought a towel, and retreated, closing the library door behind him.

Harriet sat in a fireside chair, and said, 'Come here, Peter.'

Peter came and stood before her, and then knelt down at her feet to allow her to reach his head. She cast the towel over him, and rubbed his hair vigorously dry and tousled. Then she put the towel over the fireguard, and bent to kiss him, noticing with a constriction of the heart that his straw-blond hair was streaked now with grey. In sunshine it didn't show; but when his hair was damp . . .

'You may get up now,' she said.

'I am waiting for my rebuke,' he said.

'You seemed to be saying that one death would matter less at a time when millions were dying,' she said. 'But I think that idea is likely to make the millions of deaths more possible. It loses sight of those each and every immortal souls. Or, if you are unsure about souls, those particular skeins of memory. If the murder of many could somehow diminish the importance of the murder of one, then one at a time we might diminish a massacre. A murder is an absolute crime.'

'I accept rebuke, Harriet, because you are perfectly right. Although I'm not sure that that is what I meant to say.'

'It's a running flaw in your marble thoughts, Peter,' she said. 'I know you well enough to know that you could not have spoken lightly about the death of a group of navvies, or hospital porters. It momentarily distorts your judgement that the dead were gadflies, as you called them.'

'You are right again, Magistra. And in any case, no murder was done in the Café de Paris, only an act of war. We should be keeping our minds on Mr Handley and Captain Rannerson. And on the jewel,' he added, getting up. 'Let's have Charles to lunch, and ask favours.'

16

'Sorry my dear sister can't be with us today,' said Peter.

'She's at a meeting of the Prisoners' Aid Association,' said Charles.

'How are all the children, Charles?' asked Harriet.

'All well, thank heavens,' said Charles. 'Charlie will finish his degree this summer, as you know, and is thinking of joining the RAF. His mother can't dissuade him, so far.'

'Why should Mary want to dissuade him?' asked Peter.

'She thinks it too dangerous, even in peacetime,' said Charles. 'It's all right by me. The boy is besotted by planes, and he might as well follow his heart.'

'I expect Mary is thinking about Lord St George,' said Peter.

'But it was the Battle of Britain that did for him, poor lad,' said Charles. 'Not flying routine sorties over the North Sea. I expect he'll get his way,' he added, referring to his son. 'He usually does.'

'And Polly?' asked Harriet.

'Polly has decided to follow me into the police,' said Charles.

'What does Mary think of that?' asked Harriet.

'She's envious. Keeps remarking that a proper career doing something useful is a real opportunity. And before you ask about Harriet, I haven't the faintest idea what she will opt for, and neither has she. At the moment the height of her ambition is the school hockey team.'

When the family small talk had run its course, Charles leaned back in his chair and said, 'Come clean then, you two. How is the famous sleuth doing on the trail of the mysterious emerald?'

'If we find it, Charles, you will be on the track of the murderer of Captain Rannerson, I think,' said Peter.

'Hmm. Maybe. I'm not sure at all that any crime is involved here. It isn't a crime to muddle up two nearly identical stones.'

'But, Charles, someone has appeared claiming ownership of the Attenbury one. That looks like a ruse in pursuance of theft, to me. And such a ruse must have been long in the devising, and it required cunning and knowledge to accomplish it. And probably murder along the way.'

'Your theory is that the victims, or victim perhaps, because I'm unconvinced that a motor accident involving a pawnbroker was a murder at all—your theory is that Captain Rannerson was murdered because he knew or had seen something that might have impeded this long-lasting fiendish plot? Well, Peter, you have been right before when I have been wrong, or at least slow on the uptake.'

'Come, Charles, you are not Inspector Sugg.'

'Well, it does occur to me that if you are right we have only to wait and see who turns up with the documentation and actually tries to walk off with the jewel now in the bank.'

'We have thought of that,' said Peter. 'Objection number one is that we don't know how much time it will take the mysterious Mr Tipotenios to collect his documentation and reappear. And the new Lord Attenbury is desperate for funds. But there are other potential snags. Let's make a scenario as if we were Harriet planning a novel. Mr T turns up at the bank with his documentation. I think we can take it that it will have compelling force. I think we could not rely on its being obviously forged. Can we arrest him, Charles? Can we compel him to come up with an explanation of how it is that his jewel is in the Attenbury strongbox and theirs is not?'

'Hmm,' said Charles. 'If he has a good lawyer, I don't know what we could do. It would be up to him to explain how he knows that his jewel is in Attenbury's box. But I don't see what we would do if he simply denies all knowledge about what has happened to the other jewel.'

'The devil of it is, Charles, that those stones are identical only up to a point. There is an inscription on the back of them, in Persian, and I don't think it would be the same inscription on both. So for anyone who reads Persian they are immediately distinguishable.'

'Well, not every second thief around here reads Persian,' said Charles. 'I'm surprised you don't, Wimsey, you usually have an annoying habit of knowing everything.'

'Ah, love, could you and I with fate conspire . . .' said Peter, 'we would certainly arrange for a human lifespan long enough to allow for learning Persian and Mandarin Chinese come to that, as well as Arabic, and every European language with a respectable literature to offer as an enticement. I am sixty, Charles, not three hundred and sixty.'

'We could find someone to read a Persian inscription for us,' said Charles.

'But we don't know what each stone ought to say,' said Harriet.

'Ah.'

'Can I bring this discussion down to earth?' said Peter. 'The only person likely to know that the stones had been swapped would be the person who swapped them. And that person must have had the Maharaja's stone available. So the immediate question is on what occasions was the swap possible? One such was the ten days or so during which Captain Rannerson held the stone, and was flashing it around London showing his friends. A captain in the Indian Army might have had friends who knew a maharaja or two, or he might have known them himself.

'Another such was in the débris of the Café de Paris, when there were two ladies dressed up as Indian girls. And what we were planning to ask you, Charles, is do you know any way of finding out who was sorting out the items of property belonging to the dead? Such a person might have muddled two jewels together by sheer confusion and the difficulty of the task. As we were regulated within an inch of our lives during the war, I wondered . . .'

Charles pondered. 'I can spare a WPC to see what she can find out,' he said.

Harriet felt herself blushing. 'We must invite you very soon, Charles, with no ulterior motive at all, otherwise you will begin to look very warily at any invitation from us.'

'Dear Harriet,' said Charles, 'invite me all you like. There is always interesting talk here, and good food. That salmon we have been eating was wonderful.'

'Freddy and Rachel are in Scotland,' said Harriet. 'He caught it himself in the Spey, and had it sent down to us.'

'That's the kind of friend to have,' said Charles.

'So are you, Charles,' said Peter brazenly, 'so are you.'

Charles's WPC must have been good at her job; a day or two later Harriet and Peter set out to interview a pair of sisters, now retired, who had been working in the mortuary nearest to Coventry Street on the night of 8th March, 1941. They were living in a patch of prefabs on the South Bank, just below a viaduct carrying trains in and out of Waterloo. In this unpromising setting their prefab stood out from its neighbours, having window boxes, and a rainwater butt and a dazzling garden full of marigolds and geraniums, and a tiny lawn the size of a tablecloth that looked like a yard of green velvet from Liberty's.

They had been pre-warned, and there was a packet of biscuits and a plate of cakes all ready to be brought out along with a large brown teapot. The little sitting-room was full of small ornaments, lacy antimacassars, brass fire-irons and toasting fork, fancy plates hanging all over the walls nearly obliterating the sunflower-patterned wallpaper.

The owners introduced themselves as Joyce and Susie, and immediately asked how to address a lord, never having had the need to know that yet.

'Just call us Peter and Harriet,' said Harriet hastily, fearing that the attention of the two ladies would be wholly taken up with unfamiliar protocol.

The missing titles appeared as pauses in conversation: 'Please sit down—Harriet,—Peter. Make yourselves comfy,' said Joyce. And seeing Harriet looking round the room, she added, 'You can't be doing with plain and tidy in a little house—Harriet. It looks much better with bits and pieces, we find.'

'I always wondered what these places were like inside,' said Harriet. 'It looks very bright and jolly the way you have it.'

'Would you like to look round?' asked Susie, jumping up. 'It won't take no longer than it takes the tea to brew.'

It didn't take as long to show Harriet a second room, with two beds and a wardrobe in it, a tiny kitchen and a tiny bathroom. It was all quite light and sunny. Of course it was cramped, but once you got used to the small size it was perfectly cosy. 'And a bloody sight better than the damp basement what we had before Hitler did a demolition job on it, pardon my language,' said Susie. 'After you,' and she ushered Harriet back into the front room just as the tea was being poured.

Peter was being presented with a plate of cakes. 'Camouflage cakes, those are,' Joyce was telling him.

Peter contemplated the three colours just visible through the light brown crust of the cakes. 'They look the part,' he observed.

'Home-made. Three colours in the mix, and three flavours,' Joyce told him. 'The kiddies love them.'

'Kiddies?' Peter asked, startled. There really wasn't much room for children.

'Oh, not ours. The neighbours has kiddies,' said Joyce.

'Come now, Joyce,' said Susie, pouring tea as brown as the pot itself into the teacups. 'Let people get a word in endways. They haven't come to chinwag with us.'

'We were wondering if you could remember the Café de Paris incident,' said Harriet. 'And a green jewel. Or perhaps two green jewels.'

'I can remember that all right,' said Susie. 'We won't never forget that, will we, Joyce? We was working in the East End most nights,' she went on.

'Me and Joyce here, and our friend Rita Patel. But that night they came and fetched us on account of having more bodies than they could be doing with.'

'Doing what, exactly?' Peter asked.

'Laying them out, my darling, laying them out,' said Joyce. 'Cleaning them up a bit, and putting shrouds on them to cover the wounds as much as you could. Making it as easy as possible for the poor families who came looking for them. They all had to be looked at even if they was wearing their identity discs, and not many of that lot were. Spoils the look of nice dresses, I suppose. No more than they was carrying gas-masks or identity cards in their purses. Not but what you could necessarily put the purse and the body together rightly. We was doing our best.'

'You must have seen terrible things,' said Peter. His words brought back to him in a painful flash the recollection of Mrs DuBerris sitting on a bench in the gardens of Fennybrook Hall. He had no time to work out the connection, because Joyce was saying, 'It wasn't a very nice job, no. But someone had to do it. And you know what, er, Peter, the men wasn't as good at that as the women. Not by a long way.'

'The man in charge that night said we should have had a medal,' said Susie. 'And I said to him I'd rather have a good leg of lamb!'

'But you haven't come to talk to us about bodies,

217

have you?' said Joyce. 'It's those green glass things you want to know about. Costume jewellery.'

'It would be immensely helpful if you could tell us what you remember about those,' said Peter.

'You tell 'im,' said Susie.

'Well, first we was laying out a young woman in a green sari. Pretend Indian. She was wearing one of them green things in a wire, on a ribbon at her neck. I didn't think nothing of it. I just put it in the box with her other bits and pieces, and got on with my work.'

'You put it in a box?'

'We had shoe-boxes to put stuff in. We would put everything we found on a body in one of them boxes, and chalk a number on the box, and put it on a shelf. Then we would put a luggage label on the corpus's toes, and put the same number on that before it got covered over and put on a shelf. Should have been foolproof as long as we looked what we was doing.'

'It went on all night with them bringing in bodies. Then in the morning shift some time someone brought in a couple of bags full of personal property what they had dug out while they was looking for people in the rubble. So we rummaged through that, and guess what—there was a red scarf in it and one of them green stones pinned to it on a clip to make a brooch. First we thought the green sari girl must have been wearing a stole sort of thing, but it wouldn't have looked right. So in the end we put the red scarf in the "unidentified" box.

'Then when we had a tea-break we was bitching about it,' said Joyce, 'saying what a con it was.'

'Why was it a con?' asked Harriet.

'They must of hired their costumes, see. All wearing that fancy foreign stuff. You would hire it in Covent Garden, at one of them theatrical shops. And they shouldn't of hired out the same bit of glass to two ladies for the same night. Ladies don't like to see someone else wearing the same as what they've got. Course they don't.'

'If the two jewels were the same,' said Peter, 'why did one of you ask Lady Diana, when she took her niece's things, if she had got the right one?'

'Only that one was done up as a necklace and the other as a brooch,' said Susie. 'We wasn't that fussed about them—but the costume hire want back exactly what they lend you, or you lose your deposit.'

'Course, since the lady policeman told us you wanted to talk to us about them, we have been wondering,' said Joyce, 'if they could of been real after all. Only they couldn't of been, could they, not that big?'

'At least one of them was real,' said Peter. 'Possibly both of them were.'

'Well, all I can say is coo-er!' said Susie.

'So the question is, could they have been muddled so that the one Lady Diana took home was not the one her niece was wearing that night?' asked Peter.

'I really don't think so, no,' said Joyce. 'Do you think so, Susie?'

'No, can't see how that could of happened,' Susie replied. 'We had the girl all tidied up and labelled and her things in the box before the warden brought us the bag with the other one in it. They was kept separate, all through.'

'Do you know what happened to the brooch that was with the red scarf?' asked Peter.

'Yes, I do know that as a matter of fact. I was working there about a week later, along with Rita, when a woman come in and claimed it. Said her daughter had been wearing a red turban, and had it been found?'

'Rita asked her if her daughter was all hurt bad, and she said she was shook up with a leg in plaster but she'd be all right.'

'What was this woman like?' asked Peter.

'Oh, just an ordinary sort of woman. She spoke nice. Rita said something to her about the words on the back of the stone, friendly like, but she didn't want to know. She wasn't there no more than a minute or two, and then she took her stuff and signed for it, and left.'

'If she signed for it, it might be possible to find her name,' said Harriet.

'Mrs Smith. That's what she signed. Rita said at the time, well, there's lots of those around. Wish I'd had time to have a proper look at them jewels, though. I like nice things.'

'Think where we'd be if we had nicked them!' said Joyce.

'Lying awake at night expecting to be nicked ourselves,' said Susie. 'That's where we'd be. Don't take any notice of her, she's never nicked a thing in her life,' she added, addressing the Wimseys. 'We're all right as we are. Better'n poor Rita. She copped it the very next night.'

'How did she cop it?' asked Peter.

'Fell through a manhole on her way home in the dark, and broke her neck,' said Susie. 'Broken manhole cover. Have another camouflage cake?'

'Yes, please,' said Peter. 'They are very good.'

'It needs an egg to make them,' said Susie proudly. 'But only one.'

'For all that, they plainly *could* have been muddled in the morgue,' said Peter. He and Harriet, having returned home, were putting Bunter in the picture.

'But who was the other person wearing a look-alike?' asked Harriet.

'A Miss Smith, perhaps?'

'And how did she come by a duplicate emerald?' asked Harriet.

'There was a paste copy once,' said Peter. 'I

wonder what became of that? We'd better see if anyone knows.'

'How do we find out? Do we have to ask Charles again?'

'He wouldn't mind if we did,' said Peter. 'He can see as well as we can that this is now looking like a murder enquiry. Serial murder, no less. But Bunter tells me young Attenbury is calling on us this evening after dinner, so perhaps he will do.'

'I don't like to be discouraging, Peter,' said Harriet, 'but are we getting anywhere at all with this enquiry? The emerald could have been swapped while Captain Rannerson had it; it could have been swapped accidentally at the Café de Paris . . .'

'But an accidental swap won't do, Harriet, will it?' said Peter. 'If it were accidental, the holder wouldn't know he or she had the wrong stone, and so could not turn up to claim the one in the strongbox; whatever we are looking for, we are not looking for an accident, but for an opportunity for deliberate villainy.'

'And not very plausible villainy, Peter. Our perpetrator has to have a legitimate claim on one of the stones, that will stand severe scrutiny. And then has to carry out the swap and wait; wait for perhaps many years to spring. What kind of person is that?'

'It is an advantage of crimes in your fiction,' said Peter, 'that the puzzles are designed to be soluble.

In that respect, if in no other, they do not resemble real life. But of course it seems likely that we are looking for an agent of the Maharaja of Sinorabad.'

'Haven't the maharajas all been abolished?'

'They have been dispossessed of all but their personal fortunes,' said Peter. 'I don't think democratic India has got round to confiscating family jewels. It seems rather moderate at the moment.'

'And for the moment we must be ready to comfort the victim of this implausible crime,' said Harriet. 'Peter, what can we say to him?'

'We shall give him a job to do,' said Peter. 'And he will hasten to do it for us.'

17

Edward Abcock, Lord Attenbury, appeared promptly at nine o'clock, and was made welcome with a bottle of port, carefully decanted by Bunter, and accompanied by Stilton cheese and some oatcakes. His agitation on his previous visit had subsided into an air of misery which pervaded his manner so thoroughly that it must have become the prevailing weather in his soul.

'How's it all going?' Peter asked him when he was comfortably settled with his glass in his hand.

'It's ghastly,' his lordship replied. 'Absolute hell. Do you know much about death duties, Lord Peter?'

'Not as much as you do, I'm afraid,' said Peter.

'Well, it isn't going to hit you as it has me, is it?' said Edward. 'Just die before your brother and you'll never have to know. I suppose I must have known that I would be in this pickle some day, but I wasn't ready for it. I simply can't raise the money for the tax unless I put Fennybrook Hall up for sale. I could sell the land, but it isn't getting a good price, so it would mean leaving the hall without its farms, and no income to support it. And it's in a rotten state of repair . . . In the old man's day an earldom counted for something, but now it just makes you into a class enemy or a figure of fun. And I feel a real idiot wearing those robes for the House of Lords. Like something out of Gilbert and Sullivan without the tunes. I don't suppose you've got anywhere about that emerald, have you? The family lawyer chappie tells me it was insured for a hundred thousand pounds. And that really would make a difference.'

'Well, can't you get the insurance company to pay up?' asked Peter.

'They won't pay up for a year,' said Abcock, 'if it's a question of theft. To leave time for the police to try to recover the goods. It's some sort of restriction on the policy in exchange for a reduction in the premium, which my mother signed up to a couple of years back. She was having an economy drive, and she thought the thing was as safe as it could be in a respectable

224

bank. She says she asked me and I agreed, but I can't remember. The truth is I never gave this a moment's thought while my father was alive. And after his death I just left it all to Grandfather. What a fool I am!'

'Just rather young to grasp the ins and outs of things,' said Peter. 'Don't be hard on yourself. I can tell you how far we have got.' And he proceeded to outline the quest so far. At the thought that a murder or even maybe two had been committed and were lying on police files unsolved, Edward went very pale. Peter spared him the gruesome details about 8th March at the Café de Paris, but he was looking even sicker by the time the narrative got that far.

'So the thing is,' Peter said, 'there were apparently two emeralds at that unfortunate gathering. And I know of three that would look very similar: one belonging to an Indian potentate, which we have no reason to believe is not in India; one belonging to you; and a paste copy that your grandmother used to keep in her everyday jewel box to save getting the real one out of the bank except exceptionally. And so naturally we wonder what happened to the paste copy. Could it possibly be the one that was being worn, not by your sister, but by the other woman, whoever she was? Miss Smith, apparently. Do you think you could find out if anyone in your family has any knowledge about the whereabouts of that paste copy?'

'I can give it my best shot!' said Edward.

'If you can find it,' Peter added, 'it might be useful if we could borrow it.'

'What for?' Edward enquired. He was now actually sipping his port, instead of endlessly swirling it around in his glass.

'It might jog somebody's memory,' said Peter.

'That was a neat piece of occupational therapy,' said Harriet when he had gone.

'People like to think they can help,' said Peter complacently.

'What would help now?' asked Harriet.

'Read me a poem, and I'll play you some Bach before bed,' said Peter.

Harriet took a moment or two to reach down the Nonesuch Donne, and find the place, since she was not starting at a first line to be found easily in the index, but midway.

> *On a huge hill,*
> *Cragged and steep, Truth stands, and he that will*
> *Reach her, about must and about must go,*
> *And what the hill's suddenness resists, win so.*

'Go on,' said Peter quietly when she paused.

> *Yet strive so that before age, death's twilight,*
> *Thy soul rest, for none can work in that night.*

To will implies delay, therefore now do;
Hard deeds, the body's pains; hard knowledge
* too*
The mind's endeavours reach, and mysteries
Are like the sun, dazzling, yet plain to all eyes.

Peter was already sitting at his piano, and had lifted the lid. But when she stopped reading he went on, quoting softly by heart:

Keep the truth which thou hast found; men do
* not stand*
In so ill case, that God hath with his hand
Sign'd kings' blank charters to kill whom they
* hate;*
Nor are we vicars, but hangmen to fate.

Harriet, with the book open on her knees, noticed a tiny misquotation on Peter's lips.

'It doesn't say *"nor are we vicars",*' she pointed out. 'It says *"nor are they vicars"*. It's only kings who are being called hangmen to fate, not all of us.'

'A hangman to fate is what I have often been,' said Peter, 'and if all goes well I am like to be such again.' And with that he bent his head slightly, and began to play to her.

Well, thought Harriet without resentment, he is supposed to be playing to me, but actually he isn't, he is playing to the soul of Bach.

'Keeping the truth you have found?' she said, when he finished the piece.

'Any truth I have found includes you, Harriet,' he said.

'I do wonder,' said Harriet to Peter over breakfast the following day, 'what that necklace was like.'

'I thought it had been described to you in tedious and elaborate detail,' Peter said.

'Not the eponymous Attenbury emeralds,' said Harriet. 'The original one. What sort of fit-up would look good with two large stones in it?'

'One hanging below the other?'

'Mmm,' said Harriet. 'Possible.'

'Come to that,' said Peter, 'do we know that the gems were originally a necklace? Perhaps even before the maharajas they graced the foreheads of godheads in a temple; perhaps they were in the hilt of a ceremonial sword, perhaps one each side of a golden goblet, who knows? Something to ask Miss Pevenor when we see her today.'

'And she is?'

'The scholar writing about historic jewels for whose sake the Attenbury king-stone was taken out of the bank on the most recent of those three occasions.'

Miss Pevenor lived in a large mock-Tudor semi-detached house just a step from Woodside Park, on the Northern Line. Peter and Harriet therefore set out to visit her by Tube, starting deep underground and emerging into sunlit suburbia several stops before their destination. Harriet's attention was distracted from the task in hand during the journey, because a young woman sitting opposite her was reading one of her books, *The Fountain Pen Mystery*. This woman, being rather short-sighted, was holding the book very upright and close to her face, giving Harriet a good view of the cover—she had always disliked that particular cover—and no way of seeing from the thickness of the pages left and right of the opening how far the reader had got. Harriet had to be content with seeing how rapidly she was turning the pages. At Camden Town she looked up and jumped up and squeezed between the closing doors only just in time, having obviously nearly missed her stop.

'That's a nice compliment to you,' Peter observed.

He sounds as pleased as I feel, thought Harriet.

Miss Pevenor had a large study with a bay window overlooking the garden. A smart up-to-date Olivetti typewriter stood on a table facing the window, and another table in the centre of the room was covered with documents and photographs. There were two office chairs and an armchair. The three of them sat down. But before she sat, Harriet took a step or two across the room to look at the typewriter, a model which her secretary was asking her to invest in.

'Do you type your own work, Lady Peter?' Miss Pevenor asked.

'I don't these days,' said Harriet apologetically. 'I used to have to; now I have a secretary.'

'Lucky you. I have to type up my stuff myself, and I do find the footnotes so tricky!' Miss Pevenor said. She was a rounded, rosy-cheeked woman wearing a lacy see-through pink sweater, not perhaps the best choice for her figure, but obviously hand-knitted. Harriet suspected a kindly mother or aunt. Although she was a student of jewellery she was herself wearing absolutely none—not a ring, brooch, earring or bracelet, not a necklace about her, not even a watch.

Peter told her that they were interested in exactly what had happened to the Attenbury emerald when it had last been taken from the bank. He emphasised *exactly*.

Miss Pevenor wrinkled her brow. And then she rose and fetched a large blue-bound ledger from a shelf. She turned pages. 'Here we are!' she said. 'I fetched it from the bank with a letter of authority from Lady Sylvia Attenbury on 5th September, 1949. And I returned it on 8th October that year, and here is the receipt, signed by a Mr Snader. All in order.'

'And while the jewel was in your possession, where was it kept?' asked Peter.

'In the safe every minute it was not on the desk in front of me,' she said. 'I pride myself on my security measures, Lord Peter. My insurance premiums are quite modest, considering the value of what is insured. I see you looking round for the safe,' she added. 'Let me show you.'

Miss Pevenor rose, and went to the bookcase that lined the wall behind her. She pulled out a book, and thrust her hand into the void it left. Silently a section of the bookcase slid sideways to reveal a small, but very professional wall safe.

Peter nodded. 'As long as not too many people know about this,' he said.

'The book that covers the buttons is changed every month,' she told him proudly. 'This month it is *Urn Burial*. Last month it was *Religio Medici*. And not many people, Lord Peter, would come looking for untold wealth hidden in Woodside Park. It is not as if I lived in Mayfair, or Westminster.'

Warming to her, Harriet asked, 'Can you tell us what the book you are working on is about, Miss Pevenor?'

'It is called *The Great Jewels of England*,' she was answered.

'A kind of catalogue?'

'With histories, and provenances, and descriptions, and numerous illustrations—some in *colour!* It will follow the passing of these numinous objects down the generations. A great deal can be learned, you see, about the fortunes of our proudest families, from seeing when they acquired their treasures, and when, alas, sometimes they had to part with them.'

'It sounds wonderful,' said Peter politely. 'Who is to publish it?'

'A firm called Hummerby,' said Miss Pevenor, visibly proud, 'who publish a lot of fine books and monographs for various establishments, including the Duke of Norfolk, and the Victoria and Albert Museum.'

'Splendid,' said Peter. 'I have seen some of their productions, and they make a very good job of things. We shall put our name down at Hatchard's, to receive a copy as soon as it is published.'

'How kind,' said Miss Pevenor.

'You borrowed the jewel,' Peter said, 'and kept it in your safe. May I ask you why you needed to borrow it? Was it to have it photographed?'

'Yes, indeed. There are photographs of it in a volume called *Historic Jewels, Clocks and Watches* published in 1890, but of course those are black and white. I wanted an illustration in colour. Kodachrome 25 gives excellent results. Nothing ever equals the splendour of the jewels themselves, of course.'

'It would not have taken very long to get a single stone photographed,' said Peter. 'But you kept the stone for just over a month, I think.'

'I needed to measure and weigh it. I needed to describe it minutely and accurately. I needed to transcribe the inscription on the back. I returned it the moment I had done the work.'

'You transcribed the inscription? Do you read Persian?'

'Alas, no. But in the hope that I might be able to find someone who did I copied the lettering very carefully with the aid of a magnifying glass.'

'I must ask you whether there is any chance at all that while the jewel was in your possession it got exchanged for another. Did you have any second carved emerald in your safe or on your desk?'

'Another such emerald? Good lord, no. It is surely unique.'

'There is another such. Long ago I myself saw two side by side. I have to ask you if there is any possibility that someone—a fellow expert perhaps—visited you and effected an exchange of one jewel for another.'

'What an extraordinary idea!' Miss Pevenor exclaimed. 'Of course not. Nobody visited me while I worked on the Attenbury emerald, and I showed it only to the photographer.'

'Were you present the whole time the photographer was working?'

'Yes. No—I was absent long enough to make her a cup of tea.'

'Who was she?'

'Mrs Vanderby. She was sent by the agency I use

for such work. It is a respected agency used by the Victoria and Albert. They always do very good work. I can give you their card.'

'Thank you,' said Peter, pocketing the proffered card. 'I wonder if I might also ask you to lend me the copy you made of the inscription on the jewel. I will find someone to translate it for us, and return it to you with the translation.'

'Could you really? That would be most kind. Now that I no longer have access to the jewel, I would be reluctant to part with the transcription, but by good luck I made a carbon copy, and you are welcome to that.'

'Do you ever find obstacles in the course of your work?' asked Harriet. 'I mean, do the owners ever refuse to let you see their treasures? Or object to publication of photographs and descriptions?'

'Very seldom. Usually they think that it will redound to their glory to have their property recorded in such work as I produce. They often think that their titles and aristocratic status lend lustre to their jewels, and they regard my work as though it were another volume of *Debrett's*. But I myself think the jewels lend lustre to the family names. It is certainly a great loss to their reputation when they are obliged to sell their heirlooms.'

'You don't wear any jewellery yourself,' remarked Harriet, and was astonished to see Miss Pevenor immediately blush deeply.

234

'My work has given me tastes that I cannot afford,' she said.

'Are you ever tempted, in private, to try on the glories you have been lent?' asked Harriet.

Miss Pevenor's blush deepened. She hardly needed to answer. 'The Attenbury emerald is unmounted,' she said. 'It is not in a condition to be worn. A jeweller would have to remake the golden clip that once accompanied it.'

'I wonder how you became interested in your subject,' said Harriet. She was really finding Miss Pevenor rather strange—an exotic bird in plain plumage.

'My aunt took me to see the Crown Jewels in the Tower of London when I was eleven or so,' Miss Pevenor told her. 'I have never got over it.'

'Just one thing more,' Peter said, 'and then we will leave you in peace. Was the jewel when you borrowed it damaged in any way?'

'There was a very tiny chip off the point of one of the carved leaves in the lower right-hand corner of the jewel. That is all. One would not notice it, I think, without a loupe. Considering that it had been through the Blitz, the damage was astonishingly slight.'

'Thank you very much,' said Peter, rising to go.

'I would be glad to include that ruby ring you are wearing in my volume,' said Miss Pevenor to Harriet. 'It is certainly fine enough to warrant inclusion.'

Harriet felt a shuddering reluctance—the very thought of her ring sliding slyly on to Miss Pevenor's slender finger appalled her.

Peter sprang at once to her defence. 'It is an engagement ring,' he said. 'Never to be parted with.'

'People don't always wear their engagement rings once they have a wedding ring to supersede it,' Miss Pevenor said.

'I do,' said Harriet firmly.

'No offence, I hope. It was only a thought,' Miss Pevenor said. 'I am not short of material for my volume. I'm afraid people are pressing me to include their treasures because they want to put them up for sale. Times are not good at the moment for the better sort of people.'

'Nothing as certain as death and taxes?' said Peter.

'Do you mean,' asked Harriet, 'that inclusion in your work will enhance the saleability of jewels?'

'Very much so, Lady Peter. Everyone likes a good provenance.'

As they trundled back on the Tube to Green Park, Peter said, 'Oxford next, I think. We have Bunter's photograph, and Miss Pevenor's transcription. Someone will surely be able to read it for us.'

'Any excuse will do,' said Harriet, 'for the towery city.'

'I expect there is someone in Cambridge, if you would prefer,' said Peter.

'Cambridge is very beautiful,' said Harriet, 'but it is not ours.'

'Oxford, then,' said Peter. 'Tomorrow.'

18

But as it happened, Bunter shot their excuse from under them. He was brimming with satisfaction as he took their coats and hats in the hall.

'I am delighted to tell you, my lord, my lady,' he said, the moment they were disrobed, 'that I have secured a translation of the words on the suspect emerald.'

'The devil you have!' said Peter. 'Well done, thou good and faithful servant. And how, may I ask, did you do it?'

'As you know, m'lord, m'lady,' said Bunter, almost smiling as he spoke, 'I teach a WEA course in photography on Wednesday afternoons in Fulham.'

'*I* didn't know that,' said Harriet. 'Beyond knowing that Wednesday was your afternoon off, I have never enquired.'

'Your ladyship is very considerate of my privacy,' said Bunter. 'But having had such satisfaction over many years in practising photography, and having been so often useful to his lordship in that way, I have been giving some time to helping others to the same satisfaction as I have had myself. I am completely self-taught, my lady, but of course Hope has been able to assist me in any matter in which I find myself at a loss.'

Harriet was distracted by the thought of Bunter at a loss, but Peter cut straight to the chase. 'How has this helped you to decipher Persian, Bunter?' he asked.

'A young lady in my class is an Iranian by birth,' Bunter answered, 'and it occurred to me to show her the photograph I took in Mr Snader's office, and to ask for her comments. She was puzzled at first, and told me that she did not read Arabic. But then on looking more closely she realised that the words were in Persian. She told me that having come to England as a young child she was not fully fluent in her native tongue, but she managed even so to tell me . . .' Bunter was talking on his feet as they mounted the stair together, and as they reached the library door, he opened it triumphantly, and added, 'What the words said.'

'Be done with the theatricals, Bunter, and tell us all,' said Peter.

'On the table, my lord,' said Bunter.

Two sheets of paper were lying side by side on the library table. The first one was a note made in Bunter's handwriting, so long ago.

'I will not cease striving until I achieve my desire . . .'

'That is what is on the Attenbury stone,' said Peter.

'Just so, my lord. You told me at the time, and I made a note of it. And this'—Bunter indicated the second sheet of paper—'is what is on the stone in the bank.'

The second paper said: *'or my spirit leaves my own body.'*

Harriet took up both sheets of paper, and read out: ' *"I will not cease striving until I achieve my desire, or my spirit leaves my own body."* Well, that's clear enough.'

'What do you take to be clear enough, Harriet?' Peter asked her.

'That the stones belong together. The inscriptions make perfect sense paired like this.'

'They do. But logically, the stone in the bank cannot be the Attenburys'. QED I had been wondering if the Maharaja's stone might have been floating about in England somehow, and had thought of trying some way to approach the distant potentate tactfully about it . . . Because tracking the movements of his jewel would require his co-operation. Care and diplomacy required.'

'Diplomacy comes naturally to you, Peter,' said Harriet.

'I was about to tell you, my lord,' said Bunter, 'that the potentate in question is not at the moment very distant. The court pages in this morning's *Times* indicate that he is visiting London this month and staying at the Savoy.'

'Good lord!' said Peter. 'I have occasionally

wondered if he was a real person at all. But fictional persons do not breeze into London and stay at the Savoy.'

'They might,' objected Harriet. 'They can do it more easily than real people can and more easily afford it.'

'They could also, I suppose, own fictional jewels. The problem with that is that I saw and held the Maharaja's jewel, which was too tangible by far to be an act of the imagination. But, tally-ho! Bunter, present my card at the porters' desk at the Savoy, and request an appointment to see the great man at his earliest convenience. Oh, and let Miss Pevenor have that translation in the post, would you?'

It was a foggy early evening when they set out for the Savoy. Not the white fog which from time to time enveloped their house at Paggleham but the dirty grey London fog, smelling of the coal smoke with which it was laden. In only a few yards a pedestrian would have soot-rimmed nostrils, and soot-lined lips tasting foul to the tongue. Harriet's petticoat, still one made of parachute silk from the war years, would be filthy for four inches above the hem by the time they reached their destination. The street lights had shrunk into themselves, dimly bright but casting no brightness. There were very few cars, and those were crawling along the kerb, moving more slowly than the Wimseys were walking. But there was a weird sort of beauty about it. It had the capacity to make the familiar look like a ghostly mystery. All sounds were deadened, and the two of them walked in silence, because opening one's mouth allowed the entering caustic miasma to burn in one's throat. Both of them had wrapped their scarves over the lower half of their faces. We look, thought Harriet, like bit-part actors in a Hitchcock film.

'Shall we turn back?' Peter asked her, as they passed the Royal Academy.

'No, we don't need to,' she replied, in a voice muffled in her scarf.

Peter drew her arm through his as though he thought he might lose her, and they trudged on.

'They'll have to do something about this some day,' he observed as they crossed Piccadilly Circus and headed down the Haymarket.

'People in England can't do without coal fires,' Harriet said.

'Anthracite,' Peter replied, and with that they were silent till they reached the entrance to the Savoy. A cloud of fog accompanied them through the doors and dispersed at the sight of the good fire burning in the lobby. They could see each other's breath as they both exhaled vigorously to expel the foul air from their lungs.

The receptionist phoned up to the Maharaja's room, and a resplendent servant all in white with a

241

bright red turban appeared to escort them up in the lift.

The Maharaja rose from his sofa, and advanced to meet them with extended hand. 'Lord Peter!' he exclaimed. 'After all these years I would have known you anywhere!'

Peter stopped dead in astonishment. 'Mr Nandine Osmanthus!' he said. 'Good lord! Mr Nandine Osmanthus, may I introduce my wife, Lady Peter . . .'

The Maharaja turned his attention to Harriet. A man of about Peter's age, she thought, with a lean, intelligent face. He greeted her gravely in perfect English. He was, in contrast to his servant, very plainly and austerely dressed, wearing a dark grey silk achkan, over western trousers. Then as they all sat down a sudden flash of light made her notice his only adornment—a large diamond on the buckle of his left shoe.

'Now, it will be about those emeralds that you wish to see me,' he said. Unasked, his servant placed little tables beside them, and brought green tea in paper-thin china cups. 'In what way are they causing trouble at the moment?'

'You remember, I am sure, coming many miles to confirm that Lord Attenbury's emerald was one of a pair with your own?'

'What a palaver!' said the Maharaja, laughing. 'I got arrested by the British police, my God!'

'That may not have been the only indignity you

suffered, appearing under a pseudonym, as you did,' said Peter.

'I thought it would be fun to escape my all-too-burdensome identity,' he said. 'A young man's trick. You, Lord Peter, treated me with perfect courtesy. A model English lord, I thought you. Unlike, if may say so, your host.'

'You might have had a better reception if you had appeared as yourself,' Peter offered.

Harriet listened, bemused. Why should Peter feel defensive about old Lord Attenbury's discourtesy?

'I was on his ground,' observed the Maharaja. 'It is not how we are treated in England that has been a cause of grievance, Lord Peter, but how we have been treated in India.'

'I have never been to India, I am afraid,' Peter said.

'My dear fellow! You must come, you must both come. I shall do you proud. Would you like to go on a tiger hunt?'

'I would rather hunt manuscripts,' said Peter. 'To see them; not to acquire them unless they were honestly for sale.'

'You are sure you would not like to play the English lord in my country? Shoot a few tigers and take them home as rugs? Then you can say casually to your guests, "I shot that fellow myself when I was hunting in Sinorabad."'

'Not at all my kind of thing, I'm afraid,' said Peter. 'But I would like to see the observatory at Jaipur.'

The two men sat silently for a moment, taking the measure of each other.

'And you, Lady Harriet, would like to buy jewels and silks, and ride on an elephant?'

Harriet said, 'Yes, I would like to ride on an elephant. My interest in jewels is confined to their capacity to be the crux of interesting plots.'

'As certain emeralds might be?' he asked, smiling.

'It is your own emerald we have come to ask you about,' Peter told him.

'That is my own affair, surely,' said the Maharaja.

Peter paused, like a chess player considering the next move. 'We believe it to be at this moment in the Attenbury strongbox in a bank vault,' he said.

'You are entirely mistaken,' said the Maharaja. 'The one emerald remaining to my family was returned by me to my mother's custody on my return from the mission on which I encountered you, in 1921. And since that time it has been on display in a little treasury my family established in the palace in Sinorabad for the delectation of tourists. And, of course, to collect a fee for the privilege of gawping—is that how you would put it?—at items of immeasurable value. You can read of it, mentioned in *Barham's Guide* for Indian travellers, and you shall see it when you visit me; the show also contains some very fine Mughal manuscripts. However, my curiosity is aroused; what makes you imagine that my jewel is now place-holding for Attenbury's?'

'I had better tell you the whole story, I think,' said Peter. He launched into the tale of the bank manager's mysterious visitor, and the alleged substitution of the jewels.

'The inscriptions are the key to this mystery,' said the Maharaja.

Peter unfolded from his wallet the two sheets of paper with the inscriptions written on them. The Maharaja made a great show of finding his gold-rimmed reading glasses, and holding the papers up to read them. And then his demeanour changed. Suddenly the playful, supercilious guarded manner was dropped.

'You know where the stone is that carries these words?' he cried, flourishing the paper that said: *'or my spirit leaves my own body'*.

'Indeed we do,' said Peter. 'It is the one in the Attenbury box which the present Lord Attenbury is being told is not his because another can prove ownership of it. I must ask you directly: is that other person you, or one of your agents?'

The Maharaja left that question unanswered. He said, 'At last, at last, the third stone has turned up! My father and grandfather always believed it would surface somehow, somewhere. And now it is found. And do I understand that it belongs to someone who would like to sell it? This is wonderful, wonderful!'

'A third stone,' said Peter. 'My wife did wonder what kind of setting could look right with just two. But if there are three . . .'

'The inscriptions seem to show otherwise,' said Harriet quietly. 'They are continuous. And what would the third one say?'

'My dear lady, the inscriptions you have brought me do happen to make sense together. But they are not continuous. What a pity it is,' he went on, 'that after hundreds of years of common history the balance should be so one-way. We have acquired widespread knowledge of English, and a new democracy. Good railways, and a sense of the law; our departing rulers have acquired a few tiger-skin rugs and a liking for curry. You have had the worst of it. But so few of you have learned of our culture, which is the equal of yours. If you had known a little Persian you would have seen at once that we are looking at a verse by Hafez. Look, I will write it for you in English. First the words on the Attenbury stone: *"I will not cease striving until I achieve my desire."* Then the words on my stone: *"Either my body joins my beloved"*; and finally the words on the stone so long missing: *"or my spirit leaves my own body."* Together they make up famous lines from a very great poet.'

'And they were made as a love-gift,' said Harriet, touched.

'And if I could have them together again they would be that once more. I could give them to my son to adorn his bride.'

'There is some way to go before we can achieve

that,' Peter said. 'And there is, I think, danger in it.'

'Where does danger come in?' asked the Maharaja.

'If I knew who has planted the third stone in place of the first, I could tell you that,' said Peter. 'But along the way in the track of these stones lives have been taken.'

'Take me into your confidence, old chap, and tell me everything you have been able to find out,' said the Maharaja.

Harriet wondered if Peter would be willing to do any such thing, but it seemed that he was. He began to recount the occasions when the Attenbury stone, or what everybody supposed to be that stone, had been taken out of the bank.

'I know of Captain Rannerson,' the Maharaja said. 'He was for a while a member of the Bombay Turf Club.'

'Did you by any chance offer him an inducement to acquire Attenbury's emerald for you?' asked Peter.

'My dear fellow, of course I did!' said the Maharaja. 'Or rather, my father did. And my grandfather before him. All my life it has been a determined aim of my family to reunite the stones. Announcements have been widely circulated. A large reward would be paid to anybody who could return a stone to us, or enable us to buy one of them. For the return of both the missing stones the reward would be quadrupled. My grandfather said this, my father said this, and I myself have likewise said it.'

'So when Captain Rannerson took the Attenbury emerald as a pledge, he probably intended to claim a huge reward for it,' said Peter.

'I imagine so,' said the Maharaja.

'But the interesting question is, did the person who killed him for it have a very particular motive; were they in possession of that third stone, the existence of which has so surprised me?'

'Someone killed him?'

'He was strangled within a few hours of Attenbury redeeming the pledge.'

'Now, this is very serious,' said the Maharaja.

'Yes, it is,' said Peter. 'I don't think any question of murder arises when the stone was on the rampage in 1941. Although violent death was all around it. And the person who had custody of the stone most recently returned it safely to the bank vault eighteen months ago. But about Captain Rannerson there is little doubt. If you will, sir, you must tell me all you can about that third stone.'

'It has long been lost to us,' said the Maharaja. 'My grandfather found himself strapped for cash in the middle of a terrible famine among his people. He sold two of his great jewels, in his distress, sold them to buy rice. One of them was bought by an official in the East India Company, and taken to London where it was sold to the

Attenbury family. My father had a copy of the sale catalogue in his library. The other one was taken by a military man, a compassionate fellow, who raffled it at a military banquet. It raised a decent sum of money—almost what it was worth—but the winner of the raffle was not an officer of high rank, and he was posted elsewhere very quickly. We lost track of him. We have never heard anything about the stone. And he may not have realised the value of his prize—a prize in a raffle, my God!'

'And it is this stone that has somehow changed places with the Attenbury stone. Someone in possession of it contrived to make the exchange; if they are allowed now to reclaim the third stone they will probably intend to present you with both. Is that four-fold reward still on offer?'

'It is. Of course it is; my family are honourable people.'

'You would not scruple to reward murder?'

'I would not commit a murder myself, to recover the stones,' said the Maharaja. 'But I would stop at nothing less. You must keep in touch with me, Lord Peter. I will pay you a retainer to act in my interest in this matter.'

'Thank you,' said Lord Peter, 'but I have never taken money for detective work. And I am already engaged on Lord Attenbury's behalf.'

'There may not be a conflict of interest here,' said the Majaraja. 'If I understand you correctly,

Attenbury wishes you to help him sell the stone and I wish you to help me buy it.'

'If only things were that simple,' said Lord Peter. 'But there may be a grave conflict of interest between buying and selling stones, and seeing justice done to a murderer.'

'And you would put justice before jewels?'

'A long way before,' said Peter.

The Maharaja sat contemplating Peter for a few moments, and then just perceptibly nodded, as though accepting that statement. 'Now, before you leave,' he said, 'I must show you something.' He spoke a few words to his servant, who drew back the curtains, and opened the tall glazed doors of the room. The night air blew a chilly gust, but the Maharaja led the way out on to the terrace. 'What does it remind you of?' he asked, rubbing his hands together in the cold. Harriet peered into the murky gloom. She could see, in faint outline against the night sky, the tower of Big Ben, the clock-face lit, but obscured by the drifting fog. The shape of Westminster Bridge was just discernible against the black river with faintly glittering reflections rocking in its surface.

'Monet,' said Harriet.

'Quite right, dear lady! Quite right!' said the Maharaja, as though thrilled by her perceptiveness. 'I always take the room he stayed in. They tell me there are better rooms, and I tell them that there cannot be. What paintings he made from this viewpoint! Do you know he called the London fog *cher brouillard*! He came for it specially! Can you imagine? Come in, come in,' he added. 'I will freeze you to death out here without your coats on. A little brandy to warm you up before you go?'

'So, Peter,' said Harriet in the back seat of the taxi which was taking them home slowly through fog and darkness, 'in that game who was cat and who was mouse?'

'Oh, we were the mice, undoubtedly,' he said cheerfully.

'I rather liked him,' she said. There had been a faint echo of Peter about him; a self-mocking involuntary glamour.

'Oh, so did I,' Peter said. 'But a man may smile and smile and be a villain, and all that.'

'He might be a trickster,' she said thoughtfully. 'But a murderer?'

'Probably not a murderer. But I take him to be ruthless in pursuing his aims, and he is certainly an element on the board.'

'That reward of his, you mean?'

'And the third stone. The third stone is a proverbial cat among the pigeons. Brr, I'm cold in this damn taxi. Let's to bed when we get home.'

Bunter greeted them at the door. 'Lord Attenbury called in your absence, my lord, my lady. He has left a note for you, and a parcel. On the library table, my lord.'

His lordship went leaping up the stairs, Harriet and Bunter following sedately.

Peter picked up the note. 'The paste copy has been retrieved from a dressing-up box at Fennybrook Hall. The servants believe it has been there since the old Lady Attenbury died. He has pleasure in leaving it with us for the duration.' Peter waved a hand at Bunter, who took a paper-knife, and carefully slit the brown paper of the accompanying package. It was lined with tissue paper. He lifted out of the paper the entire paste copy—the rivière of emeralds and tiny diamonds, and the great green stone hanging from it.

'Of course,' said Peter, 'this is a copy of the stones as they used to be. Before they were re-set.'

'Strewth!' said Harriet. 'These are dazzling! Whatever can the real ones have been like?'

'Oh, quite terrific,' said Peter. 'Real hit-you-in-the-eye. But I think I prefer the phoney ones.'

'It's not like you to go for the ersatz, Peter. Why?'

'These fakes arc innocent,' he said. 'They have lain unregarded in a box with old curtains, old-fashioned frocks and hats and stage cutlasses for a generation. There is no bloodshed to lay to their account.'

19

Harriet surfaced from deep sleep, dreaming of a phone ringing. Had she dreamed it, or had there really been a phone call? She turned over and looked at the pretty little alarm clock at her bedside, with luminous spots round the dial and on the hands. Two thirty. She must have dreamed it. The house was now silent, the room dark. Sometimes it was flooded with moonlight, but tonight a slender crescent moon hung in an upper pane of the window glass, surrounded by a sprinkle of stars; these astral bodies kept their light for themselves. She could hear Peter's steady breathing where he lay beside her. Nothing had wakened him. She turned over, buried her face in her pillow and tried to return to sleep. She was cross with herself; how could she work tomorrow if she could not sleep through the night? Here she was, warm and safe and in a silent house . . . But no, the house was not silent. There were stealthy noises, someone moving about quietly, a brief whisper, a door being gently opened and shut. She was now completely awake, and listening intently for every slight sound. She heard in the quiet street outside the sound of a motor car. A car door being opened. Nothing and nobody should be stirring at two thirty. And then a light tap on the bedroom door.

Bunter's familiar voice: 'My lord; my lady . . .'

Before she could answer him he entered, and put the lights on. She sat up, blinking. Peter woke cleanly and completely; he said, 'What's up, Bunter?'

Bunter was holding Peter's shirt and trousers. 'There has been a phone call from Duke's Denver, my lord,' he said.

'Is it my mother?' asked Peter, in a voice in which Harriet heard terror.

'No, my lord, it is the house. There is a fire in Bredon Hall. The Duchess has asked if you can come at once.'

Peter shook his head, as if to shake off drowsiness. 'I'll get dressed right away,' he said.

'When you are ready, my lord, the car is at the door, and your case is in the boot,' said Bunter.

'I'm coming too,' said Harriet.

'Yes,' said Peter, discarding his pyjamas, and pulling on a vest. 'If you would, Harriet. And Bunter, you too, I think.'

Bunter nodded, like a man vindicated. 'I have taken the liberty of packing overnight cases for her ladyship, and for myself, my lord.'

Harriet dived into her dressing-room, and got rapidly into old clothes. She ran downstairs. The front door was standing ajar and the car with engine idling was at the kerb, Peter at the wheel. A triple thump of the front door closing, followed by the car doors, and they were on their way.

'If my mother asked for me, then I take it she is herself all right?' asked Peter as they sped along Oxford Street towards the Clerkenwell Road.

'I have no reason to think otherwise, my lord,' said Bunter. 'But it was not your mother who called. It was the Duchess, not the Dowager Duchess.'

'*Helen* summoned me?' said Peter. 'Good God. What did she say *exactly,* Bunter?'

'That the house was burning down. Would you come at once. That's all, my lord.'

There seemed to be not another car on the road. Peter drove straight through all the traffic lights on Old Street, and they turned on to the A10. Peter put his foot down, and Harriet closed her eyes. They sped through north London, Enfield, the miles to Cambridge and then Ely. Out on to the vast flatness of the Fens, where the first light of tomorrow was drawing a just visible faint line of grey light between earth and sky, far away on their right. They did not speak; until they reached their destination there was nothing to be said. Sitting beside Peter, Harriet sensed his tension. Saw his hands that usually lay lightly on the steering wheel clenched on it now.

The nearer they got to Duke's Denver, the huger the load of dread she felt. She imagined a scene like that in *Jane Eyre*, when Jane had looked towards a stately house and seen a blackened ruin. They reached the park gates, which were standing open and unattended. And what met their eyes as they rounded the woodland plantation and had a clear view to the house was more like a scene from *Rebecca* than one from *Jane Eyre*. It looked as if an enormous party was being held in the house, with every window on two-thirds of the great Palladian frontage brightly lit. It was blinding; it took Harriet a moment or two, blinking, to discern the scene on the lawn and carriage drive in front of the house. There were fire engines, hoses running into the fountain basin, people running about backlit everywhere. The torches they were holding looked like frantic fireflies darting through the darkness.

Peter flung open the car door and a smell of burning engulfed them. As they got out a fireman ran up to them. 'Are you family, sir?' he said. 'Can you get these people to keep out of the house now? They are in mortal danger.'

The scene resolved itself as Harriet's eyes got used to the dark. Servants were carrying pictures and furniture out of the house and stacking stuff on the lawn. The great pictures, with two or three struggling porters carrying them, waved like the sails of ships at sea in the draught created by the fire. Peter ran forward. She heard his voice—it carried unexpectedly well considering its light timbre—giving orders. She heard him say, 'Where the hell is Gerald?'

And then 'Bunter!' Bunter had parked the car as

far from the house as the drive allowed him, and was now running towards Peter.

It was unclear to Harriet what she had best do herself. Looking away from the house she saw that there was an ambulance, which had come up the drive behind them, now slowly crunching across the gravel towards the west wing. She followed it. It stopped beside a little group of people. At first she thought that something from the house had been laid on the grass at their feet. When the ambulance men knelt down one on each side of it she realised that it was a person. The ambulance manoeuvred so that its headlights lit up the scene. Gerald. Gerald lying quite still under a blanket. Her mother-in-law was kneeling beside him, wearing a fluffy dressing-gown, and holding his hand. Helen stood rigid behind her, shaking. Gently the ambulance man removed the Dowager Duchess's hand from that of her son, and asked her to make way. They were taking his pulse, and then pounding his chest. But not for long. 'I'm so sorry,' they were saying. 'Nothing to be done, I'm afraid.' Nevertheless they lifted Gerald into the ambulance.

The Dowager Duchess looked up at Harriet and said, 'Is Peter here? Find Peter.'

Looking round, Harriet saw a group of the servants, standing close together, and silently watching their world disintegrate. 'Go and find Lord Peter,' she said to the nearest one. He was just a boy, holding a handkerchief over his right hand. 'Are you hurt?' she asked him.

'It's not bad,' he answered. 'I'll find him.'

But it was Harriet who was on the spot here. She thought that Helen must be in shock; she realised that Helen's whole world, her status and her wealth lay dead with her husband at her feet. God knows which of her losses would hurt her most. Harriet thought that she herself was the last person to help Helen. She said to her mother-in-law, who must be in deep distress herself, 'Will you stay with Helen exactly here, Mother, while I go and get the car? We need you both in the warm somewhere.'

She walked back to the Daimler, hoping that Bunter or Peter would be in sight, but she could see neither of them. The fountain basin had run dry, and the firemen were dragging their hoses round the house to the lake, a quarter of a mile away. She got into the driver's seat, and turned the ignition key, left in the lock, luckily. She had never driven the Daimler before and she had to find the lever that allowed her to slide the seat forward. Time had frozen; everything seemed to be taking a long time. But it was probably only minutes before she reached the two women, and got them into the car. Then she drove towards the Dower House. The carriage drive took a long elegant curve to get there; Harriet drove straight off the drive, and across the lawns in a direct line to her destination.

At the door of the Dower House she found her

mother-in-law's scatty maid, Franklin, standing wringing her hands. At the sight of her mistress she let out a positive wail of relief, and ran forward. Harriet said, 'Helen needs hot sweet tea, and a warm bed as soon as possible. Will you help your mistress manage that? And then see that she is herself all right. I'll be back as soon as I can.'

It was the Blitz that had taught Harriet that in an emergency you give the less injured a useful job to do. But nothing had taught her how to deal with this—the dreadful immediate calamity that had befallen Peter. While she got his mother and sister-in-law into a warm house, somebody would have told him. Was Gerald already dead when Helen phoned for them? Someone would have told him, and she had not been at his side.

She rejoined the mêlée in front of the house, and found herself beside the boy she had sent to look for Peter. 'I couldn't find him, missus,' the boy said. 'I've only been here a month, and I dunno what he looks like.'

'What happened to your hand?' Harriet asked him.

'It got bit burned, missus. It's nothing much. There's others worse hurt.'

In the dirty grey light of early dawn, muffled in fenny mist, she saw Bunter, carrying books. Then she heard Peter's voice. 'Thomas, can you get to a phone? I think we might be able to reach one in the east wing. I want an ambulance to take people into

King's Lynn. I want all these burns and cuts properly seen to. We'll round up the walking wounded while we wait for it to come.'

'Won't we be wanted here?' asked the Denver butler.

'Don't argue, Thomas,' said Peter. 'Just make sure everyone with an injury gets in that ambulance.'

'Yes, Your Grace,' said Thomas.

Peter flinched as though he had been struck in the face. 'Much too soon for that,' he said.

Harriet went and stood beside him. A fireman approached them. 'No more getting chattels out of the other end of the house, sir,' he said. 'The whole thing may firestorm any minute. Not safe.'

'Are we sure there is nobody left inside?' said Peter. Harriet wasn't sure he had noticed her standing beside him, until he slipped his hand into hers. They stood together, watching the party lights in the blazing windows burn on. Bunter came running towards them, carrying, Harriet noticed, a last armful of books.

'Get back, get back,' the fire chief was calling. 'It'll blow in a minute. Get back!'

'Blow?' said Harriet, standing her ground until Peter moved.

There was a loud crack and rumble. Across two-thirds of the house the roof had fallen in. Liberated, the fire leapt skywards, in a flamboyant display of flames and sparks. No longer contained within the building, it roared loudly. They could feel the warmth on their faces, and they began to edge away across the gravel. And as they went the great façade suddenly collapsed. It fell from low down, like someone flexing at the knees. It went down with a thunderous roar, and fell inwards, across the inferno behind it. It gave the fire pause; for a moment the light and warmth of the conflagration was halted. The appalled watchers on the drive could see that the back wall of the house had already partly fallen; they could see sunrise catching the surface of the lake beyond the house.

The fire drew breath; then it began to re-emerge from the rubble pile that had damped it, not in the one huge blaze with which it had burned before, but in dozens of little flames, licking through the surface, and beginning again. Unheard in the huge sound of the fire the ambulance had arrived. Peter turned and walked away to make sure his orders about injured people were being observed. Bunter seemed to be busily directing the removal of furniture and pictures from the drive to safety in the stable block.

Harriet thought she had better return to the Dower House to comfort Peter's mother. It must be a terrible thing to lose a son. She felt an irrational urge to rush home and make sure her own sons were all right. The rising light showed her everyone around her covered with smuts like chimney sweeps. And surely Peter must need some rest.

'Peter, come back to the Dower House, and get some rest,' she said to him.

'Later,' he said.

Did he mean to stand there until the last object had been put in the barn, the last servant put in the ambulance, or ordered to get some rest?

She tried a ruse. 'Peter, *I* need some sleep. Come with me and rest.'

'Sorry, Harriet,' he said, walking away from her.

'Peter, your mother must need you very badly,' she said, catching up with him. He turned towards her a face streaked with soot, lined and inexpressibly tired. 'My mother will expect me to see to things here,' he said. 'Tell her I will come as soon as I can.'

'Yes, of course,' she said. And walking away she realised that although Peter had told Thomas that it was too soon to be calling him 'Your Grace' it was *de facto* who he was now. In the last hour she had seen him becoming the Duke, like it or no. And with a further shock she saw that in that same last hour she had herself become the Duchess.

A family doctor was in the Dower House when Harriet reached it. A pleasant, grey-haired gentleman in a three-piece suit with a gold watch on a watch chain who reminded Harriet immediately of her own father. He had, Franklin had told her, sedated Helen, and was now in the drawing-room with the Dowager Duchess. When Harriet entered the room he was taking her mother-in-law's pulse, one hand on her frail wrist, the other holding his watch. She was sitting in her favourite chair, still in her sooty dressing-gown, steadily and silently weeping.

'Hot tea for you too, Duchess, and a bath and a rest,' he said, releasing her wrist.

'But I don't know what is happening out there!' she cried.

'Nothing is happening that will not wait for you,' he said.

'What happened to my son, Dr Fakenham?' the Dowager Duchess asked him.

'Ah,' he said.

Peter appeared in the doorway, and stood there, listening.

'I had warned him twice,' Dr Fakenham said. 'He took no notice, I imagine. But his heart was dicey. Standing outside on a cold night wearing only a silk dressing-gown over his pyjamas, and watching his house burn down triggered, I think, a heart attack. I will sign the death certificate to that effect. Now will you yourself, Duchess, please take my advice, or shall I expect to be called out again shortly to another avoidable calamity?'

'My dear Honoria,' said Harriet, 'please . . .'

'Come, Mother,' said Peter. He stepped forward, picked up his mother in his arms, and simply carried her away and up the wide, winding staircase towards her bedroom.

'Now there's a man who keeps himself fit for his age!' said the doctor admiringly. But Harriet thought her mother-in-law, frail and bird-boned as she now was, was not much of a burden.

'Is there anyone else needing attention before I go on my rounds?' Dr Fakenham asked her.

Harriet said, 'Perhaps you would be kind enough to see if any of the firemen have been hurt?'

'Certainly, Duchess,' he said.

She must have flinched as visibly as she had seen Peter flinch.

'Come now,' he said to her. 'These things happen to the best of us. Only to the best of us, of course. Common folk have other hazards in life.'

'My father was a family doctor like you,' Harriet told him.

'Well, doctors breed a good line in sensible daughters,' he said. 'I wish you luck.'

20

Harriet dragged herself upstairs. She found a hot bath ready for her, clean clothes laid out on a chair, her sponge bag in the bathroom, and a wide bed in which Peter was lying already asleep. It took a while to scrub herself clean. When she emerged into the bedroom again she found coffee, eggs and toast on a tray waiting for her. Bunter appeared and said, 'Is there anything else you require, my lady?'

'Nothing thank you, Bunter. Get some sleep yourself; this cannot be a good day ahead of us.'

He thanked her and left. She got into the bed beside Peter and was instantly asleep.

When she woke Peter had slipped away quietly. The tray of uneaten breakfast had been removed. She looked at her watch: ten thirty! She dressed rapidly and went downstairs. She found Peter and his mother in the yellow drawing-room, talking quietly.

'My poor Gerald!' said the Dowager Duchess. 'I know he was a pompous man. A man for all the stuffiest conventions you could find. But he didn't have a happy life. The responsibilities weighed him down. And I don't think Helen looked after him properly. There should have been another son. He never got over Lord St George's death. Not even when you had a son to supply the need, Peter. And the one time he did break out and look for some happiness it all went desperately wrong. He never left the beaten track again, as far as I know. My poor son. And now it will all land on you, Peter. And I shan't like to see you and Harriet bearing it.'

'We'll manage,' said Peter.

Harriet slipped away. She went to telephone the children's schools and make sure her sons heard the news from her, and not from hearing about the inevitable fuss in the newspapers.

Coming back, she found Helen in the room, still shaking, though with anger this time, not shock. 'Your outrageous manservant has been giving servants all the bedrooms!' she said to Peter. 'When I told them to get themselves to the servants' quarters at once, they said they had been assigned the guest rooms to sleep in. Damned insolence!'

'I don't suppose they know who they are to take orders from at the moment,' said Harriet carefully. 'And there wasn't enough room in the servants' quarters here for all the people from the Hall as well.'

Helen went on speaking to Peter. 'You see what you get for marrying out of your class, Peter,' she said. 'A damn fool thing to do. Now a woman will be in charge of all this who hasn't the first idea how things should be done. Not a clue. We may expect disorder and vulgarity on every side. And I must remind you all that this is my house now. Your mother will have to take herself off to her London flat as soon as possible, and I shall decide how the bedrooms here are disposed of.'

Peter said, 'Do you think we might bury my brother with calm and dignity before you start quarrelling over houses and bedrooms?'

Thomas arrived at the door and said, 'Lady Mary has just arrived, my lord.'

'Oh, my God,' said Helen. 'My sister-in-law the policeman's wife. And I suppose she has brought her children with her. And where are they to sleep? In the stables?'

Harriet said, 'Helen, you are overwrought. We shall all assume that you do not know what you are saying, and will speak more gently when you have recovered yourself.'

'Are you being *kind* to me, Harriet?' said Helen, and abruptly burst into tears.

'When did you last have anything to eat, Helen?' Harriet enquired. She rang the bell, and when Thomas arrived she ordered breakfast for Helen in her room.

And that done, suddenly desperate for the open air, Harriet made her escape and went for a walk in the park. The air still smelled of bonfire, and she could see wisps of smoke rising from the fallen part of the house. The fire engines had gone. Instinctively she turned the other way and walked into the wood that covered a gentle rise behind the Dower House. The birds were callously singing as usual. What time was it? When would she have a chance to talk properly to Peter? No knowing. How would her son Bredon take to being a lord? It wouldn't be good for him. Well, perhaps at a really posh school nobody would be impressed, and it could pass unnoticed. How did people manage heavy responsibilities who had not been raised to expect them? Well, the present King had not been raised to expect the crown, and he made a good job of it. Being raised in the expectation of a dukedom had made poor wild and wonderful Lord St George attempt to endanger his own life in every way he could think of, and overspend his allowance in dozens of imaginative ways. If he hadn't been killed in the Battle of Britain he would probably have managed to kill himself driving or riding to hounds. And Peter? A carefree second son. While St George was alive, Peter had been safe. But for the last few years he must have known this might happen.

Harriet made the circuit of the path through the woods and turned back. And here was Peter, coming towards her.

'All right, Domina?' he asked her.

'I just ran away for a bit. As you see, I'm on my way back.'

'Can't tell you how much I'd like to run away myself,' he told her. 'But I'm tied like Gulliver among the Lilliputians. The estate manager wants to see me. The lawyers want to see me. Gerald's accountant wants to see me. The fire officer wants to see me. The vicar wants to see me. Bunter has put them all off until tomorrow, and made appointments for them in sequence. But there's also the undertaker; I must see him this afternoon. You should return to London and leave me to get on with it.'

'I'd rather stay with you,' said Harriet firmly.

They had reached the door of the Dower House, and they hesitated there. 'Hope Bunter is coming up on the morning train tomorrow to take photographs of the ruin for the insurance claim,' Peter said. 'Shall she bring your typewriter and manuscript folder?'

'Perhaps she'd better,' said Harriet. 'And I'd better find a cubby-hole to work in.'

'And in the meantime, come and say hello to Mary and Charles,' he said.

Charles said, 'So sorry, Peter. Let me know if there's anything I can do.'

Peter said, 'Not up your street, I think, Charles. The fire officer-in-chief thinks it was an electrical fault, and God knows when the place was last re-wired. All the old gaslight pipes were still there. But thank you.'

Lady Mary flung her arms round her brother and said, 'Hard on you. I know I'd simply *hate* it.'

They were all avoiding the Hall. They could still smell it on the air; they could see the ragged, blackened, partly collapsed structure on the gentle rise out of all the windows, for the Dower House faced the Hall. But somehow nobody felt like walking across there to have a closer look. It was as if they were all waiting for each other. After lunch, when Peter has seen the undertaker, Harriet thought.

When they did set out, the family all came too. 'You don't have to do this just yet, Mother,' Harriet said.

'Better face it, dear,' the Dowager Duchess replied.

'Wrap up warm, then,' Harriet said.

As the little group walked up the hill, Harriet fell back, and walked beside Charles, leaving Lady Mary to walk in step with Peter. Their childhood home, she was thinking. They were not alone when they reached the drive in front of the house. A solitary helmeted fireman remained.

'You can't go too near, sir, I'm afraid,' he said to Peter. 'The stone bit will be safe when everything has cooled down, in a day or two. And the part beyond it.'

'The stone bit?' said Peter. 'It's all a timber-framed Elizabethan house, behind the Jacobean frontage.'

'The fire hit solid stone, sir, and stopped. You can see for yourself.'

And so they could. There was a blackened stone wall standing two storeys high. On one side of it all was a pile of scorched rubble. Beyond it the last stretch of the frontage stood almost unscathed. The blackened wall had a ground-floor arcade in it, and an upper storey of arched windows all filled with rubble. In the heat of the fire one of the blocked arches had disgorged its filling, and they could see that the wall was four feet thick. They could see also that the Jacobean frontage had been built in front of this stone building, simply sweeping past it left and right to make the immensely grand façade that until yesterday had been the glory of the house.

'Good God!' said Peter. 'It looks Norman.'

'Peter, do you remember that doorway that was like a little corridor, between the drawing-room and the green bedroom?' Mary asked him. 'It was all panelled in oak—and we thought it was too thick, and it must have had a priest's hole in it? Do you remember?'

'Yes, I do,' he said. 'We never found the priest's hole. And now we seem to have found the original house; the one that Margaret Bredon brought into the family in the fourteenth century. Scorned and neglected, and covered over . . . and look what it has done for us now; it has saved the east wing, and, above all, the library.'

'You awful Wimseys!' said Helen. 'All that fuss about pictures and books and the blasted library; and I'll bet my socks that nobody has given even a passing thought to the jewellery.'

'I'm afraid if you didn't think of it yourself, Helen, probably not,' said the Dowager Duchess.

'Oh, I don't mean my *own* jewels,' said Helen. 'I grabbed those as I left my bedroom. I mean the family jewels—all that Tudor stuff. Unwearable and worth a fortune.'

Harriet paid no heed to this exchange. She was

seeing in her mind's eye—and she had a very agile mind's eye—a little stone house, gable end on to the old frontage. She saw that to the east of it a wing of the Elizabethan half-timbered house still stood. She imagined it all cleaned and made good. It would be very curious and unsymmetrical. And in the stumps of the walls of the ruined part of the house she could imagine a formal garden; a physic garden such as a medieval doctor might have planted. She stood there bemused, and in love, as she had once as a small girl been bemused by the odd, elaborate house called Talboys, that Peter had bought her for a wedding gift.

They all looked their fill, and then quietly, one by one, turned back to the shelter of the Dower House, standing elegant and undamaged under the cool autumn sky.

'Bunter, where is *The Times*?' asked Peter the following morning. 'Is the death notice in?'

'It is, Your Grace,' said Bunter. He produced a sheet of newsprint, and laid it carefully on a side table in the breakfast-room, alongside the usual display of copies of *Punch*, *Tatler* and *Country Life*. The birth, marriage and death notices were on the page.

Gerald Christian Wimsey, 16th Duke of Denver. Suddenly, on 31st of October . . .

Peter picked up the page. 'Where is the rest of the paper?' he asked.

'I took the liberty, my lord, of withdrawing the rest of the issue . . .'

Just then Mary and Helen entered the room, and advanced to the breakfast table. Peter caught Bunter's eye, and the two men left the room without a word spoken.

'Is it very bad?' Peter asked, when the door had closed behind them.

'I'm afraid it is, Your Grace.'

'I had better see it. Can you bring it to my room where we can look at it quietly?'

'There are stories in all the papers, m'lord.'

'Bring them all. We'd better know about it.'

Banner headlines. MURDER TRIAL DUKE DIES IN FIRE . . .

The Duke of Denver has died during the evacuation of Bredon Hall, the family seat, which caught fire on the night of 31st October. Violence and sudden death are not new to the Duke and his family. He inherited the dukedom on his father's death in a hunting accident in 1911. In 1924 he was tried for murder, and acquitted, being the only person in modern times to have been tried by a full session of the House of Lords, thus exercising the right of every British citizen to be tried by a jury of his peers. The Duke at first declined to defend himself, saying that it was on a point of honour. The trial was a sensation at the time, and brought the Duke worldwide notoriety. On his acquittal he retired to his family seat, Bredon Hall in Norfolk, and devoted himself to managing his estates. His experience in the House of Lords did not prevent him from frequently attending to speak on rural affairs. He was sixty-six. His only son, the Viscount St George, has predeceased him, killed while serving as a fighter pilot in the Battle of Britain.

The title will devolve upon his brother, Lord Peter Wimsey, whose reputation as a private detective was enhanced by the evidence he gave in his brother's trial, leading to the acquittal. The family name, however, will not be free of scandal, because the new Duchess, alias the novelist Harriet Vane, was also tried in 1929 for the murder of her lover, Philip Boyes. There was a hung jury, and by the time a second trial was convened Lord Peter Wimsey had assembled enough evidence against another suspect to secure her release without a stain on her character. Lord Peter now becomes the 17th Duke of Denver . . .

Peter laid down the paper. 'Are the rest of them like this?' he asked Bunter.

'The rest are far worse, I'm afraid, Your Grace,' he said.

'Do they all pick on Harriet?'

'They all mention her, even the ones mostly interested in the House of Lords.'

Their voices must have been heard by Harriet, who walked through the communicating door and said, 'What's up, Peter?'

Helplessly he indicated the papers. 'I would have spared you this,' he said.

'I would soon have heard,' she said crisply. She picked up *The Times*, and read it. 'Let me see the gutter press.'

Bunter said, 'All here, my lady.'

Peter flinched as he saw her reading. 'Why do they have to drag up all that stuff?' he said.

'Nature of the beast,' she replied.

'Horrible for you,' he said.

'Never mind me,' she said, 'what will it be like for the boys when all their classmates get wind of this? And do they even know they are the children of a murderess? Acquitted, of course. Have we ever told them?'

'I suppose I was going to tell them some time. They must have heard rumours, but now it will be wildfire.' Then, suddenly decisive he said, 'Let's get them out of there. They will have to be here for the funeral anyway. I'll ring both the schools and get them to put the boys on trains. Is that the right decision, Harriet?'

'Yes,' she said. 'It's the best we can do.'

Bunter's ruse with the papers did not work for long. The papers were asked for.

'Carrion crows!' said the elder Duchess in disgust. 'Carrion crows is what they are.'

Helen said, 'It's no good wringing your hands over the newspapers. Peter's ludicrous occupation and ludicrous marriage lay us open to all this. Touch pitch and be defiled.'

White as a sheet, Peter stalked out of the room. The Dowager Duchess said, 'Would you rather, Helen, that there had been nobody to help Gerald save his life?'

Helen said, 'I would rather he had not got himself into such a demeaning situation.'

While this conversation was going on Charles looked at the paper. 'They'll be besieging the gates by now,' he said. 'I'll see if I can drum up a bit of support from the local constabulary to keep them at bay. But then I'll have to go back to London.'

A phone call from Bredon's housemaster. 'I have young Peter Bunter in my office, Lady Peter. He tells me that he is part of the family, and asks if he may accompany your son to Denver. Shall I send him with Bredon, or keep him at school?'

'Send him,' said Harriet.

'How very gentlemanly of young Peter,' Harriet said to Bunter.

'Presumptuous of him,' said Bunter stiffly.

'No, Bunter,' said Harriet. 'Just accurate. Of course he is part of the family.'

• • •

Paul and Roger arrived from their prep school by lunchtime. The boys from Eton arrived in the early evening. They looked both solemn and uneasy. Bunter immediately divided them, sending young Peter to help his mother with the photography, and taking the Wimsey boys to their father in the Dower House.

'Ask Harriet to join us, would you, Bunter?' said Peter.

Harriet arrived, and hugged her sons in turn. They permitted this unresponsively with the lordly condescension of the young.

'Sit down, boys,' Peter said. 'Your mother and I need to talk to you. Have you seen the newspapers this morning?'

Bredon blushed scarlet, and Paul looked down at his hands. Answer enough.

'It is not your uncle's history that we need to talk about,' said Peter. 'That can wait. It is the part of the news reports that concern your mother.'

Paul looked up, and said brightly, 'Were you really tried for murder, Mother? I knew Dad had got you out of some scrape, but . . .'

'He did indeed,' said Harriet. 'He got me out of the hangman's noose.'

The misery in the room was almost tangible. 'Your mother and I would like to tell you about it now, very fully, so that you know the truth and will be defended against the sort of thing in the papers this morning. I think you must know that your parents are very happy together. What you now see is that the past can jump up and upset things at a moment's notice. Now shall I do the telling, Harriet, or will you?'

'You, I think, Peter.'

Peter began by telling them how he had first seen their mother in the dock at the Old Bailey, on trial for murdering her lover, and how he had at once been unshakeably convinced of her innocence. Quietly and carefully, he explained that some of the jury had disbelieved her account. They had not been able to understand why she had left Philip when he offered to marry her, if she had been willing to live with him while he declared that on principle he didn't believe in marriage. He explained why she had bought arsenic. Being well used to their mother's research for her detective stories, they would find that perfectly credible?

The boys nodded. Peter continued to tell them how the jury had not been able to agree, and there had been a retrial. That had given him the time he needed to solve the crime. He went through all the stages of the detection, to how he had found the real culprit, and entrapped him. How Harriet had been told that she left the court without a stain on her character. Six years later Harriet had accepted his proposal of marriage. Did they have any questions?

Bredon said to Harriet, 'Why did it take you such a long time to marry Father? Couldn't you see he'd make a jolly sort of husband?'

'It was very stupid of me,' Harriet said, 'but after the trial it took me a while to clear my head.'

'It must have been so awful for you, Mother!' said Paul. He had tears in his eyes.

'It was perfectly dreadful while it lasted,' Harriet said. 'But I don't regret it. If it hadn't happened I would never have been brought together with your father. I would not now be married to him, and I would not, could not, have you, my dear sons.'

Roger got up and went to Harriet and hugged her. Immediately his older brothers did the same. Harriet was encircled. Peter looked on ruefully; he felt as if his tenderest feelings had been put through a cheese-grater, and he was longing to embrace Harriet himself.

'I say, Father,' said Bredon in a while. 'I suppose Paul is still Paul, but am I now Lord Bredon?'

'Paul is now Lord Paul. You can use the title of viscount—Lord St George as your cousin was.'

'Christ!' said Bredon. 'Do I have to?'

'No,' said Peter. 'True courtesy requires people to call you what you wish to be called.'

'I'll just be Mr Wimsey, then,' Bredon said.

'You can avoid using a title, if you like, Bredon,' said Peter. 'But you cannot in the long run avoid the responsibility that goes with it.'

'You mean all the stuff that's hit you now?' said

Bredon. 'I expect a Labour government will take it all from you before I get in the hot seat.'

And then he favoured his parents with something he had inherited already—the crooked Wimsey grin—and said, 'At least you two are *interesting* parents. You've no idea how boring other chaps' parents are!'

'Get along with you!' said Peter. 'There's really no point in your going back to school when we shall need you up here again for the funeral. You're on furlough. Try not to get in the way.'

'Thanks, Father,' said Paul. 'Does that apply to Peter Bunter too?'

'You must ask Bunter that question. But I don't see why not. Saves a train fare.'

'But aren't we all immensely rich now?' Paul asked.

'I rather think,' said the new Duke of Denver, 'we may find we have all been ruined.'

21

The Duke was buried in the family vault in the parish church of Duke's Denver, on a grey and rainy day. It was a large parish church, having benefited from the generosity of dukes down the centuries, who had added wide aisles, and an extra bay to the nave. The church stood on the perimeter wall of the park, where the dukes could reach it without leaving their own purlieus, and the parishioners could reach it without setting foot in the park. It was packed; the great families of two counties turned out for Gerald, and many friends from London as well. The indoor and outdoor servants of the Hall stood at the back of the aisles, among the parishioners. The service went strictly by the book:

Ashes to ashes, dust to dust, in sure and certain hope . . .

Peter read the first lesson, and Bredon read the second. Peter, having fortunately seen the order of service proposed by the vicar, had ruled out 'The King of Love My Shepherd Is'—the line *Perverse and foolish oft I strayed,* might seem rather too apt for Gerald—and settled for 'The Lord Is My Shepherd', and 'I Vow to Thee, My Country'. Then everyone returned to the Dower House for the usual refreshments.

Like most funeral parties it started sombre, and cheered up a bit as it went along. Since everyone had passed the stump of the Hall as they walked between the church and the Dower House, there was a lot of talk about what Peter should or could do about that. Nice, neutral talk that didn't upset anyone more than they were already upset. There were many people button-holing Peter and telling him gruffly that his brother had been a good sort of chap. The old school. Man of honour, and all that. Passing of an era. Don't envy you taking over, Peter; hard act to follow.

By mid-afternoon they were all driving away, and the rain had stopped. The assembled family found themselves alone together.

'You read beautifully, dear,' the Dowager Duchess said to Bredon. 'Just as well as Peter, which was more than could have been expected of you. I was proud of you. Your Uncle Gerald would have been proud of you too. It's an odd thing, isn't it, how at funerals one always thinks that the dead person should have been there; how they would have been pleased to see everybody and hear what was said.'

'Ridiculous,' said Helen.

'Yes, Helen, I am ridiculous,' said the Dowager Duchess. 'But I shall be out of your way for a bit now. I think, Peter,' she said, turning to her son, 'I would like to go to New York, to visit my dear friend Cornelia.'

'If you think you can manage it, Mama,' he said.

'I have it all worked out,' she told him. 'You shall drive me down to London and put me on the train to Southampton, and Franklin has telephoned and found there is a nice cabin available on the *Liberté*. I can manage very well. I shall stay for a month.'

She's a clever old bird, thought Harriet. By the time she gets back we can have worked out where she will be living.

Helen said suddenly, rather gruffly, 'Yes, you did read well, Bredon. Thank you.'

Bredon looked astonished, as well he might, thought Harriet. He put his hands in his pockets and took them out again. 'Er . . . you told us to keep out of the way . . .' he said to Peter.

'Yes, I did,' said Peter, 'and you made a good job of that, too. Haven't clapped eyes on any of you since you first arrived. What have you been up to?'

'We'll show you tomorrow,' said Paul, 'when we've all got out of best clothes.'

'Helen is a person who doesn't know who she is,' said Harriet to Peter as they prepared for bed.

'Do any of us know that, at the moment?' he asked.

'No, I don't mean accepting or rejecting new roles—I mean she hasn't properly decided what sort of person to be; whether to be a pleasant, or a harsh and unkind one. She is the most spectacularly snobbish woman I have ever met, but I realise she thinks it is up to her to maintain standards of a kind. She keeps changing tack and surprising everyone. Did you see Bredon's face when she praised his reading?'

'She has as much adapting to do as any of us,' Peter admitted. 'But I can't bear the way she treats you. It makes me so angry I can't trust myself.'

'Don't waste rage on it, Peter. I'm pretty watertight to Helen. How do you think the boys took your sudden revelations?'

'They're turning out all right, I think,' said Peter, offering an indirect answer.

'They really have made themselves scarce, these last few days,' said Harriet. She considered telling Peter something, and then thought better of it. Since Roger still liked it, she had gone up to his bedroom to tuck him in and kiss him goodnight, something that both he and she missed when he was at school. Very shortly he would fend her off, she thought, so she took her opportunities.

'What have you been up to, darling?' she had asked him three nights ago. 'Hope you haven't been bored?'

'Bored?' he had said. 'I should jolly well say not! But it's secret, Mummy. Can't tell.'

With so much going on Harriet had not had time to worry about the secret.

'I expect it had occurred to them that if we noticed they were around we might want to send them back to school,' said Peter.

You could trust boys to be fascinated by fire, and ineluctably drawn towards soot, that most dramatic form of dirt. The morning after their arrival at Bredon Hall the disappearing sons had set out in a posse to explore. Even the elder two were impressed.

'What a mess!' said Paul joyfully.

'A relief for the old man, I should think,' said Bredon insouciantly.

'Why?' asked Paul.

'I shouldn't think anyone will want him to break

the bank putting a roof on that,' said Bredon airily, waving his hands towards the pile of black rubble that was most of his ancestral home.

PB said, 'I wonder how much they got out?'

'What do you mean?' asked Roger.

'Oh, you know, books and pictures and things.'

'Oh, that stuff,' said Bredon. 'I wouldn't take it as a gift myself.'

'It's all your ancestors, you posh lot,' said PB.

Bredon put up his fists at PB, and they all laughed.

A lanky young man with a wheelbarrow was working near them shovelling up ashes and debris. 'The stuff is in the barn,' he said. 'I'll show you if you like.'

The barn had been part of the buildings of the home farm. It stood empty these days, the land having been attached to the next farm, and being worked by the tenant farmer there.

They all trooped inside. It was full of objects: pictures leaning against the walls, small pieces of furniture, books in great tottering piles, tapestry wall-hangings just tossed to hang bundled up over the sides of the stalls, various porcelain jars, silver candlesticks and bric-à-brac simply piled at random on a pile of hay-bales; but it was even more full of a choking and repulsive stink of scorch.

'Ugh!' said Paul.

'Let's open it up,' said Bredon.

285

They unlatched the great cart doors, and trundled them open.

'Now the trap in the hay-loft,' said Bredon. Roger scrambled up to do it. Cold, clean air swept through the building. A few cinders spun away on the up-draught.

Bredon said, 'Could we do anything about all this?'

Paul said, 'Where the heck would we start?'

'We could bring everything into this big central space and empty all the stalls,' said PB. 'And then use the stalls like filing boxes and put things back in some sort of order. We could do with some trestle tables to put small things on, and for a writing desk to make lists.'

'I can make lists, PB,' said Roger. 'I've got good clear handwriting.'

'We'll take you up on that,' said Bredon, ruffling his younger brother's hair.

'Would you know where we could find trestle tables, by any chance?' PB asked the gardener, who was standing by, watching them.

'There's some in the tack-room,' the boy said. 'They get set up to put the wage packets out on come pay day. I'd help you fetch them . . .' he added uncertainly.

'What's your name?' asked Bredon.

'Jim, sir. I'm Jim Jackson.'

Bredon looked levelly at him for a moment. 'Do you think we can borrow you, Jim?' he asked.

'You couldn't normally, sir,' said Jim, 'without you asked the Head Gardener. But he's in the hospital with the back of his hands burned quite bad, and almost to his elbow one arm, we're told. And it's all at sixes and sevens, sir, so I don't think anyone would notice what I'm after doing.'

'Well, Jim, do as you like, then,' said Bredon. PB was looking at Bredon with a flicker of a smile.

'I'm game to help out if I can, sir,' said Jim. 'I can do what you tell me, but I haven't a clue what all these indoor things are, mind.'

'Would you be kind enough to get out a couple of those trestle tables, Jim, please,' said Bredon sweetly. 'Paul will help you carry them.'

They all set to work willingly enough. Even Roger could carry small pictures and objects. But they quickly discovered that it was hard work.

'It uses different muscles from rugger,' said Bredon ruefully, after an hour's work. He leaned against a post, stretching his legs and arms.

'I never knew that soot was greasy,' said Paul. But so it was proving: everything blackened that they had touched had fingerprints in the grime; everything relatively clean that they had touched had grimy fingerprints, and they themselves were beginning to look like sweeps.

'Bredon, I think this is too much for us,' said Paul.

'Oh, never say die,' replied Bredon. 'This is the hardest bit. Tomorrow we will be moving things back into the stalls, and that will be one by one. Cheer up, Paul.'

Jim, who had been quietly helping with the biggest pictures, slipped away at this point.

Bredon thought he had given up on them, but he was back quite soon with two rather larger gardeners, one of whom was a grown man. 'This here's Bob,' said Jim.

Bob walked around a bit. Then he said, 'Do you boys have permission from the house to be doing this?'

'No, Bob,' said Bredon. 'We are showing initiative. We are always being told at school to do that.'

'Oh, ah,' said Bob. 'Well, the garden men will help you, but only if you give me a formal order that they are to do it. Understood? Anything gets broken, and you takes the blame, not one of us.'

'Of course, Bob,' said Bredon, unruffled.

'Only, young master,' Bob said, 'we don't know how things stand no more. The old Duke ran a tight ship and he had a short temper. He was very fair, mind, but we watched our steps. We don't know what the new Duke will be like at all. By rights I ought to get all three of us out of here fast, only I can see you could do with a bit of a hand.'

'I think you'll find my father is pretty fair,' said Bredon.

With two more hands to the job they moved everything into the central space by mid-afternoon.

Bredon offered thanks, and said the work would be easier from then on, and he thought could be managed without more help.

'Those lists we are going to make will be the filthiest lists known to man,' said Paul, holding out to Bredon his spectacularly blackened hands.

'We'll keep Roger clean,' said Bredon. 'He can sit at the table and do the actual writing while the rest of us do the scene-shifting.'

As he spoke they realised that Bunter had come into the barn and was standing listening and looking.

PB took the lead. 'We are hoping to sort things and make lists, Dad,' he said.

It seemed a long time before Bunter answered. They all knew that if he disapproved the work would stop at once.

'Good idea,' he said at last.

'I thought, Dad, we would need kinds and grades,' said PB.

Bredon raised an eyebrow.

'Kind of things listed separately—as in pictures, prints, tables, jars,' said PB. 'And grades as in how damaged, like a little, a lot, totally destroyed.'

'What are you going to make these lists *in?*' asked Bunter.

'Haven't thought yet, Mervyn,' said Bredon, flashing the Wimsey smile at Bunter.

Bunter left, and they stood around surveying the next day's work. But he was soon back, carrying an armful of leather-bound folio ledgers, which he put down on the trestle table. 'Some distant duke bought in enough of these to last the house till doomsday,' he said.

'Thank you,' they said in ragged unison.

'And now to clean you up,' said Bunter. 'You will need hot baths, and you may need help scrubbing down to get that soot off. You cannot possibly tramp through the Dower House looking like that. I shall organise baths for you in the servants' quarter. No arguments.'

Feeling as sheepish as naughty children, they obeyed.

The day after the funeral, at breakfast, Bredon offered to show his parents what their sons had been up to. He led the way across to the barn. Within the barn Peter Bunter was waiting. It was clear at a glance what had been happening. A little makeshift table carried a row of ledgers, in which the boys had been listing the items. Harriet picked up the first ledger. *Pictures, undamaged,* she read.

'Anything in that list is over here,' Paul told her eagerly. 'The number in the book corresponds to the label on the frame.'

The next ledger was labelled *Pictures, damaged.* The damage was carefully described. Harriet read: 'Frame scorched in lower right-hand corner, three small holes in canvas,' and 'picture blackened over whole surface, frame broken on opposite corners.'

She put down this ledger and picked up the next: *Books, damaged*. She handed it to Peter. The three boys were standing around, eagerly waiting for parental reaction.

'We thought this might be useful, for insurance or something,' said Paul.

'There's hours of hard work here,' said Peter, 'and of course it's useful. Thank you.'

'We couldn't have done it without Peter Bunter,' said Bredon. 'He dreamed up the system.'

'And we got help moving these big pictures around,' said Paul. 'The gardeners helped us.'

Harriet realised that Peter was struggling with emotion. She knew full well what it was, but Bredon misread it.

'Most of this isn't as bad as it looks, Father,' he said. 'A lot of it is smoked rather than scorched. We thought we'd better leave cleaning anything to the experts, but I bet a lot of these pictures will clean up as good as new.'

'I'm very proud of you,' said Peter. 'Of all of you.'

'We think these lists will take us another three or four days, Father,' said Bredon. 'May we finish the job?'

'What? Oh, more time off school, is that it? Yes; another week.'

'Bunter says PB must go back tomorrow,' said Paul. 'He said: "My son has got to make his way in the world."'

'We all have to make our way in the world,' said Harriet. 'One world or another.'

'I'll have a word with Bunter,' said Peter. 'But when it comes to what PB does, what Bunter says, goes.'

'I'll think he'll ask my mother,' said PB. 'And she will ask him if he knows what you think.'

Going back to London, when at last they were free to do so, felt like putting on again clothes that one has not worn for a while. Deep familiarity overlaid with recent unfamiliarity; welcome and strange at once. Harriet had not written a single word during their absence; too much to do, too many interruptions. And Peter, she thought, had not given a thought to detecting anything. In that she was wrong, it turned out. Having seen his mother safely on to the Southampton train, complete with Franklin and many suitcases, he came home, and, unusually for him, tapped lightly on the door of Harriet's study, entered, and sat in the armchair facing her.

'I am returning to you, Miss Vane,' he said, 'in the persona of Lord Peter, the notorious sleuth, and, moreover, a sleuth with an unsatisfied client, and an undetermined investigation on his hands.'

'I am glad to see you back, Peter,' she said. 'What will you do next?'

'Bunter says there is something I ought to read,' he said. 'I shall go and read it. And I believe young

Attenbury has twice left his card here, and is likely to call at around three.'

'Would you like moral support?'

'If it doesn't bore you overmuch. I'll leave you to get on with your own work now.'

But he was soon back, holding in his hand a magazine with an austere, academic-looking cover. 'Look at this,' he said.

Harriet took it from him. '*The Proceedings of the Society of Antiquarian Jewellers*,' she read.

'Page thirteen,' he said.

Page thirteen carried a report of an address given to the society by one Miss Pevenor. She had been offering an account of her researches, including a description of the Attenbury emerald, and the translation of the inscription.

'Quite interesting, Peter,' said Harriet, puzzled at his agitation.

'Don't you see?' he said. 'That woman has just put herself in mortal danger.'

'The reason being?'

'The heart of the matter is those inscriptions,' he said. 'If you can read those, and you know anything about Persian poetry, you know there are three stones. And that's a very dangerous thing to know. Look, I'm going to see if Charles can give her some protection.'

Peter left the room. Curious, Harriet continued to inspect Miss Pevenor's article. She skimmed it rapidly. 'The inscription upon the back of the jewel, *or my spirit leaves my own body,* is clearly incomplete. Possibly the stone was once part of a collection . . .'

She did not look up as Peter entered the room. 'Peter, surely this is all right,' she said. 'Miss Pevenor doesn't know anything about the Maharaja's stone. It's all speculation. She doesn't even know that what she thinks of as the Attenbury emerald isn't the right one.'

When Peter didn't answer, she looked up. He was standing in front of her, quite still.

'It's too late,' he said. 'Charles tells me she was murdered last week.'

'Horrible,' said Harriet. 'That poor woman! What had she done to deserve to die terrified and helpless?'

Peter had just finished describing to her what he had learned when he and Charles had visited the Middlesex Constabulary to discover what they could about the death of Miss Pevenor. It had in fact been reported in the copy of *The Times* that carried the stories about the death of Gerald; not even Bunter had spotted it, in small type way down the page. On a normal day it would have rated headlines, but it had been more fun to harass a great family with a scandal or two. The local police had been a bit bemused to find themselves visited by a senior officer in the Met and a famous amateur, over what James Vaud, the detective in

294

charge, described as 'a squalid case. Run of the mill'.

Someone had talked their way in to the house. No sign of forced entry. And the victim had felt secure enough to sit down at her desk, spread out some papers in front of her. 'Must have intended to show the visitor something,' Inspector Vaud had said. 'And then she was attacked from behind. Bit of picture wire round the neck. Tightened with a paper knife being turned in it.'

'Obviously the local force knew she was working on valuable things. There was a bit of disturbance in the house—books flung on the floor, broken china, dressing-table drawers all emptied. Motive, robbery, they thought. And they couldn't find anything worth taking, so they reckoned it had all been taken. As to *what* might have been taken, they could read her ledger. She should have had the Marshal pearls, and three diamond tiaras. They had circulated descriptions.

'They were gratifyingly amazed, Harriet, when we asked if they had found the safe. Remember she told us the book in front of the buttons to reveal it was *Urn Burial*? Well, I had a quick look roughly where I remembered *Urn Burial* to have been when we visited her, and it was a complete give-away. There was *The Garden of Cyrus* on the shelf, completely out of order—not another Thomas Browne anywhere near it. Wonderful moment! I took the book down, and in seconds I had the panel opened and the safe revealed. I haven't felt so prestidigitous since I learned how to get a rabbit out of a hat when I was a boy.'

'So what was in the safe, Peter?' Harriet asked.

'They couldn't open it. So I called up Bill Rumm, and he trundled up on the Northern Line, and cracked it for us. It contained the Marshal pearls, and three diamond tiaras,' he said.

'So nothing had been stolen?'

'Not a peppercorn. But Inspector Vaud stuck firmly to his guns. The mere fact that a robbery had not occurred did not mean that robbery was not the motive.'

'You can't blame him for that, Peter. Logically he is quite right.'

'Oh, logic . . . I think he might have noticed how desultory the ransacking was. Not a very serious search. But why should I trouble to enlighten him? It would have taken till the middle of next week to explain to him what we thought the real motive might have been.'

'Peter, you should face the fact that it really might have been a botched burglary. Quite a few people probably knew she wrote about jewels, and might have thought she might have some around.'

'It doesn't really look like that to me, Harriet. Thieves do sometimes assault a householder in the course of a crime. They have been known, even, to kill them. But it's very unusual. After all, burglary carries a prison sentence; but murder leads to hanging. You need a professional for a jewel heist, because you have to know how to convert the loot safely into cash. And professionals, in my experience, take very good care not to go armed, in case the situation gets out of hand and they incur the death penalty.'

'So what do you think would happen, Peter, if the Royal Commission on Capital Punishment which is under way at the moment abolished hanging? Would burglars go armed?'

'They might,' he said. 'An unlooked-for result of such a decision might be more murdered householders. Whether anyone would identify a length of picture wire as a homicidal weapon unless they found it actually round the neck of a garrotted victim is another thing.'

'What do you think about the death penalty? Would you like to see it abolished?'

'Charles told me once,' he answered, 'that he had a friend who was a prison governor. And that man told him that he thought capital punishment was more merciful than a life sentence. And yet . . . there are too many mistaken verdicts. Think what a near thing it was that you . . .'

'I think, Peter, that the man who really killed Philip Boyes deserved to die. And therefore, you see, that if I had really done it I would likewise have deserved death.'

He shook his head. And then he indulged himself in the urge to hug her.

'I'll tell you one thing, though,' she said, in a voice muffled in his shirt. 'If they abolish the death penalty it will mar detective fiction.'

'Why?' he said, releasing her. 'Wouldn't all that puzzle-solving retain its charm?'

'Charm,' she said, 'but not bite. The public is gruesome and vengeful. Life imprisonment may be a worse fate, but from a fictional point of view, it won't be anything like such a good ending.'

'Ghoul!' said Peter.

'Peter, did you find out what was on the table in front of Miss Pevenor? Exactly what did she seem to have got out of her files to show her visitor?'

'Oh, the description of the Attenbury emerald, I'm afraid,' he said. 'Dammit, Harriet, if I hadn't been railroaded by a dukedom that woman would still be alive!'

22

Lord Attenbury was agitated. Peter offered him a rueful apology for having so little to report, mentioning that family affairs had been taking up his attention recently. Whereupon the young man exploded.

'*You'll* be all right!' he cried. 'But what about me? What am I to do? Do I preside over the ruin of my family with nobody to help me?'

'Believe me, I am trying to help you,' said Peter. 'But with the best will in the world we may not be able to get this sorted out in time for the Inland Revenue. You'd better find a bit of stoicism to meet the situation.'

'Stoicism? That's damned easy to say when you don't need it yourself!'

'I would have thought our situations are uncannily parallel,' said Peter.

'Do you, Wimsey? Do you indeed? As I understand matters, at the moment your brother died the house was on fire? What do you suppose is the value of a burning house? Might even be negative! So you will escape duty on that, collect the insurance and make a neat escape. Where will it be? A handy tax-free haven like Bermuda? Or Switzerland perhaps? But my family will be ruined, I tell you, *ruined!* We shall live out our lives in poverty!'

Harriet said quietly, 'Lord Attenbury, many people, *most* people, live without hunger or misery on a fraction of what you will have left even if you must indeed sell the house to pay the duty. I have lived with barely twopence to rub together myself, and although it was hard at times, it was not demeaning. You won't really be reduced to indigence.'

He sat down abruptly, facing Harriet. 'That's the devil of it,' he said. 'I suppose it depends what you're used to. Or perhaps, what your womenfolk are used to. They are making such a *fuss,* Lady Peter! Such howls at any economy I suggest. They expect a way of life that I cannot see how to maintain for them, for any of us. And it's not like selling a semi-detached villa in Finchley; selling Fennybrook Hall would humiliate us. Whatever you say.'

'Let's hope it doesn't come to that,' she said. 'But, Edward—may I call you Edward?—I think that most women manage whatever life throws at them. They may make an awful fuss when difficulties are in prospect; but when it comes to the point, they manage.'

'They haven't ever had to,' he said, speaking quietly now. 'I wish any of them were as sensible as you are. My girlfriend has given me up, and my mother says she doesn't blame her. "What have you to offer her?" That line of talk.'

'If the love of a good husband was not enough for her, then she was prime among the extravagances you cannot afford,' said Harriet. 'Forget her as quickly as you can.'

'Bloody Denver has all the luck,' he said, rising to go. 'You'll let me know, I suppose, if you come up with anything?'

'We'll run along immediately with anything of the sort,' said Peter.

'What did he mean by that last remark?' said Harriet, when the door had closed behind the departing guest.

'Let me decode it for you,' said Peter. 'By bloody Denver he meant me; and in that last comment on my luck he was complimenting you. Only for the most basic of your virtues, I'm afraid: your Johnsonian bottom of common sense. You made a good job of that, Harriet. You calmed him down admirably. I was seriously tempted to have him thrown out.'

'I take it that we are not actually planning on pocketing the insurance money and making off with it where the remote Bermudas ride?'

'Would you like that?' he asked.

'I would positively hate it.'

'I thought so,' he said. 'Then we'll stay here. And let's see if we can get these pestilential emeralds laid to rest.'

'Where, Peter, if all were solved and sorted, do you think they should be laid to rest?'

'They should all three be in the Maharaja's museum. Attenbury should have the value of his; and the wicked owner of the mysterious third stone should hang for murder. Now let's see if we can bring all to come about according to the words of the prophets. A council of war this evening, I think. We shall be ourselves again, as if the glories of our blood and state really were shadows.'

'Oh, let's!' said Harriet.

They dined early, and Peter invited the Bunters to join them. A bottle of Cockburn's had been decanted, and Mrs Trapp, the cook, had managed to find a small triangle of Stilton. Not, of course, the way Stilton should be bought or served, but many times better than no Stilton at all. Harriet hoped that Hope Bunter wouldn't find the talk too boring. She was vaguely aware that the pleasant, easy-going way of life that the four of them had adopted during the war, and which had survived six years of peace, was threatened now. It was much easier to imagine, and indeed to achieve, this party sharing a modest treat together in the London house or at Talboys than at Duke's Denver.

'Right,' said Peter. 'I thought we might try to eliminate any that we can of the three occasions since 1921 when the jewel has been out of the bank. *If* we can. We'll start with the matter of the expensive horse in 1929. You first, Harriet.'

'Well,' said Harriet, 'we know Captain Rannerson was holding the jewel for quite a while. Showing it to all and sundry. Supposing one of his Indian friends said, "I've got one just like that!" and supposing they compared the jewels and advertently or inadvertently muddled them up, and the wrong one came back to Attenbury when he found the money.'

'Hideously plausible, Harriet. But the mistake would have to be deliberate to account for the unknown person turning up now and making the claim on the bank.'

'Okay, so it's deliberate.'

'And this little twist to the tale just didn't happen

to happen where anyone who has talked to Freddy got to hear of it.'

'But such a small thing might not get reported to all and sundry. Two people just showing each other the jewels, each one holding the other's for a minute or two. Put them down on the table, shall we say to pick up a drink, and bob's your uncle,' Harriet said.

'And this happened in 1929,' said Hope, 'and the perpetrator hasn't made any move to get the advantage of it all this time? The wrong emerald has just lain in the bank?'

'It's pretty unlikely, Peter,' said Harriet in agreement.

'Well, something that he or she does seem to have done is to send a few people to their maker,' said Peter, 'starting with Captain Rannerson.'

Bunter, sitting at the end of the table, was holding a pencil, and had a notebook in front of him.

'I am recording a possibility that the exchange was made during the time that Captain Rannerson had the jewel,' said Bunter. 'Do you consider, Your Grace, that the motive for that murder was to recover an emerald that had been swapped for the Attenbury one?'

'That would be odd, wouldn't it?' said Peter. 'Why kill someone when one has just achieved the cuckoo in the nest trick that will let one at any time recover the jewel?'

'There was a huge reward on offer to anyone who could present the Maharaja with both,' said Harriet.

'But if the swap had been effected then both might be obtainable without going to the trouble of killing anyone,' Peter said. 'On reflection I can't see that we can rule out anything as a result of this story. Can any of us?'

There was a general shaking of heads.

'No progress on that one. Let's move on to consider the Blitz.'

'Well, that's a terrible story of confusion and death, isn't it?' said Harriet.

'Death but not murder,' said Bunter quietly. 'Not a targeted death.'

'And much confusion,' said Harriet. 'However certain our ladies are that they could not have mixed up the stones, and all that system of shoe-boxes, it plainly could have happened.'

'The interesting question there is: who was wearing the rogue emerald? If we knew that we would be hot on the scent,' said Peter. 'All we know is that they were both there together, Attenbury's and the third stone.'

'And if the cuckoo trick had already been carried out, they were the wrong way round,' Harriet pointed out. 'Verity would have been wearing the third stone, and the unknown Miss Smith Attenbury's. Very odd.'

'Yes, but we are running ahead of ourselves. We

don't know that the trick had already happened.'

'I shall record the possibility that it happened in the morgue, Your Grace,' said Bunter.

'Now what about Miss Pevenor?' said Harriet. 'Killed in the course of an unsuccessful burglary?'

'The other way about,' Peter said. 'A fake burglary used to cover up a murder. We need to think what, if anything, these occasions have in common.'

'This sounds like an eleven-plus question,' said Hope. 'I saw a sample paper while I was doing some school photographs last week. Underline the odd one out—peat, wood, coal, gas, bricks.'

'Gas,' said Peter. 'All the others are solids.'

'Bricks,' said Harriet in the same breath, 'all the others are fuels.'

Hope laughed. 'Who knows which of you passed and which failed that question?' she said.

'Well, we are all failing this task,' said Peter. 'The Blitz is the odd one out, in that two jewels were involved; only one put in an appearance on the other two occasions. The Blitz is also the odd one out in that nobody was murdered, unless Rita was pushed down that manhole . . . The horse trading is the odd one out in that Rannerson had an Indian connection absent on the other two occasions.'

'Unless the Indian costumes being worn by the ladies make that connection,' said Harriet.

'I suppose they might,' said Peter, 'but it's a bit

thin compared to a rank in the Indian Army. Miss Pevenor is the odd one out in that she was interested in the back of the stone instead of only the front . . .'

'Didn't Susie say that Rita had made some friendly remark to Miss Smith about the writing on the stone?' said Harriet.

'Yes, she did,' said Peter. 'I think we had better find out a bit more about Rita. Would you like to see what you can dig up for us about her, Bunter?'

Bunter did not quite manage to conceal his delight at being asked.

'I have taken the liberty of looking up what I could find about the lady already,' he said. 'I was a little uneasy when you mentioned to me that the lady who had actually returned the second emerald had met with death a short while afterwards. She was not difficult to find. I visited the British Museum newspaper library on a remote chance that the lady had merited an obituary. And there she was.' He opened his notebook and read his notes: 'Rita Patel, Anglo-Indian origin. Lecturer at the LSE in developing economies. Accidental death on 9th March, 1941. Great loss to oriental studies . . . fine linguist . . . devoted herself to war work . . .'

'Bunter, you are a marvel!' said Peter.

Harriet contemplated Bunter with astonishment. 'What put you on to the idea she might have an obituary?' she asked.

'I thought I remembered her name, my lady, in an article about the London School of Economics.'

Is Bunter thinking of taking a degree? Harriet wondered. Then, No, of course, it is Peter Bunter that he is thinking about. That's how he sees his son making a way in the world.

'How very clever of you, Bunter,' she said.

He acknowledged her with the very slightest inclination of the head.

'It provides an Indian connection with the Blitz occasion,' he said.

'So now Miss Pevenor is the odd one out. No Indian connection arises in her case, as far as we know,' said Harriet.

'But it's staring us in the face now, isn't it?' said Peter. 'It's about the inscriptions. The inscriptions not only allow one to distinguish one stone from another, they allow the deduction that there are three. Miss Pevenor had obtained a transcription of the lines from us, and told the world that she had done so. The owner of the third stone will kill to keep its existence secret.'

'Then it should have been too late to kill her—the news was out,' said Harriet.

'Not exactly, my lady,' said Bunter. He picked up the copy of the account of Miss Pevenor's speech, and pointed out to her a paragraph.

'The inscriptions will merit further investigation,' Harriet read. 'I will attempt to find someone who can identify the source . . .'

'That wouldn't have been too difficult,' Bunter offered. 'And with the identification the third stone would have been hypothesised. And the owner was determined to keep its existence secret.'

Peter said, 'But now it is being used as a decoy to swindle Attenbury out of his, its existence must come to light.'

'But long after the event,' Harriet said. 'When it is very difficult to follow trails; when reconstructing what happened has become impossible with the blurring of memory. Let's try another tack. Let's make a mental picture of the villain in all the detail we can command. It's what I do when I begin to write a detective story—anatomise the murderer in my own mind. One must have a clear view of the villain, otherwise the clues are impossibly muddled.'

'Well, to start with, our murderer is holding the third stone, and is intending to use it as a decoy. He or she is able to form a long-term plan, and pursue it over many years,' said Peter.

'What is the motive? If it's just greed, why defer the *coup de grâce*? Why not claim the emerald in the bank any time sooner?'

'I don't know,' said Peter, 'unless . . . unless the timing is not coincidence; it has been delayed in order to cause the maximum difficulty to Lord Attenbury.'

'So this person is consumed with hatred of the Attenbury family. Why?' said Harriet.

Peter shrugged. 'You know how I hate why questions,' he said. 'When you know how you know who. Sometimes the who in question will tell you why, but that's a tale you won't hear till you have your hands on the villain and it's all over.'

'There's a further point: exactly what makes the killer strike?' asked Harriet. 'He is afraid that the person who has the stone out of the bank will cotton on to the fact that it isn't the right one?'

'I suppose that might lead to a search for the Attenbury stone, and the foiling of the plot,' said Peter. 'But how was it known when the stone was taken from the bank? That wasn't announced in the newspapers.'

'Perhaps there was an accomplice in the bank,' said Harriet.

'Wickedness in a temple of rectitude?' said Peter, smiling wryly.

'Perhaps it wouldn't seem very wicked for somebody simply to tell a friend when the emerald had been borrowed.'

'They must at the very least have supposed themselves to be assisting theft,' said Peter, 'which is a fairly grave matter in a bank.'

'Or perhaps the villain is friendly enough with the Attenbury family to know of at least one occasion when they reclaimed their emerald.'

'We've moved on from that, though, Harriet. We are no longer looking for one occasion on which the jewel could have been swapped; we are looking for someone who intervened on every occasion on which it was out of the bank.'

'I don't know enough about this sort of thing, Peter. Would the insurers be told when the jewel was out of the bank?'

'Yes, they would,' said Peter. 'Of course they would. Let's get the firm's name from Attenbury, and go and sniff around the insurers. Brilliant, Harriet.'

23

Messrs Abraham, Farley, Van der Helm and Bird had offices off Fetter Lane. Peter and Harriet paused to pay their respects to the statue of John Wilkes, and entered the little side street of Georgian frontages. There was a small gate at the far end into a cemetery, now containing as many park benches as headstones, and profusely overgrown, mostly with what a gardener would have called weeds. Having looked over the railings at this pleasing sight, Peter and Harriet retraced their steps a little, and climbed the few steps to the front door with the long-winded brass plate beside it. The conversion of a Georgian house into offices, although there are many hundred such in London, seems never to have been mastered, and always produces a haphazard, rather random effect. So it was here. The first door on the right was labelled 'Reception'. Peter knocked and they went in.

The room, under a fine plastered ceiling, and within tall windows through which the light poured in, was darkened by a thicket of tall filing cabinets. In clearings in this thicket there were two desks with harassed-looking young women working at typewriters. One of these desks was near enough the door to serve as reception. Peter asked for Mr Abraham.

'Dead,' said the girl at the front desk. 'Long ago.'

'Mr Farley?' Peter asked.

'Same,' said the girl.

'Then we must ask to see Mr Van der Helm.'

'Retired. Lives in Holland since the war.'

'Mr Bird, then?' asked Peter.

'He's retired too,' the girl replied. 'Mr Buxton is in charge here now.'

'How long has Mr Buxton been in charge?' asked Peter.

'Nearly a year,' the girl replied. 'You'll find him very competent, Mr . . . Mr?'

Peter handed her his card.

'Coo!' she exclaimed.

'What is it, Beryl?' asked her colleague, weaving her way through the filing cabinets to lean over Beryl's desk. 'You're famous!' she said to Peter.

'I do try not to be,' said Peter, favouring her with his most ingratiating smile. 'I was hoping to talk with somebody in the firm who has been here a long while.'

'It's Mr Bird you want,' the girl said. 'It's Mr Bird he wants, Beryl.'

'Retired?' asked Peter.

'Doesn't like it,' the second girl said. 'Comes in to the office several times a month. He's been retired five years, and he still calls it "tidying his desk"! And,' she added triumphantly, 'he's here now!'

'Would you be kind enough to ask him if he could spare the time to see us?' asked Peter.

'I'll take up your card,' the second girl said, manoeuvring round Beryl's desk with some agility, and disappearing up the stairs.

Peter and Harriet waited sitting on a hard bench in the hallway, but luckily did not have long to wait.

Mr Bird occupied a large elegant room on the first floor, with a view over the churchyard outside, and a skyline enhanced by the heavy elegance of a Hawksmoor church spire. Peter deduced immediately that Mr Bird, retired or not, still had a controlling interest in the firm. He was a very small man, who had obviously once been taller, exquisitely tailored, with a shock of unruly white hair. He was beaming at his visitors.

'The Duke of Denver!' he exclaimed. 'And the Duchess! How *exciting!* Whatever can this be about, I ask myself; my firm has never, I think, had the pleasure of insuring the Wimsey family. Although perhaps, if in your present trouble you are dissatisfied with your current insurers . . . That would be Messrs Balstrom, would it? Do sit down.'

Mr Bird's leather armchairs were worn, deep and comfortable. Harriet settled down in one of them, and listened, and looked, watching Peter at work.

'This is not about my own family, Mr Bird,' Peter said. 'I am here to ask you about a certain emerald that you have insured for Lord Attenbury.'

'We do have the Attenbury family's property covered,' said Mr Bird. 'May I take it that you have their permission to discuss it with me?'

Peter reached for his wallet, and produced the letter of authority that had introduced him to Mr Snader.

Mr Bird nodded, and said, 'How can I help?'

'Would you tell us what exactly you insure the famous emerald against?' asked Peter.

'Loss, damage, or, with reservations, theft,' said Mr Bird.

'And you are informed when the stone is taken out of the bank?'

'Always. Otherwise the insurance policy would not hold it covered.'

'So when it is returned to the bank . . .'

'We are told. There is a maximum number of days out which the policy covers. It has never been out for anything like that number of days during my time here.'

'When you are told that the stone has been returned to the bank, do you take measures to satisfy yourself that it is the stone itself, and not, for example, a paste copy, that has been returned? And that it has not been damaged during its excursion?'

'Naturally we do, Your Grace! We are not a very large firm, as insurance firms go, and the sum assured is immense. The Attenbury emerald is by far the most valuable single object on our books.'

'Who inspects the stone for you?' Peter asked.

'It always used to be Mr Van der Helm; now it is a colleague of his in Hatton Garden. But, Lord Peter, this conversation is taking a turn that I find chilling indeed. Is there a problem with the emerald?'

'I'm afraid there is,' said Peter.

'Will you excuse me a moment?' said Mr Bird, as he rose and left the room.

He returned visibly agitated. 'Attenbury has indeed raised the question of an insurance claim on that jewel,' he said. 'Mr Buxton did not see fit to tell me about it. In case it troubled my mind during my retirement, indeed! This could ruin us; but of course there are the reservations, and Mr Buxton thinks we should be able to see off the claim by citing the family's duty of care. I am upset, Lord Peter, upset.'

'What are the reservations, Mr Bird?'

'They are what we sometimes write into the

314

policy in the case of theft of an item of value. That is that we will pay out after a year, to allow a police enquiry to bear fruit.'

'So Attenbury has to wait for his money?'

'Yes. But I am very afraid for my firm . . .'

'Help us then, Mr Bird. Let us see the reports on the jewel that have been rendered by Mr Van der Helm, or his colleague.'

Mr Bird picked up the phone on his desk and asked Beryl to bring the Attenbury file to him.

It was a thick file. But it was orderly. Mr Bird extracted a report on the state of the stone for each of the occasions when it had been returned to the bank. They were careful documents: one sheet of paper headed with the company letterhead, and the qualifications of their valuers. They all said simply that the stone had been inspected. The troy weight was given. It was recorded that there was no damage, except that when the stone was returned in 1941 a slight scratch was noticed on the back, below the inscription. This scratch was recorded again when Miss Pevenor returned the stone. The flaw in the stone was described each time: small inclusion with moss-like jardinière towards right-hand edge, at about two o'clock on the circumference . . .

'How far back do those go?' asked Harriet.

'To the foundation of the firm, in 1890,' said Mr Bird proudly.

'Can we see some earlier ones?' asked Harriet.

'You'll find they are all in perfect order,' said Mr Bird.

'That one looks longer,' said Harriet, picking it up from the desk. It was of two pages clipped together. It was dated 1921, and signed 'Van der Helm'. It recorded the flaw in the stone. But it added that Mr Van der Helm had not seen the stone before. He was unable to precisely match the description of the flaw made by the previous valuer with his own observation, although there were strong similarities.

Mr Bird picked up this document and regarded it fondly. 'Van der Helm was a devil for detail,' he said, 'when he first joined us. We were newcomers here together. He showed me, I seem to remember, and I couldn't at all see what he meant. No two people see things just the same way, don't you think? And the emerald was unique. Not as people say nowadays rather unique, or very unique. Unique is an absolute, Your Grace, isn't it?'

But his two guests were looking at him in consternation.

They couldn't wait to thank him and make their escape and think out the implications.

However the two secretaries were waiting for them below. Beryl and her companion shot out of the reception room when they heard steps on the stairs, and blocked their way. 'Oh please, Lady Peter,' said Beryl. 'My friend here thinks you are the same person as Harriet Vane; could we have your autograph? Please? We just adore your books!'

Mr Bird, who had walked down to see them out, tutted audibly behind Harriet, but she put on her professional smile, produced her fountain pen and inscribed the two autograph books she was offered.

'Don't you ever get tired of that?' asked Peter as they walked away.

'It is silly, isn't it?' said Harriet. 'But so long as I haven't got tired of being read . . .'

'We'll call on Freddy on the way home,' said Peter. Freddy's office was in Chancery Lane and they took a cab there.

'What ho!' said Freddy. 'Jolly nice to see you both. Haven't a biscuit to offer you—Rachel has forbidden them. I'm getting tight in my suits.'

'You are indeed looking well,' said Peter. 'Never mind biscuits, it's information we're after.'

'At your disposal, old chap,' said Freddy, leaning back in his chair and looking fondly at his old friends.

'Freddy, do you remember telling me, and quite a few other people, that an emerald could always be identified again by someone knowledgeable who had seen it once? By the flaws?'

'When did I tell you that?' asked Freddy.

'At that party when Charlotte Attenbury got engaged to Northerby.'

'That's going back a bit,' said Freddy. 'Can't

remember a thing I said so long ago. Well, I can remember proposing to Rachel, but what you're asking about is even further back than that. Bit much to expect of me.'

'Well, I wasn't asking you to remember your long-ago words, I was just wanting you to verify the information you gave.'

'About telling emeralds apart?'

'Yes. Is it true that someone who had seen a stone before could reliably identify it again?'

'Well, you know how young men assert themselves, Wimsey. It would depend on how distinctive the flaws were . . . but usually, yes, I'll stand by what I said.'

'Righty-ho. Now what about it if the person who had seen the stone before has retired, and someone else takes over, relying on the description left by his predecessor?'

'Well, obviously it would be a bit more difficult. But it should be all right. Look, Wimsey, this happens quite a lot. People do retire, or die or run off to South America. And someone else takes over. Doesn't usually raise any waves. Did this retired chap leave a good description?'

'Yes. So the second chap records that he cannot precisely match the flaws in the stone he is looking at with the first chap's description.'

'Are you asking me if there would be anything fishy about that?'

'Exactly.'

'Well, describing flaws is not an exact science. Bit subjective. But it doesn't usually come to that. Stones are normally identified by weight, colour, cut, provenance—the flaws aren't the only thing. If everything else was right, your second chappie probably thought that he was simply taking a different view from his predecessor.'

'He was troubled enough to record his difficulty.'

'Who was he, may I ask?'

'Van der Helm.'

'Mmm. Van der Helm was the best in the business. Are you going to tell me what all this is about?'

Peter launched into the tale of the decoy jewel.

Freddy whistled. 'Well, in that position, ladies and gentlemen, the discrepancy in the flaws being all you have to go on . . . I would say that the wrong stone came back to the bank just before Van der Helm took over. But look here, Wimsey, it isn't fair to blame *him*. Unless you knew that there was more than one of those socking great carved emeralds you'd think you were seeing things if it didn't seem to be the same. Have a heart.'

'It is very far from our minds to blame the valuer,' said Wimsey. 'We shall leave Van der Helm at peace wherever he may be, growing tulips or fixing windmills. But thank you, Freddy. That makes the matter clear enough.'

- - -

'Peter, you were cheating!' said Harriet in mock indignation, once they got home. 'You led me to believe that the swap of the stones must have happened after the events of 1921. That you were certain the right stone had been collected from the pawnbroker, and by you in person.'

'I didn't mean to cheat,' he said. 'I believed what I was saying. But it doesn't look like it now, does it?'

'One of only two possibilities now,' said Harriet. 'A mix-up at the pawnbroker's, or a mix-up at Charlotte's engagement party.'

'One of the two stones at the pawnbroker's was the Maharaja's,' said Peter. 'And since he could read the inscription we can trust him to have redeemed the right stone.'

'But, Peter, didn't you tell me he had the Attenbury stone taken out of its mount, so that he could read that inscription? If there was something wrong with the Attenbury one at the pawnbroker's, surely he would have known. He would have realised he was looking at the third stone.'

'Yes, of course he would. If Handley let him handle and turn over the Attenbury stone. We must ask him.'

The Maharaja had left the Savoy, and was steaming homewards on a liner via the Suez Canal. The complications of a phone call to a ship at sea were deputed to Bunter. It was going to take some time.

'Aren't you sick of all this, Harriet?' Peter asked her.

'Of a fuss about a jewel? I am somewhat. Aren't you?'

Peter considered. 'I can't help myself as to what I worry about,' he said. 'I suppose I could sleep at night knowing that someone had pulled off a clever fraud against Attenbury, and was likely to get away with it . . .'

'They will be apprehended when they show up again to collect their own jewel,' said Harriet.

'But they might not show up. Not the least of the puzzles is why they haven't shown up already. As I was saying, I might be able to live with an unsolved fraud; but an unsolved murder? Two murders? Perhaps as many as four if we rule out all coincidence? To get sick of it all and potter off leaving that unresolved would be a dereliction of duty.'

'A duty to whom, Peter?' she asked. 'To the dead?'

'To the dead we owe only the truth,' he said, 'but I was not thinking of them. I was thinking of the next prospective victim. Murder is addictive; each one seems easier than the last.'

It was nearly midnight before Bunter appeared and called Peter to the phone. The Maharaja's voice was distant, and accompanied by bursts of static crackle. But Peter could understand him well enough. He had not been allowed to handle the stone other than his own at the pawnbroker. He had not had sight of the inscription on the back of it. As far as he knew it could have been either the Attenbury emerald, or—a thought that had not crossed his mind at the time—the other stone that his family had not heard tell of for the best part of a century.

24

'We are back to the beginning,' said Peter the next morning. 'Back to the time when my wits were awry, and I was in Bunter's custodianship. Bunter had better sit in on this arm of the discussion.'

'Okay,' he said, when they were settled together, as usual at the library table. 'To rethink. Osmanthus, so-called, turned up at Fennybrook Hall before lunch, with his own jewel in his pocket. He had to wait for Mr Whitehead to come from the bank in London with the Attenbury jewel. Since up to that time the jewel had been verified for a generation by Mr Van der Helm's predecessor, I think we may take it that it was the right stone that he brought. There has to be solid ground somewhere. Mr Whitehead arrived at about three o'clock.'

'Later, Your Grace,' said Bunter.

'Bunter, do you think you could possibly simply address me as you used to when I was just Lord

Peter, while and when we are playing the old familiar game, and detecting? I would feel more comfortable with a pen-name in my professional life. Let the dukedom be a private sorrow. Unless, that is, you might be ready to call me simply Peter.'

Bunter looked down at his hands while he considered this request.

'Mr Whitehead came at four, my lord,' he said.

'All right, at four. Then there was a little power struggle in the library, and eventually we had to call on Lady Attenbury, and the comparison of the stones was made. Fifteen? Twenty minutes maximum. Then Osmanthus pockets his stone and departs. Mr Whitehead departs with him. Osmanthus gets to hear of the uproar in the house he has left, and pawns his stone for safety. Meanwhile, the other stone is taken to Lady Attenbury's bedroom, and put in her safe until five, when Jeannette comes for it, for them, because we are still talking about the complete set of jewels. Am I on track so far, Bunter?'

'Perfectly, as far as I know, my lord.'

'Jeannette puts out the set of jewels on the stand in Lady Charlotte's room. Little Ottalie and her friend 'borrow' them from there, and take them back to the nursery. A few minutes later they also take the paste set from the open drawer in Lady Attenbury's room. Jeannette finds them fooling about with a king's ransom, and hurriedly puts the kit back as it should be, and returns it to Charlotte's room. They muddle things; what goes on to the stand in Charlotte's room the second time is the paste rivière and the real king-stone. Pity it wasn't the other way around, really.'

'Not such a good story,' remarked Harriet.

'We are coming up to six o'clock,' Peter continued. 'Charlotte comes up to dress, with Northerby with her. They step just inside her room for an embrace. Northerby pockets the king-stone. By the time Charlotte looks round it is gone, and she summons Jeannette and the panic starts. All clear so far?'

'Both clear and puzzling,' said Harriet.

'Murky, isn't it?' said Peter. 'Let's keep following through. That evening Charlotte is wearing the real necklace, that she thinks is her mother's paste copy; the paste copy is abandoned in Charlotte's room, the paste king-stone is hanging on the lovely rivière round Charlotte's neck in the dining room, and the real king-stone is in Northerby's pocket. How did he get it out of the house when all the bedrooms and all the luggage were searched?'

'I have wondered that, my lord,' said Bunter. 'And I have come to the conclusion that it must have been concealed in Mr Northerby's bag of golf clubs. I remember his man having that bag in the hall when Sugg declared his curfew.'

'But it would have been harder to hide a golf bag than it would have been to hide a jewel,' said Harriet.

'Perhaps not, my lady, if everyone is looking for a jewel and nobody is looking for a golf bag. I have asked myself where one would hide a golf bag, and I have supposed that one would hide it among other such. I think it must have been put in the hall lobby alongside Lord Attenbury's own.'

'Excellent, Bunter,' said Peter. 'So Northerby departs when allowed to with the loot in the bottom of his golf bag, and he pawns it at once in his desperate need for the money. And then by and by I go and get it back. Since when it has been the wrong stone. Somehow Northerby pawned the wrong stone.'

'Are we imagining that all three stones were actually present in the house on that day?' said Harriet. 'That's rather far-fetched, Peter.'

'But we don't know anything about the wrong stone. We don't know who had it or when or why or how. We can't tell how far-fetched this train of reasoning may be.'

'I think,' said Harriet, 'that there is something we ought to know, that neither of you have mentioned in your accounts. Were those two children playing about alone, or was there somebody with them?'

'Ottalie,' said Peter. 'We had better go and find Ottalie.'

• • •

Lady Ottalie Attenbury lived in Eaton Square. Her side of the square stood in beautiful run-down grandeur, facing the sun. At the top of the steps to the front door a row of doorbells indicated that the house was divided into flats. One of the bells was labelled 'OA top floor'. Peter rang this bell. When nothing happened they tried the front door, found it open and began to climb the stairs. These were wide, carpeted in worn and shabby Axminster, and lit by a roof-light far above. As Harriet and Peter ascended they heard music above them. Someone was playing and singing, in a fine soprano voice.

'Mozart,' said Peter.

They stood on the landing for several bars, listening. Then Peter tapped lightly on the door, the singer fell silent, and the door opened. Harriet would instantly have realised that this was Charlotte's sister; the facial likeness was marked. But this woman was shorter and slightly frail-looking. If the fashion of the day had allowed a woman of thirty-plus to be pretty, she was still pretty, and she was wearing the New Look—a full skirt and tight sweater. Her music had made her radiant, and she took a while to react to her unexpected visitors.

'Yes?' she said, looking at them blankly.

'You might remember me,' Peter said. 'Peter Wimsey.'

'Oh, lord, *Peter!*' said Ottalie. 'Step in here off

326

the gloomy landing where I can't see who you are.'

Peter did so. He introduced Harriet. The flat was very light, and the large room they stepped into was nearly empty of furniture, containing mostly a Steinway Grand. Nevertheless it was a spectacularly untidy room, with piles of books and music all over the floor.

'We are sorry to have interrupted your music,' Harriet offered.

'Oh, God, did you hear that?' was the reply. 'I'm sorry. It needs a lot of work yet.'

Harriet didn't know what to say. If she said, no really, it was beautiful, she risked sounding like an ignoramus; and she hardly knew how to explain to a person considerably more musical than herself the effect it had on her to hear a piece played imperfectly. It made audible the difficulty in the music; it made audible the demands made on the performer. It was moving in a fashion that a perfect performance never quite seemed to be.

Peter said, 'A little more practice on that low note, perhaps.'

'This one?' she said, touching a note on the piano keyboard.

'No,' he said, 'a few bars later. I'll play it for you.'

'Can you really?' she asked. 'The accompanist is very late this morning.'

'I can after a fashion,' Peter replied, taking off his coat, casting it on to the floor over a stack of books, and sitting himself at the piano.

Harriet watched and listened. Peter's playing sounded a bit hesitant at first. After all, it wasn't Bach. Ottalie opened her mouth and sang full voice.

'Dove sono i bei momenti Di dolcezza e di piacer?'

When they finished the piece they were both silent for a few seconds.

'You could do that if you practised,' said Ottalie. 'But it can't be what you came for.'

'Of course not,' said Peter, 'I didn't even know you were a singer.'

'Well, I trained at the Royal College,' she said, 'but I didn't make it professionally. I just sing in the London Bach Choir, and I do a few weddings and funerals when I'm asked. The perfect dilettante, that's me.'

'Diletto, after all, is the Italian for pleasure,' said Peter. 'Look, is there anywhere we can sit?'

'Through here,' Ottalie said, and led them into a much smaller room with a settee and armchairs and side tables, all deep in clutter. She made room for them to sit by simply throwing stuff on to the floor. 'I'm no good at this,' she said to Harriet. 'Are you any good at this? It's growing up with servants that does the damage.'

Harriet said, 'I'm very lucky.'

'Of course I had help before the war,' Ottalie said. She was standing in the middle of the room with a volume of *Grove* in her hand, looking around for somewhere to put it. Harriet was glad she wasn't going to throw it down in the corner—

it was a thick book that might break its binding if treated roughly.

'Mind you, I *adored* the war,' Ottalie said. 'It was very easy to be useful. Fire-watching and first aid and then, when someone found out I could do Italian, transcribing Mussolini's broadcasts for our people. When I started out all the Italian I knew was from Da Ponte libretti; with a touch of Verdi for good luck.' She giggled.

'May we sit down?' said Peter, doing so. Harriet sat also, and Ottalie slipped down on to the floor in front of a still encumbered chair, and leaned against it, looking up at Peter from somewhere near the height at which she had looked up at him all those years ago.

'You know your nephew is in trouble?' Peter asked her.

'Yes; and how!' she said. 'And you are sleuthing for him. Jolly kind of you. He hasn't a spare bean to pay you with.'

'I've known your family since I was a boy,' said Peter.

'So you have. Peter, I can't imagine how I can be the least help to you. Your jolly wife here would be far better at detecting than I can be.'

'She is a great help,' he said gravely. 'It was Harriet's idea that we ought to come and talk to you. It is what you may be able to remember that we need.'

'I have a lousy memory,' said Ottalie.

'Except for songs, perhaps?'

'Oh, songs . . .' she said. 'That's different. They have music to go by.'

'Cast your mind back, Ottalie, to that evening when Charlotte's engagement party was in progress, and you were playing with the emeralds. You and a friend.'

'Ada DuBerris,' said Ottalie. 'Still a friend as it happens.'

'And the maid Jeannette found you . . .'

'God, was she angry!' Ottalie said. 'I'd never heard a grown-up talk to another like that.'

'But that is just what we have come to ask you,' said Peter. 'If you and Ada were playing alone, or if there was somebody else there.'

'Just Ada's mother, popping in and out,' said Ottalie. 'She was showing us how to wear the stuff, and how to preen in the mirror. And then Jeannette arrived in a high dudgeon, and started attacking us all, especially Mrs DuBerris. A lot of ought to know better at her age, and how the gems were Jeannette's responsibility, and how it was unfair for a guest who couldn't be held to account for anything to risk the livelihood of a servant . . . well, you can imagine. We were all very abashed, and crept around doing just as Jeannette said. Didn't I tell you all this at the time? I seem to remember confiding in you.'

'You didn't confide in me about Mrs DuBerris,' said Peter quietly.

'She asked me not to tell anyone. I thought she didn't want the grown-ups to know she had been ticked off. I used to try to keep it from Mummy when I had been in trouble, so I knew how she felt.'

'How did she take being stripped off by Jeannette?'

'She was as timid as a mouse. Said sorry a couple of times. Thoughtless of her . . . that sort of thing. But look here, Peter, I really don't see how this has any bearing on what happened next. On that awful Northerby man's box of tricks. That can't have had anything to do with who was in the nursery. I don't get it.'

'You are being more helpful than you know, Ottalie,' said Peter. An undertone had entered his voice, audible to Harriet, though perhaps not to Ottalie.

'Did you say that you still know Mrs DuBerris?' he asked.

'Well, not exactly *her*. But Ada is a friend, yes. She's a bit musical; couldn't afford to train, but she plays the fiddle a little, and we often go to concerts together. I sometimes take her along when I need a companion on a trip. We've known each other since childhood, after all. And I sometimes give her things. So does Charlotte.'

'What kind of things?'

'Oh, you know, when we clear our wardrobes some of the clothes fit her. Nothing valuable.

Charlotte says she is a hanger-on and a scrounge, but then she was too old to play with Ada as I did. And I don't think Ada is into horses as she is into music, although she always tries to please. She doesn't have much in common with Charlotte.'

'And even less, I imagine, with Diana?'

'Poor Diana,' said Ottalie. 'No, no love lost there at all. I don't see where all this is getting us.'

'Tell us more about Ada. She never married?'

'No. Various boyfriends in the war that didn't last. You know what that was like. She's quite good-looking, but she doesn't have a penny piece to her name, and to be honest, I think it's her mother that's the trouble. When I was very little I thought it was wonderful for Ada to have a mother who was always close, and put her above everything else. I thought my own mother was distant and cool. The servants did a lot for us that Ada's mother did for her in person. But later Ada's mother was a bit much. Is a bit much, actually. Always knows exactly where Ada is, and who she is with. Imagine that for a woman who is my age! Like having a cobra round your neck. I'm sure that's what frightens the men away, and I don't blame them.'

'You don't like Mrs DuBerris, I see.'

'No,' said Ottalie, 'I don't like stranglers.'

'*What* did you say?' asked Peter.

'Oh, I only mean that she is choking the life out

of Ada. Ada ought to cut free, but she doesn't seem able to.'

Peter said, 'Ottalie, would Ada have known, do you think, when the family emerald was taken out of the bank? Could she have got to hear of it?'

A shadow passed across Ottalie's face. 'So that's what you're getting at,' she said.

'I'm afraid it is.'

'Well, Ada certainly knew when it was all about a horse. She and I were with Charlotte over the weekend when the bet was made. She was one of the party.' Ottalie paused, frowning. 'I really don't see how she could have known when my sister-in-law borrowed it for Verity. I didn't know about that till long afterwards. Charlotte wasn't in London, and Ada has never been on talking terms with Diana. I think you're barking up the wrong tree, Peter. Because she couldn't have known about letting Miss Pevenor have it, either . . . Oh, God, hang on a mo, I think she could. Father was getting a bit doddery by then, and he wanted to ask Edward what he thought about it, and Edward was round here having supper, and Father rang to ask if I knew where Edward was . . . and of course we talked about it. Edward couldn't see why we shouldn't lend it to the Pevenor woman; Father had said it would be a good thing when Edward came to sell it. And Ada was here that evening. We had been to a matinée at the cinema.'

There was another pause while all this sank in.

Then Ottalie said, 'Peter, this has *got* to be wrong. Whoever is playing tricks with us has got one of those emeralds of their own. And in all the years I've known them Ada and her mother have been really, really hard up. It doesn't make sense. They don't even *like* jewellery, so if they had an emerald they would have sold it, and done themselves a favour with the money.'

'Why do you say they don't like jewellery?' asked Harriet, chipping in.

'Well, they speak very contemptuously about wearing what they call baubles,' Ottalie said. 'And we've learned not to offer them jewellery. I gave Ada a diamond pin once; I thought if she didn't like it she could sell it and buy a frock. But it came back the next day with a note from her mother.'

'Perhaps what is known to them is told to another,' said Peter. 'Perhaps we are looking for a friend of theirs. Now, Ottalie, I must ask you not to let a word of this conversation get to Ada. Can I trust you for that?'

'I suppose so,' Ottalie said. 'I usually tell her everything.'

'I will keep Ada out of this if I can,' said Peter. 'But if she has been warned of this conversation I may not be able to. It's in her own best interests not to know what we have been saying.'

'Okay,' said Ottalie.

As they were leaving, Peter said to her, 'Your mother was one of the best women I have known.'

'I understand that now,' she said. 'I try to be like her.'

'Good for you,' said Peter, kissing her lightly on the cheek.

'So that's how it was done,' said Harriet, when they were walking away down the street.

'Yes,' he said. 'All clear now. And when you know how, as I said, Harriet, you know who.'

'Well, it's not all clear to me,' said Harriet. 'Anybody who had seen two stones at once was in danger . . . presumably because they might deduce the existence of the third stone. The Maharaja had seen two at once—he had arrived to do just that, but there was no point in attacking him, because he was the source of the reward. But you had seen two stones at once also—why have you been immune from attack all this time?'

'I have wondered that,' he said. 'And I have dredged out of memory the fact that there was someone once whom I told that I could not read Persian. And you see, Harriet, that train of thought leads to the same place. It was Mrs DuBerris that I told.'

25

'Discovering that someone could have done something falls a long way short of proving that they did,' said Peter. Harriet was sitting down beside the fire in the drawing-room, and Peter was pacing up and down like the unfortunate tiger in the London Zoo.

'So what do we do now?' Harriet asked him. 'Do we consult Charles?'

'It's out of our hands if we do that,' said Peter, coming to stand in front of her.

'What is making you so uneasy, Peter? You have achieved a triumph of deduction. Or are you worried that it might not be right?'

'I think it's right, provable or not,' he said.

Harriet looked at him with concern. 'Are you afraid of what you will go through if someone hangs whom you have incriminated?' she asked softly.

'Yes, I am,' he said. 'I always am. And afraid of what it imposes on you when I impersonate a jelly. But it has never so far stopped me doing what I should.'

'Then it mustn't now.'

'No,' he said, 'no,' and he resumed pacing.

Harriet got up and began to walk beside him. The room was not large enough for two people to pace up and down in; he grimaced at her, and sat down, whereupon she did too.

'So the problem is?' she asked him again.

'It's taking me back painfully to the very beginning of all this,' he said, 'when I didn't know whether I was helping a friend or apprehending a thief. Forgive my deplorable vanity, Harriet, but I don't want to take to Charles after all these years another divided loyalty. He and I have been batting for the same side all this time . . .'

She waited for more.

'What am I doing, Harriet?' he asked her. 'Am I helping a friend get his property back, or am I an angel of justice?'

'Do I have to tell you that, Peter?' she asked.

'What will you think of me if my intervention decisively and permanently robs Attenbury of his emerald?'

'What will I think of you, or what will young Attenbury think of you?'

'I can live without his good opinion if I have to; the loss of yours would destroy me.'

'You seem to me to be a good friend, to your friends and to mine, and that's a pleasant virtue. It's nice to live with. But when it comes to the crunch, Peter, blessed are they who hunger and thirst after justice.'

'Justice will seem very like vengeance,' he said.

'All those lost years,' she said. 'Years of the life of the strange but harmless Miss Pevenor, of the doubtless deplorable Captain Rannerson, possibly of the admirable Rita Patel, of the pawnbroker:

337

how do you weigh those in the balance against wealth?'

'All right, Harriet,' he said. 'Your firmness makes my purpose just. It's the dish best eaten cold then. I shall confront her without telling Charles, and entrap her if I can.'

'I'm coming with you,' said Harriet.

'No,' he said. 'It will be dangerous.'

'I'll wear that stout dog-collar you gave me once, if you like,' she said.

'My God, have you still got that?' he said.

'I thought it might come in handy if we ever got a dog,' she said, and their conversation dissolved into laughter.

Mrs DuBerris lived in Mortlake, in a shabby terrace of houses with their doors straight on to the street. The trains racketed past, very close; but beyond the track there was a patch of allotments giving a view to another such terrace row. An iron footbridge gave access to anyone this side of the line who had an allotment the other side. The allotments were neat and growing food in rows, but all the houses had that post-war look of near dereliction. Bunter was with them. Peter drove past the house first, and then parked the Daimler a quarter of a mile away, well out of sight. Bunter went off on a recce, and came back to report.

'There is a narrow path along the ends of the

gardens behind the houses, my lord,' he reported. 'The garden ends have rickety fences, and the gardens are small. I can position myself at the gate from the garden of number fifty and prevent an escape by that route. I notice also, my lord, a window open at the back of the house. I think I would be able to hear a loud cry of alarm and respond accordingly.'

'Will you be unseen there? Is there cover?' asked Peter.

'Sufficient, my lord. Give me a start of five minutes.'

The woman who opened the door to them startled Peter. Surely Mrs DuBerris was of about his own age, but she had a deeply lined face. She had dyed her hair a bright chestnut colour, which covered every grey hair and looked odd framing the ageing face. A pair of brightly glittering eyes looked out at him.

'You!' she said. 'What do you want?'

'To talk to you,' Peter said.

'Well, *I* don't want to talk to *you*,' she said. 'Push off!'

'I thought I should talk to you before I talk to the police,' said Peter mildly to the closing door.

Mrs DuBerris opened the door again and stepped back in her narrow hallway to let them in. She marched into a small front room, and sat down abruptly in a fireside chair. 'Say what you have to say and get out,' she said.

'I believe you are in possession of the Attenbury emerald,' Peter said.

'I don't give a damn what you believe,' she said.

'I can get a search warrant,' said Peter.

'I don't deny I have an emerald,' she said.

'You have the one that rightly belongs to Lord Attenbury.'

'So what?' she said. 'Fair exchange is no robbery. Those things are easy to confuse.'

'Unless you read Persian,' he said, his voice smooth and quiet. He had not sat down. 'And I see that you do,' he added, reaching for a book on the shelf in the fireside alcove, and holding out a book in Arabic script.

'It's not a crime to read a foreign language,' she said.

Harriet had posted herself in a corner of the room beside the window. She saw another, much younger woman come down the street carrying a violin case and a string bag of groceries, and stop at the front door to let herself in.

'Fraud is a crime,' said Peter, 'and so is murder.'

The front door opened quietly.

'Murder?' said Mrs DuBerris. 'Ha! You'll have trouble pinning that on me, won't you? No signature on those deaths—a different method of killing every time!'

'But, Mrs DuBerris, how do you know about the murder methods? How do you even know what murders I refer to? Unless you know everything about them, that is?'

'You're a fool, Lord Peter,' she said venomously. 'I'm not going to call you "Your Grace", it would choke me. "Your meddling interfering busybody" would suit you better. What do you hope to gain by trapping me? I'll tell you what you will not gain, and that's your friend's emerald. Look, here it is.' She reached for her bag which was hanging over the arm of her chair. 'I'm going to throw it in the fire.' And she held out her hand towards the burning grate. 'Do you know what will happen to it in a fire?' she asked. 'It will be cracked open by the heat. That will fix Edward Attenbury, won't it? But the stone in the vault will still be mine! I shall be hanged for murder, do you think? Then what do I have to lose? But it warms my heart to think what Attenbury has to lose!'

Peter said, 'It is also a crime to be an accessory to murder. Do you care for what your daughter might have to lose? Give me the stone, and I will keep your daughter out of it if I can.'

Mrs DuBerris had already raised her arm for the gesture that would have cast the stone into the flames. Now she slowly let it fall to her side.

Ada DuBerris had been standing silently in the room doorway, behind Peter's back, during the last few exchanges. Now she stepped into the room. 'What is all this about, Mother?' she asked. She went to her mother, stood behind her, and put an arm round her. Very gently she took her mother's hand, bent the fingers back, and released the jewel from her grasp. Then, holding it, she said to Peter, 'I have always understood this was ours. Inherited from my father. Isn't that true?'

'The one you have inherited is perfectly safe, Miss DuBerris,' Peter said. 'But that is not it.'

'Take it then,' she said, holding it out to him.

'No, Ada, don't!' cried Mrs DuBerris. 'Hold it over the fire till I can make an escape!'

'Mother,' said Ada DuBerris, 'there's a man at the back gate, and a police car in the street.' And she handed the emerald to Peter.

Harriet looked out of the window. 'There really is a police car in the street, Peter,' she said.

'I must speak to Bunter on the subject of ignoring instructions,' said Peter. 'Harriet, would you go outside and ask the Constable driving that car to come and make an arrest.'

The Constable conferred with Peter in the hallway. Then he entered the little room, in which they were now all crowded together.

'Ethel DuBerris,' he intoned, 'I am arresting you for attempting to defraud one Edward Attenbury; and on suspicion of the murders of . . .'—here he looked down at his rapidly scrawled notes— 'Captain Alan Rannerson, Muriel Pevenor, and others. You do not have to say anything, but anything you do say . . .'

'Say?' exclaimed Mrs DuBerris. 'Do you expect

me to cave in and incriminate myself like a character in one of that woman's stupid mystery stories? I'm not saying a damn thing.'

Suddenly there were policemen everywhere. A detective inspector stood in the doorway and said, 'What is going on here?'

'This Constable has just made an arrest,' said Peter.

The scene blurred for Harriet. Across the press of people in the room she was looking at Ada DuBerris, standing in the corner behind her mother, white as a sheet, her hand over her mouth. Across the room she met Harriet's eyes with an expression of pure horror. Then they were taking Mrs DuBerris away in handcuffs.

Ada said, 'Mother, tell me you didn't kill anyone!'

But she was given no answer.

The police Constable asked who Peter was, and then thanked him for allowing him to make the arrest. 'It will go in my records, sir,' he said. 'Most people would have called for a more senior officer.'

'You did it perfectly well,' said Peter. And from the timbre of his voice Harriet knew at once that the Attenbury affair had entered that always-to-be-expected aftermath that meant sleepless nights, and sudden departures abroad and a time of edginess and unhappiness. One thing Peter could never do was enjoy his triumphs. To the Detective

Inspector who had appeared, Peter said, 'Keep a close eye on your prisoner, Inspector.'

'Do you expect self-harm?' said the Inspector.

'She has lost what she has been living and planning for these thirty years,' said Peter. 'Just watch her.'

'Point taken,' the man said. The bevy of policemen were leaving.

Harriet said across the room to Ada, 'Are you all right?'

It was a silly question. Ada was shaking like a person with a fever. Harriet went through to a little kitchen in a lean-to at the back of the house, to make tea. She found sugar and added it lavishly. Then she brought the cup through to the front room and offered it to Ada, who shook her head. 'I think you should,' said Harriet softly. 'Do you have a friend who could come and keep you company for the next few hours?'

Ada looked at her dumbly. Then: 'I'll ask Ottalie,' she said.

26

It was ten in the evening. Peter had been glum and restless ever since they left Mortlake; now he was fiddling with the arrangement of some books in the library.

'Are we going abroad?' Harriet asked him.

'Would you like that?' he said.

344

'Only if you would.'

'Where would you like to go?'

'I have never been to Greece.'

'Mmm,' he said. 'Might be rough comfort. It's only a year or two since they were fighting a civil war.'

'Wouldn't some heroic travel be good for us?'

He smiled at her. 'For me, you mean? To take my mind off other things?'

At that moment they heard the doorbell ringing in the hall below. They stood and listened—had Bunter gone across the garden to his own mews house? They heard the back door open and shut as Bunter returned to duty—the doorbell rang in his hall as soon as it rang in theirs. There was the murmur of voices, and then Bunter appeared.

'Lady Ottalie Attenbury and Miss DuBerris, Your Grace. Will you see them? They appear, my lord, to be in a distressed state. So much so that I did not ask if it would wait until the morning . . .'

'Yes, Bunter, wc will see them,' said Peter.

'Will you bring tea, Bunter, please, and something simple to eat—biscuits, bread and butter and jam—whatever you can find at this hour,' said Harriet.

'Do you expect them to be hungry?' asked Peter.

'Distressed people often forget to eat,' said Harriet.

It was Ada DuBerris who appeared first in the room; she was being propelled from behind by

Ottalie. Ada was weeping, swollen-eyed, hardly able to see where she was going. Ottalie had that bright-eyed, flushed, alert appearance that excitement, good or bad, confers. 'Peter! Please— you must help us!' she said.

'I will help you if I honourably can,' said Peter.

Harriet was surprised by the chill in his tone. 'Please sit down, both of you,' she said. 'Bunter is bringing tea.'

'Oh, tea!' said Ottalie dismissively.

Ada said, very quietly, 'Please, Lord Peter, tell me what my mother is supposed to have done . . .'

Peter in sombre tones launched into the tale of the substitute emerald.

Ada said, 'I didn't know she had done that. But . . . no harm has been done, has it? We can just swap the things back. What sort of punishment will she get for that?'

'I'm afraid that isn't the worst of it, Miss DuBerris,' said Peter, and he proceeded to tell her about the deaths.

As he spoke a desperate calm descended on Ada. 'Why should anyone think all that had anything to do with my mother?' she asked.

'It has to be someone who over many years knew when the Attenbury family took their emerald out of the bank,' said Peter. 'You and your mother fit that bill. It's hard to think who else does.'

'Me?' said Ada. And then, 'She was furious with me when I borrowed our emerald to go to the Café de Paris in fancy dress. I've never known her so furious. But, but as God's my witness, I didn't know why she was so interested in gossip about the Attenburys, I really didn't . . . Oh, God, are you saying I helped her commit murder?'

'I think you did,' said Peter, 'although I have no idea whether you knew what you were doing. No; don't answer that. You urgently need a lawyer, and your mother needs one even more urgently. The less you say to anyone in the meantime the better.'

Ada ignored him. 'She was angry enough for that,' she said, 'but I wouldn't have thought she could be brutal enough.'

'Believe me,' said Peter, 'you should say nothing till you have spoken to a lawyer.'

'We couldn't possibly afford a lawyer,' she said.

'You could sell your emerald.'

'She wouldn't agree. She would die first . . .'

A horrified silence hung in the room at that remark.

Ada uttered a choking sob. 'Will you talk to her, Lord Peter? Will you persuade her she needs a lawyer? I'm sure she won't listen to me, she never does.'

Harriet thought that Ada's mother had listened to her all too well, but she left the thought unuttered.

'Yes; I will talk to her,' said Peter. 'No—don't thank me. Go home and get some sleep if you can.'

'You'll spend the night in my place, Ada,' said Ottalie. And then, already standing up to go, she said, 'What was your mother so angry about, Ada? We always tried to be so kind to her, to both of you.'

'That's it,' said Ada bleakly. 'Your kindness made her angry. And you know what, Ottalie? I don't entirely blame her for that.'

When the two women had left Harriet surprised herself by taking a sandwich from the plate as Bunter bore it away. Peter had left the room, and she could hear his voice on the phone.

'Lawyer all fixed up?' she asked him when he returned.

'Not till the morning. But I've got a couple of names from Impey Biggs of rising talents who might take it on. Unless she confesses it will be very hard to pin the murders on her. But it'll be hard to clear her of fraud. Some bright young fellow will be glad to try.'

'And is it up to you to find him?'

Peter looked shamefaced. 'Everyone in jeopardy deserves a decent defence,' he said.

'Do you think I could argue with you about that?' she replied.

'It's so hard on you when I throw a wobbly like this,' he said, turning away from her.

She said to the back of his head, 'It's when I love you best, Peter.'

Peter went out early the next morning, leaving Harriet to her novel. Few people appreciate that

348

authors have deadlines; that they owe a completed book somewhere in the expected window for it in a publishing schedule. The image of the writer staring into space waiting for inspiration, which when it comes will not entail labour, but merely writing something down, as if taking dictation, is wide, wide of the mark. Harriet's publisher was expecting something from her in time for the autumn list; indeed he had already announced it under a provisional title in his catalogue. But not surprisingly, she found it difficult to concentrate. At an average of one thousand words to four pages of typescript, she was some twenty thousand words short of the gratifying moment when she could begin to unwind the tightly coiled turns of the plot and let the reader see an outline of the denouement. Clever readers, of course, would already have seen through the entire thing, and for them the ending would lack surprise. But Harriet knew from experience that the pleasures of having guessed it all, with the concomitant pleasure of feeling clever, would make up for that as long as matters were not humiliatingly easy to guess. This present work had been interrupted—no, positively invaded by life; and she would have much ado to get it back on course. The invasions and interruptions promptly arrived in battalions to sit in the front of her head, and divert her attention.

She fought for the direction of her thoughts, and had so far succeeded that when Peter came in at about midday she was lost to the real world, and so reluctant to surface that she did not emerge from her study until an hour after the usual time for lunch. The two places set on the little breakfast table were both untouched. Peter was sitting at the window, with a copy of *The Times* in his hand.

'Goodness!' said Harriet. 'You needn't have waited for me. You must be starving, Peter.'

But the moment he looked up and their eyes met she said, 'What's wrong? Was she horrible to talk to?'

'The lady won't see me,' he said.

'Can she refuse?'

'Oh, yes. One of the few liberties remaining to an incarcerated prisoner is the right to accept or refuse a visitor.'

'I didn't know,' said Harriet.

'You didn't know? And there was I all those years ago taking comfort from the thought that you could have, and did not, refuse to see me. Such slender strands of hope were all I had.'

'We've made up to each other for all that long ago,' said Harriet crisply. 'What's wrong this morning?'

'She refuses to see me, but says that she would see you,' he said.

'Ah.'

'Harriet, you absolutely don't have to do it. She has no right, no claim in the matter at all. It isn't in the least like that visit you made to Harwell; you

350

had something personal to tell him—with this woman you have no connection at all.'

'Hush, Peter,' said Harriet softly. 'You know that I will do it. Define for me exactly what the mission is.'

'To talk her into saving her daughter's skin, and just possibly her own, by hiring a good lawyer.'

'A lawyer that you are paying for?'

'No. The sort of lawyer she needs would cost the wages of three gardeners at Denver for several years. I will help her find the right man; but why should we pay for it when she has a huge sum of money at her own disposal if she will only see sense and sell her emerald?'

Harriet observed, but did not comment on, the minting of a new currency: value determined by what it would pay for at Denver.

Mrs DuBerris sat at one end of a scrubbed deal table, and Harriet at the other. She was, to her own surprise, rather distressed at her surroundings. Or perhaps her discomfort arose from her dislike of the other woman . . .

'There is a good deal about your situation that I do not understand,' she began.

'That's a bad start,' said Mrs DuBerris calmly. 'I cannot think of anyone better placed to understand me. You too have married above yourself—streets above yourself. How would you feel if you had been despised and rejected by your husband's family? If you had been made to feel that he could have married you only as a result of some trick, some exploitation of his illness? If nothing had been done to assist his child; if you had been left to struggle in poverty for years? If his family had even got at the College of Arms to deny you the title that should have belonged to his wife?'

Harriet considered that. 'I shouldn't have approved their conduct,' she said, 'but I could have got along with my own life, I think. I should have despised them in return.'

'That's it. I knew you would comprehend me.'

'Remember that I came on the scene long after all this, and have only heard tell of what happened. But don't I understand that the Attenburys—Lady Attenbury particularly—were kind to you?'

Mrs DuBerris was suddenly suffused by rage. Fists clenched, eyes flashing, she practically spat the word. '*Kind?* Oh, yes, they were kind! If you call occasional invitations and gifts of cast-off clothes kindness. Everything they gave us I gave away again at once! It was intolerable, you understand, *intolerable*. Lady Attenbury should have compelled her brother to accept me, not merely wrung her hands at him and given me cups of tea. We needed money and a place in society, not hand-me-downs. And that was William's *right*. It was his daughter's *right*.'

'Yes, it was,' said Harriet.

'He was entitled to marry whom he chose!' Mrs

DuBerris continued. 'And what was wrong with me? There's many a vulgar chorus girl married into the aristocracy and prancing around playing the grand lady. They never asked, they never knew where I came from, they just assumed I was dirt because I was nursing common soldiers. How we hated them!'

'But you had that emerald,' said Harriet.

'It was William's plan. When he was dying. We were living in a squalid lodging house in Dover; I couldn't safely get him any further, and his family wouldn't come; wouldn't help. We got cold letters. When the one came that told him he was disinherited we made a plan. Swap the emerald, and wait for the right moment for revenge. William knew the Attenburys well. He thought they lived beyond their means. He thought the time would come when they needed to sell their baubles. And then our day would come!'

'But wouldn't you be avenged on the wrong person? The Attenbury family weren't the main offenders, surely, however little you liked their cast-off clothes.'

'Oh, they all stick together, those toffs. We could have threatened the ruin of one branch of the family unless the other branch changed their tune.'

'So you swapped the emeralds.'

'That was easy, although that fool Northerby nearly spoiled it. No sooner had I swapped it than he lifted it. Couldn't wait. Greedy bastard; he was supposed to be in it with me, and then he thought he could take it and cut me out. But it was my jewel he took. At first I thought he had wrecked the plan, but I just sat tight, and by and by your Lord Peter had got it back, and it was in the bank.'

'How was it that William had one of the emeralds to give you?' Harriet asked.

'An old soldier gave it to him. His father had won it in a raffle, he said. He gave it in exchange for a new coat.'

'I don't understand you, though. You waited all those years, and you killed people—what was all that about?'

'I wanted to choose my time to strike. The longer I had waited the more I had to lose if anyone saw it was the wrong stone in the Attenburys' box. That wasn't likely unless someone saw it who could read Persian. But that kept seeming possible. So I did what I had to do. For William; it was his idea. In his last few nights he was feverish, and he thought we could buy Fennybrook Hall, and eject the Attenburys, and live in it ourselves. And I thought if I waited and watched, I might manage to do that.'

'You did it with the aid of a Mr Tipotenios, I understand. Who was that?'

'An out-of-work actor. He borrowed a theatrical costumier's suit. Not hard.'

Harriet was coming to the firm conclusion that

354

the woman she was talking to was mad. And that that would be her best defence.

'You needn't think you have got me to confess,' said Mrs DuBerris. 'Hearsay is not evidence, and this conversation would be your word against mine. I shall deny every word of it. And I haven't been read my rights.'

'Did you mean to incriminate your daughter? William's daughter?'

Mrs DuBerris shook her head.

'But you have done. Someone will have to defend her from the obvious conclusion that she was your accomplice in murder. I am here, since you won't see my husband, to persuade you, if I can, to hire a lawyer, for Ada's sake if not for your own.'

'I can't . . .'

'You must sell your emerald.'

Silence.

Harriet continued, 'You may have felt justified all those years in keeping your jewel as a means of revenge, and living in poverty as a result; it's another thing, surely, to hang on to it now, when any confusion is sorted out, and Ada risks a prison sentence for something she knew nothing about. Do you love your daughter, Mrs DuBerris, or is hatred all that you feel for anyone?'

Mrs DuBerris gestured to the prison officer, looking at them through the grille, and the interview was abruptly at an end.

• • •

'Failure,' said Harriet to Peter when she returned home. She recounted the interview as well as she could remember it.

'And did you sympathise?' asked Peter.

'I allowed myself a moment's complacency at the thought that I had never felt homicidal when being chipped at by Helen,' said Harriet. 'And then I remembered that I had my husband at my side when being snubbed and insulted. She was alone.'

'I don't think you needed me to avoid becoming murderous,' said Peter. 'And I don't think a defence of insanity is an easy wicket. A plan devised and pursued for so many years is going to look to a jury more like wickedness than lunacy.'

'Such a ramshackle and improbable plan,' said Harriet. 'And I need you for everything. But, Peter, it's a bitter sort of irony, isn't it, to realise that that woman has sold her soul, embittered her whole life, and become homicidal to get something that we have simply been landed with, and would so gladly be without!'

27

'We seem to have averted the ruin of the Attenbury family,' said Peter. 'And we have ruins of our own to attend to. I can't put off going to Denver a day longer.'

'I'm coming with you,' said Harriet.

'Only if you would like to.'

'As it happens I would like to; but I would expect to go with you whether I liked it or not, except in the face of an imperious conflict of duty.'

'The duty is mine . . .'

'With all your worldly goods you me endowed. Don't you remember? If Duke's Denver is yours, it's mine.'

'I'm not quite getting the hang of this, am I?' he said wryly.

'You are severely disorientated. You'll get used to it.'

'That's what I am afraid of,' he said. 'Keep me grounded, Harriet.'

'Well, Your Grace, if a blackened ruin in Norfolk is not heavy enough to ground you, I probably can't manage it. When are we leaving?'

'If we went with the hour we could be there by lunchtime.'

'Driving?'

'Of course, driving. The trains take much longer, and one needs to be met at the station.'

Harriet resigned herself.

'Does Bunter come too?' she asked.

'Bunter has gone ahead,' he said.

The man who came out to meet them from the lodge, and to open the wrought-iron gates for them was Dick Jenkins, old Bill Jenkins's younger son. Harriet remembered her first arrival here, newly married, out of her depth, being gravely greeted by Bill Jenkins, and that Peter had asked after his sons. Bill was dead now—how many generations of Jenkinses had served the Duke? And how few could so continue? Grief and sadness ahead . . .

As if the cosmos shared their dejection, a light drizzle began as they drove towards the house. Bunter came out to meet them holding an umbrella at the ready as they pulled up at the front door.

'I have taken the liberty of booking a room for you and her ladyship at the Denver Arms,' he said.

'Is that necessary, Bunter?' said Peter. 'Isn't the east wing undamaged?'

'There is no water supply, my lord. The fire melted the lead pipework. And perhaps, when you look round . . .'

'Lay on Macduff,' said Peter, with unnecessary accuracy.

The intact part of the house was structurally sound enough; anything wrong with it was wrong before the fire. But it was all looking sad and dirty. The smoke had penetrated nearly every room, and left a greasy film of soot on everything. And it smelled of smuts. As they walked round it became more and more depressing. The housekeeper, Mrs Farley, and Gerald's butler Thomas joined them.

'We are at a loss, Your Grace, as to how to clean many of these rooms,' said Thomas. 'I have cleaned the silver; and Mrs Farley has washed all the ceramics.'

'I ceased to wash the curtains,' Mrs Farley offered, 'when the first pair we dealt with simply disintegrated.'

'You washed things?' Peter asked. 'With no water?'

'There is a water supply in the stable blocks, Your Grace,' she answered.

'Thank you for trying,' Peter said. 'But we shall need expert help to deal with this. We shall have to recruit some professional restorers.'

'We didn't know what to do, my lord,' said Mrs Farley and promptly burst into tears. 'All these lovely things, that we've looked after since I first came here when I was thirteen, as a kitchen maid . . .'

Thomas said stiffly, 'Control yourself, Farley!'

Harriet intervened. The woman's whole life's work, she thought. She very briefly and lightly put an arm round Mrs Farley's shoulder and said, 'We shall make this liveable and bright again; it will be comfortable and clean, and not everything will prove to have been spoiled. You shall see; and you shall help us.'

'Leave it all untouched for the moment,' Peter said. 'The insurance assessor is coming tomorrow, and when we have talked to him we shall have a plan.'

'Of course, we need a plan of our own,' he added, as they walked away towards the stable block, with Bunter following a step behind them.

They ran to ground in the tack-room, where there

was a table and chairs, and sat down to confer.

'I shall be in the adjacent room when you need me, Your Grace,' said Bunter.

Harriet said, 'Bunter, won't you stay and help us? Anything we decide will involve you as much as anyone.'

Bunter looked at Peter, who leaned over and drew out a third chair.

'Gerald had seen to it that it was all heavily insured,' Peter said. 'We could have it put back as it was. Perhaps we should do that. But as to being able to run it as it was . . .'

'If we put it back as it was it will be mostly fake,' said Harriet. 'Whereas every stone and beam that remains is genuine.'

'Your most excellent opinion is?'

'That we should keep what we have, and demolish what we have lost. Clear up the mess, and plant a garden in the outline of the burned-out walls.'

Peter stared at her, thinking about it.

She went on, 'We would have a curious, beautiful house with ten bedrooms and an attic range. A library, a drawing-room, a hall, a truncated gallery, but a gallery all the same: a good-sized house, Peter, and plenty for a family our size. Less ruinous to run.'

'Where does my mother live?' he said.

'There is easily room for an apartment for her and Franklin in the remaining house.'

Peter gave her a quizzical look. 'While Helen lives in greater splendour in the Dower House?' he said.

'Helen will enjoy that,' said Harriet emphatically.

'May I ask what you think, Bunter?' asked Peter.

'Her ladyship's plan seems sound to me, my lord. Practical. If we need more space in the future, it would be possible to convert this stable block.'

'So it would,' said Peter. 'Item one, decided, then. Item two: death duty. I think we can pay it if we sell off most of the land.'

'Does that mean turning off an ancient tenantry?' asked Harriet.

'Yes. Some of them will buy their holding from us. But of course, the future income from the land will be lost.'

'What about the servants?' Harriet asked. 'Do we have to send them packing?'

'The war has done a lot of the work for us,' said Peter. 'Most of the staff joined up, leaving just the older ones running the show. Only two of those who went have returned, both of them gardeners. We shall have to pension off most of them.'

'That won't be any fun,' she said.

'It will be like eating toads,' he said bitterly.

'If I may suggest, Your Grace,' said Bunter.

'Suggest by all means,' Peter said.

'Since I accompany you on your migrations you can dispense with Thomas. And I understand he would like to retire from serving the family to help his brother run a pub in King's Lynn. But I think you should retain Mrs Farley, who seems an efficient sort of person.'

Peter said, 'Fine. Fiat. Have you been interviewing the whole establishment, Bunter?'

'I have, my lord. Here is a list, together with a note of what the people on it would like to have happen. They are quite realistic, Your Grace. They have little plans of their own.'

'Whatever would we do without you, Bunter,' Peter said.

'There is a task which I cannot assist you with, Your Grace,' said Bunter. 'And that is to sort the pictures into those that you would wish to hang in the remaining house, and those that will have to be sent for sale. All of them will be familiar to your lordship from childhood; I cannot surmise which will be of sentimental value to you.'

'Harriet shall help me choose,' said Peter. 'She will be living with the relicts.'

When they returned to the house a message was handed to them by Thomas. A message from Charles. Peter went into the tack-room to the telephone and Harriet lingered in the pale afternoon sun, and stared at the house, seeing it marred, and imagining it mended.

Peter came briskly out to her, almost running. 'Mrs DuBerris has made a clean breast of it,' he said.

'Good lord!' said Harriet. 'She seemed determined that she wouldn't do that, when she was talking to me. To what has she confessed?'

'The whole charge sheet except for Mr Handley. Denies all knowledge of that.'

'Well, accidents do, after all, happen,' said Harriet.

'Yes. Maybe. Anyway she has admitted killing Rannerson and Patel and Pevenor. And malicious hanky-panky with the jewel. Case closed.'

'Will she hang?' asked Harriet.

'Maybe not. It's getting controversial to hang people. Her lawyer will try his best. I think they won't charge her with Patel.'

'Peter, why not? I liked the sound of that woman. A really useful life was taken there.'

'Tactics, Harriet. The woman fell down through a broken manhole cover, in the blackout, late at night. No witnesses. Sort of thing that happened every night in the Blitz. The only evidence that she might have been pushed is our old friend coincidence and that confession. Any defence lawyer worth his salt can demolish a confession. We think it's an odd coincidence, but as you just said about Mr Handley, coincidences do happen, let Aristotle say what he will. A defence lawyer will make a huge meal of it: groundless charge, cock-and-bull story about an exotic jewel, pure coincidence, charge brought against his client out of malice . . . Nobody suspected foul play at the time, no police file was opened, no postmortem considered necessary . . . I could write the brief myself. You could do it even better.'

'You mean, they couldn't make it stick?'

'I don't see that they could, no. And they will then be thinking about the effect on a jury of bringing a charge that won't stick alongside others that should. The motive for the other murders is also associated with that jewel. Weakens the whole case.'

'But she has confessed.'

'She could, and indeed should, change her plea.'

'Why should she change it, if it is true?'

'It's always better to have the evidence spelled out in court, especially if someone is to hang on the basis of it. *Bono publico*, and all that.'

'So what do you think will happen?'

'Touch and go. A jury won't like the sound of those jewels and inscriptions that nobody can read. If she withdraws her confession it might be that none of it could be made to stick.'

'I can't read her mind,' said Harriet. 'She is very disturbed. Mad, I think. So we may never know whether poor Rita Patel was pushed, or just coincidentally fell?'

'It's the nature of coincidence, isn't it?' said Peter. 'It doesn't amount to certainty. And it won't make any difference to DuBerris. One hangs just as decisively for a single death as for three.'

Harriet wondered how severe Peter's solved-case depression would be this time. But this time he had other matters on his mind.

A discussion with the insurers, for example. At first the assessor declared that although his firm would have to pay every penny entailed in the total reconstruction of Bredon Hall as it was the night before the fire, they would not pay a penny towards any lesser plan.

'He thinks we are deliberately planning to do very little, and pocket the difference in cash,' Peter reported to Harriet.

'Well, aren't we?' she asked him.

'Another way of looking at it would be to say that what we propose will save the insurers money; and then discuss the division of the spoils. The fellow today acknowledges that a full restoration would risk bankrupting his firm, but nevertheless is adamant that whatever we do we shall not pocket a penny piece above what we spend on repairs. I sent him off declaring that in that case we would demand a restoration of the whole lot. He has gone back to London to think about it. My brother must be turning in his grave.'

'So perhaps no cash?' said Harriet. She felt on uncertain ground, never having discussed his family finances in this way before, only their own resources. 'How badly do we need cash?'

'We have to find the death duty,' Peter said.

'And we can't find it?'

'I am about ten thousand short,' Peter said.

'After I have thrown most of our personal wealth at it, as well as selling a lot of land.'

'We should sell Talboys,' Harriet said.

Peter looked at her hard. 'I promised you once no one other than us would ever set foot in it as the owner as long as I lived,' he said. 'Had you forgotten?'

'I was only thinking that it would be hard to live in three houses,' she said. 'There aren't enough days in the year.'

'Are you actually asking me to break a promise to you?' he said ruefully.

'Well, no . . .'

'We could let it if we haven't time to live in it, and save my battered honour in that way.'

'What could we get for it?' she asked. 'How many gardeners' wages here would the rent cover?'

'You never fail to amaze me, Harriet,' he said. 'Age has not withered you nor custom staled your infinite variety.'

'Idiot!' she protested. 'I get your drift. Be aware there will no asps at the breast for me; you're stuck with me.'

'I thought that was the other way round,' he said.

Peter and Harriet stayed at Denver for nearly a month. Helen assigned them a room in the Dower House, so they were not at the Denver Arms for very long. There seemed to be an endless list of

366

chores, decisions, negotiations. The insurers had agreed their plans, but the Ministry of Works was taking an interest in what would become of a half-burned-down important house; an architect was needed to plan the alterations required, an engineer to assure them of the stability of the walls that had been licked by fire. Harriet had taken a fancy to opening up the stone arches that had once supported the upper storey of the stone house. She thought they would look splendid filled with large windows, giving on to the new garden. And the new garden was what she was putting her mind to, leaving the more immediate problems to Peter. It was in a garden book that she found a shrub called *Osmanthus Nandina*. Smiling, she carried the book through to Peter, who had set up an office in the stable block.

'If all those years ago you had been a gardener, Peter . . .' she began, but then she saw that Charles was with him. She had not heard the car come up the drive.

'What's up?' she asked.

'Mrs DuBerris has hanged herself in Holloway Gaol,' Peter said.

'Those idiots let her have bed sheets,' said Charles. 'They seemed to think that if a prisoner has confessed he or she will be perfectly happy to be hanged by the powers that be. And I understand you warned them at her arrest, Peter, that you thought she was a risk.'

'Yes, I did. But I thought she would do it sooner.'

'So she escapes justice,' said Charles, clearly still angry.

'Well, she hasn't exactly *escaped* justice,' said Harriet. 'Just administered it herself. I suppose it might be easier to be the actor rather than the acted upon.' She was remembering the fierce pride and rage of Mrs DuBerris.

'Believe me, Harriet,' said Charles with sudden ferocity, 'some things are best done professionally.'

That evening Peter said, 'I've had as much of this as I can bear. Let's go back to London.'

'Tomorrow?'

'I thought perhaps tonight,' he said, looking at her hopefully.

'As Your Grace pleases,' she said, causing him to shake a fist at her. He drove even faster at night, making Harriet ride in terror of an unlit cow on the road; but they reached home safely, yet again.

London, however, was no longer a kingdom apart. Peter was still largely occupied with Denver affairs. An enquiry from Black Rod was received, asking him when he intended to take his seat in the Lords. Peter at first said that he would not take up his seat; but when Charles learned of that he pointed out that there was no voice in the Lords with any knowledge of crime except from the judiciary viewpoint. They were talking over dinner, with the Bunters present. Charles spoke warmly of how good it might be to have someone with practical experience of the nature of forensic evidence, of the nature of ordinary police work, to speak when laws were being drafted. 'A morsel of common sense, Peter,' he said, 'and, of course, expressed with wit and elegance.'

Peter sighed. 'Oh, very well then,' he said, 'Gilbert and Sullivan without the music for me, too.'

And Hope offered to take a portrait of him in his robes of state.

By and by Ada DuBerris presented herself. 'I didn't make an appointment,' she said. 'I thought you might not see me if you knew I was coming.'

'You had no reason to think that,' Peter said.

'Well, you wouldn't be the only one,' she said. 'Most of my friends somehow don't want to see me right now.' She was pale, and had lost weight.

'What can I do for you?' Peter asked. 'Other than to suggest to you that fairweather friends are good riddance.'

'I want to sell this,' she said, taking a twist of tissue paper out of her handbag, and putting it down on the sofa table. She flicked the tissue paper open to reveal the emerald. 'And I don't know how. I'm afraid of being cheated.'

'That's a not unjustified fear,' said Peter. 'But I can help you. You must go to see Lord Attenbury at once. He is certain to be selling his, and there is a reward available if both stones are offered together.'

'*He* won't see me,' Ada said.

'Have you tried?'

'Yes.'

'Although you are his second cousin once removed or something,' said Peter.

'What a ghastly thought!' said Ada.

'I rather agree with you,' said Peter. 'That young man takes after his father, I'm afraid. Shouldn't speak ill of the dead, of course. Look, I think you need an intermediary. Someone to negotiate a deal with the Maharaja for both of you. And I know just the person, as it happens. I think you should go to see Freddy Arbuthnot. Tell him I sent you and all that.'

'Thank you, Lord Peter,' said Ada. 'Can I still call you that?'

'Certainly you can. Or just Peter. Cuts the fuss a bit. And I did, after all, first meet you when you were a tiny little thing in nursery frills.'

'You're nothing like as horrible as my mother said you were,' observed Ada. 'You're being very helpful.'

'Well, do me a favour in return,' he said. 'Leave that jewel on the table while I see if Harriet is free. She has heard so much about it, or them, that I'm sure she'd like to see one of them.'

Harriet was indeed free. She looked with great curiosity at the dark stone lying on the table.

'Pick it up if you want to,' said Ada.

Harriet picked it up very gingerly, and held it to the light. The intaglio carving gave it a differential density, the thinner parts gleaming with river-green translucence. She could even see the faintest shadow of fragments of the inscription on the back showing through. She was struck with a sudden wave of emotion; of longing to possess this stone, to stare at it and lose herself in its depths, as though the heartbroken yearning of the Persian poet whose words it carried had been twisted into desire for the stone itself.

She put it down abruptly. 'I should sell it as soon as you can,' she said to Ada.

'I don't exactly want the money,' Ada said. 'Or at least I don't want much of it myself. I want to make a fund to give bursaries to train musicians. Poor young people who can't afford the teaching they need. And I don't know how to do that, either,' she added.

'I can't help you with a trust fund,' Peter said, 'but I know a man who can. I'll post you off in the right direction as soon as you've got the money.'

'So what did you think of it?' Peter asked Harriet when Ada had left them.

'What a perilous thing, Peter!' she said. 'I found an intense admiration for the man who long ago dispossessed himself of it to feed the poor.'

'It got to you, too?' he said. 'I thought you might have been immune to it.'

She shivered slightly. 'I am gladder than I can tell you that it isn't ours,' she said.

A week later Freddy Arbuthnot showed up, dropping by at the cocktail hour, and accepting gin and It.

'I've come to talk to you about the reward that Maharaja fellow is offering,' Freddy said. 'He's putting up a handsome price for both the jewels, and an even more handsome reward of some kind, and he thinks the reward is due to you.'

'The emeralds aren't mine,' said Peter. 'Nothing to do with me. The reward was for anyone offering them both together, wasn't it? The two owners should share it.'

'Point of view, certainly,' said Freddy. 'Just thought you might be glad of a few thousand at the moment.'

'What makes you think that, Freddy?' Peter asked.

'Oh, it's got about that you are selling some shares; that's all.'

'Buy some, sell some.'

'Oh, come on, Wimsey, I can work out the position you are in, and so can a lot of people.'

'The emeralds are not mine,' Peter repeated. 'Harriet said just the other day that she was glad of that. I rather agree with her.'

'You're a silly fellow, Wimsey,' said Freddy.

'And I'm dashed fond of you. All right, have it your own way; I'll see the Maharaja off. Just let me know if I can help, won't you?'

Bunter appeared with the breakfast tray the following morning, bringing with him not *The Times*, but *Country Life*.

'I thought you would like to see this, Your Grace,' he said. He handed Peter the magazine open at a full-page announcement of the sale of Fennybrook Hall.

Ancestral home of the Attenbury family, never before on the market . . . main house by Sir John Soane . . . extensive park-land, stables, home farm, offered for sale furnished or unfurnished . . .

'Well, well,' said Peter. 'Take this to show to Harriet at once, Bunter. I expect a visit from Lord Attenbury before the day is out, and we should be prepared.'

It was actually the following day that Lord Attenbury appeared, having the grace to be rather embarrassed, and full of exculpation and explanation.

'You see,' he offered, 'it seemed for such a long time that we couldn't possibly keep the house, that we should simply have to sell it, and we rather got used to the idea. Well, my mother and my aunts did, that is . . . I myself, of course . . . well, as I was saying, then when the emerald business was all sorted out—eternally grateful, of course—it occurred to us that now we had the money we didn't necessarily want to blow it all on keeping the family pile. White elephant, really. The women thought it would be fun to have a little place on the Riviera for the winter, and to go to New York now and then; they let me off the hook, you see. And in the modern world we don't have to live like fuddy-duddy old landowners. Nobody respects that any more, after all. You should do the same, Peter. It's quite liberating really.'

'Thank you for your advice, Attenbury,' said Peter. 'I shall not take it.'

At Denver again. The house now habitable, beginning to show its lopsided charm. Even the new formal garden taking shape. Harriet in gum-boots with planting lists in her hands.

Peter came towards her, emerging through one of the new garden windows with a telegram in his hands. 'My mother is coming home at last,' he told her. 'Arriving in five days.'

'Hurrah,' said Harriet. 'And her part of the house is all ready for her, Peter. I saw to that.'

'Thank you,' he said. 'Harriet, I . . .'

'What, Peter?' she asked, when he paused.

'I wish I had found a way of not dragging you into all this. You didn't bargain for this.'

'For better, for worse, for richer, for poorer, Peter? I think I did. Considering that you told me quite recently that there's no such thing as a forgetful sleuth, you seem a remarkably forgetful husband.'

'You found it hard enough to stomach my position as it was,' he said sadly. 'And when you married me my nephew was alive, and I was safe from the succession.'

'It was the glamour and privilege I bucked away from,' she said. 'If I had realised all the burdens and responsibilities that went with them I would have accepted you much sooner. And, Peter, since I am now the Duchess of Denver whether we would or no, I intend to be a good Duchess.'

'Don't you want to be Harriet Vane?' he asked her.

'Yes; but I am large. I contain multitudes.'

'Have you reckoned a thousand acres much?' he asked. 'If every atom belonging to me as good as belongs to you . . .'

'You see?' she said, smiling at him. 'I shall still be Harriet Vane, and you shall be the only duke in England who can play ping-pong with quotations.'

'Oh, yes,' he said, 'I can still do that! Do you think I can still detect?'

'I'm sure you can, if the need arises,' she said. 'I haven't noticed dukedom softening your brain.'

'There is something intrinsically absurd,' he said sadly, 'about a ducal detective.'

'You have been too much in Helen's company,' said Harriet. 'If I can be a duchess, and Harriet-Vane-the-writer, then you can be the Duke of Denver, and Lord-Peter-the-detective.'

'Can I still be Peter, naked and unadorned, and your friend and lover?' he said.

'Well, evidently,' she said. They caught each other's eyes, and stood smiling for a moment. Then they walked on a little. 'Peter?' she said, sliding her arm through his, and walking him along the newly laid gravel path. 'There is a consolation in all this, you know.'

'I'd like to know what it is,' he said.

'I've been so happy with you, all these years,' she said, 'but in a way what I was afraid of did happen. Except while the war was on everything I was doing was voluntary. I didn't have to write unless I wanted to; I didn't even have to look after my own children unless I wanted to. Or lift a hand to any domestic task. There were no constraints about anything at all. And now I once again have things to do that are needful, and are my duty. Don't try to protect me from it, let's just get on with it. Let's do our best. Content, Your Grace?'

'I shall be if you are,' he said.

From Honoria, Dowager Duchess of Denver, to Cornelia Vanderhuysen, in New York.

Bredon Hall, 21 April, 1952

My dear Cornelia,

Please forgive me for taking so long to write to you upon my return, after all your hospitality to me over so many weeks. This is the sort of letter that used to be called a bread and butter letter, but in your case it should be a caviar and champagne letter, so generous you were to me. I know you were worried about me on the voyage home, and in a way you were right—we had terrible weather the moment we left the Hudson, and Franklin was so sea-sick that she could not do anything for me and I had to rely on the cabin staff. They were perfectly kind and efficient, and you know, dear Cornelia, I had to come home some time. Well! You'll never imagine what I found when I got there! As you know I was expecting a cold welcome from Helen, and a lodging of some kind in the Dower House, but I found instead that I am to have a very nice set of rooms in the Hall itself, all ready for me with fires burning, and many of my own pretty things already installed. So odd, really, Cornelia, to think of Harriet getting things ready for me, when I remember so well all the fun I had on Peter's marriage getting the Audley Square house ready for her. I have to say that although there is still a lot to do, the poor old lopsided house is really quite charming, and when Harriet asked me if I thought they had done the right thing in not rebuilding the whole stately pile, I said yes very sincerely. Just the same, I shall have to remember where the house now stops, and not go sleep-walking into the garden . . .

I'm sure you will be wanting me to tell you about more important things, and not go running on about bedrooms and sitting-rooms and such like, although really, dear, such things do matter more than we like to admit. As you know I have been very anxious about Peter being squashed flat by his dukedom, and losing that devil-may-care exuberance that made us all love him so dearly. I thought he might turn into another version of Gerald, although I could not imagine Harriet playing Helen; Bunter was the only one of the three that I thought would be like a duck in the water . . . Or should that be on the water? They do tend to float on the top, don't they? But you know, dear, I had been underestimating my son. He always was a chimera—or do I mean a chameleon? Always playing about with disguises. All that man-about-town he used to go in for, it was always a mask for the real man; I did know that. And now the dukedom is a cover story, and he's playing it really rather well, though with a much lighter touch than Gerald, of course. And the real Peter is still there, and even managing moments of the old

378

panache. It's Harriet that is the big surprise; she seems so competent and rather in her element as if she was as much in charge as when she is writing a novel. When I asked her how she was managing she said, 'I'm just making it up as I go along, and when in doubt I ask Bunter.'

Helen is very grumpy and cross about it all. I rather think she was looking forward to Harriet making a mess of things, either so that she could take over and run everything herself, or so that she could snipe from the sidelines. I am very relieved that I am not under the same roof as her, although I think she will spend a lot of her time in London. Even Peter's fortune won't do everything as it used to be done, and a lot of his property in London was flattened in the Blitz. Things certainly will have to be scrimped a lot according to the past. I shan't mind that, and neither will Harriet.

So all's well here, Cornelia, and you needn't worry about me one bit. In fact you had better plan to come and visit and see it all for yourself. I should like that very much.

Always your affectionate friend,
Honoria

PS: You'll never guess what has just happened, not if I gave you a hundred tries!
That Maharaja person who bought the

379

emeralds—remember we were looking at a report of it together in the <u>New York Times</u>— has decided to give Peter a present. A sundial, he said, and Harriet, I understand, thought it would look good in the middle of her new garden. But yesterday, it came in three lorries! You would call them trucks, dear. And a team of Indian masons to put it together, following the lorries up the drive in a coach. And two Indian astrologers, and the Astronomer Royal no less, our very own Harold Spencer Jones, to get the thing properly lined up. Harriet fled into the kitchen, and she and Mrs Farley managed a sandwich lunch, while Bunter produced some rather nice white wine, so the house held its head up in a manner of speaking. Luckily the Indian masons were provided with their own lunch, because some of our sandwiches were roast beef. They have been building the thing for two days now, and it's very strange. It's all pink and white marble, and it has a crescent moon shape, lying on its side, and a little flight of steps rising in the middle, which casts a shadow left or right as the sun goes by. It's a sort of prefab, with all the stones numbered and ready to put together.

The experts were all saying it wouldn't be very accurate because it's too small—my dear it's twelve feet high! But the Maharaja said the one it is a copy of is one hundred and twenty feet high! His will tell the time by the second, ours will only do it to the right six seconds. But then, dear, whoever really tells the time by a sundial? Peter said something about making a botch of something done much better by a watch, but he said it just to me when the Maharaja was out of earshot.

As I write the workmen are putting a little cupola on the top of the steps to crown the whole thing, and I do think when we have great-grandchildren they will love running up and down those steps, though I am probably far too old to be around to see that.

PPS: By yesterday evening I still hadn't posted this letter—so sorry, Cornelia, you will think me bad-mannered—the Maharaja and the Astronomer R had all gone home, and just the masons and the astrologers were left. Mrs Farley has been feeding people like a one-woman British Restaurant; nicer food, of course, but the same feeling of emergency numbers, so I'm sure she's glad to see the back of everybody. Anyway, after dinner Bunter came in with the coffee and told us that everybody had now gone—the masons' bus had taken them off while we were eating, and it was a lovely moonlit evening, so we all went out into the garden to have a look. Harriet said, 'Oh, Peter, it works as a moon-dial as well!'

and she went forward to look closely, and she saw that there was some funny writing on the white marble curve where the ruler marks are for reading the time. Peter came to look, and he said, 'I think I can guess what that is,' and then they were kissing like newlyweds, so I scrambled away to the other side of the thing, and watched the moon by myself for a minute or two before we all went in to bed.

I shall ask Bunter in the morning what the words on the sundial say—he will know. He always knows everything.

But by then this letter will at last be in the post.

PPPS: You really will have to come to visit, Cornelia, if only to see the sundial for yourself.
Always your loving friend,
Honoria

Center Point Publishing
600 Brooks Road ● PO Box 1
Thorndike ME 04986-0001 USA

(207) 568-3717

US & Canada:
1 800 929-9108
www.centerpointlargeprint.com